I0652388

QUEST FOR THE DRAGON'S EYE

WRITTEN BY
JODY SLYMAN

"Quest for the Dragon's Eye," by Jody Slyman. ISBN 1-58939-658-8 (softcover).

Published 2004 by Virtualbookworm.com Publishing Inc., P.O. Box 9949, College Station, TX, 77842, US. ©2004 Jody Slyman. All rights reserved. No part of this publication may be reproduced, stored in a retrieval system, or transmitted in any form or by any means, electronic, mechanical, recording or otherwise, without the prior written permission of Jody Slyman.

Manufactured in the United States of America.

This book is dedicated to my friends, Zackary and Stephanie Seitles. May your life together be long and full of happiness.

INTRODUCTION

PRINCESS ALEXANDRA ROMLAY, a beautiful young woman of 22 years with straight shoulder length, fiery red hair and milky jade green eyes, is sitting in a dark brown saddle atop her snow white horse. She stands near 5'5" tall and her thin yet incredible build is about 120 pounds. She is dressed in a thick padded cloth, long sleeve top with varying shades of brown. The Princess is wearing long padded cloth trousers also in varying shades of brown and she has on dark brown leather boots that come up to just below her knees over the trouser legs. She is carrying a short sword, with a golden handle and two foot silver blade, on her left hip and a golden handled, silver eight inch bladed dagger on her right hip. Both weapons have been tarnished and blood stained from the long journey she has made. Her face, a little dirty, has a weary yet poised look about it as she appears to be in deep thought, staring blankly.

Princess Romlay is atop a small hill gazing across the barren, charred black lands known as the Island of the Dead. The dusky cloud that hangs over the island making it appear to be at constant darkness has impaired her vision some. The smell of old death hangs in the air as she reaches down and touches a small brown pouch tied around her belt on the front of her waist. Her mind wanders to all the days that she and her friends, yes, she would consider them her friends even though she is the

Princess, given what they have been through, have spent on this noble quest and to be so close only to face what they now must face.

Princess Romlay knows the horrifying truth, that her small party may not make it through what they are about to encounter. She watches as the glow of hundreds of torches light up the distant horizon continue towards them, as the army of the undead, no doubt led by the Lord of the Undead, draws more near with each passing moment.

As she awaits their scout's return, Princess Romlay speaks out loud with tired determination, not wanting the others to know what is really going on in her head, "No matter what happens, one of us must make it back with the pouch."

Princess Romlay's eyes narrow and continue to gaze at the uncertainty that lies ahead.

CHAPTER 1

TWO MONTHS EARLIER, in the Kingdom of Glenfin, a birthday celebration in being prepared. Glenfin is a large town surrounding the castle. The town is hundreds of stone and wood buildings with stone roads. The town covers a good ten square miles. Most of the buildings in the middle part of the town near the castle are either tailor shops, taverns or blacksmiths. Numerous horse stables line the outer roads as the land surrounding Glenfin is mainly grasslands with emerald green rolling hills. Small huts and homes dot the grasslands around the main town of Glenfin.

People are walking everywhere. They are dressed mainly in tunics and dresses of all different colors and designs. The streets are also littered with the poorer type that wears mainly rags and wanders the streets begging for whatever they can get. Also walking the roads of the town are knights dressed in shiny plate mail armor from head to toe. Most of the knights are carrying a sword on their hip and a shield in their hand.

The castle is surrounded by four huge stone forty foot high walls shaped in a square that protects the four square miles of noble land inside. Each corner of the castle wall has a circular tower that extends towards the sky at sixty feet. On the southern wall is a large wooden gate that is twenty by twenty feet. The courtyard surrounding the castle is plush grass with beautiful flowers lining the stone walkways as the smell of jasmine and rose petals fills the air. On the northern side of the castle grounds is the royal family's horse stables.

The tops of the walls are dotted with knights in their armor and archers wearing chain mail armor and carrying a bow with thirty arrows on their backs. Each tower has two lookouts that are also archers. The courtyard is dotted with men and women of nobility. They are dressed in formal tunics and dresses of many bright and full of life colors. Walking among the nobility are more castle knights and archers.

Banners hang everywhere around the castle grounds. Each banner wishing the Princess, Alexandra Romlay, a happy birthday. The banners are bright and full of color. There are numerous banners hanging in the town surrounding the castle as the people show their love for the royal family. However happy the scene is, there are many more knights and archers out and around as the security has been increased for the upcoming birthday party the King is throwing for his daughter.

King Romlay, a regal man in his late fifties with black hair that is showing some gray as well as his well trimmed beard and mustache, stands in his throne room. He stands a noble 5'10" tall and weighs about 180 pounds. King Romlay is wearing a dark blue tunic and trousers that is covered with his blue and gold royal robes.

The throne room is a large two hundred by two hundred foot room that has incredibly beautiful drapes hanging on each wall. The floor is open so that there is plenty of room for dancing. Tables line each of the walls except for the wall across from the door. Twenty feet out from the wall across from the door is a level that rises up ten steps. On top of the level is the king and queen's throne.

The thrones are purple velvet and felt with lavish gold trim. Next to the throne on the left is a small hang carved table and upon the table is a jeweled crown.

At that time, Princess Alexandra Romlay walks in. She is wearing a nice lightweight purple dress that hangs close to her nice physical shape. The Princess walks up to her father.

King Romlay speaks in a smooth yet powerful voice, "My daughter, the day has arrived. Tell me, what would you like for your birthday?"

Princess Romlay sighs as if the answer is obvious, "The chance to get out of the castle and maybe a little adventure."

King Romlay replies in a tone that says we have been over this before, "It is far too dangerous for you out there."

The Princess debates her case, "But nothing ever happens in the castle and all the training you demanded that I have is for what?"

King Romlay stands firm on his point of view, "The training is for if you ever need it. We have many enemies out there. I lost your mother because of my foolishness; I will not risk losing you." He decides to change the subject, "So, when are you going to find a husband?"

Princess Romlay rolls her eyes, "Not this again father. I told you, not until I am ready."

King Romlay decides not to press the issue, "Is your elf friend, Robin, going to be here tonight?"

Princess Romlay nods, "Yes." She decides to leave before anything else comes up, "I better go and get ready."

King Romlay nods as the Princess walks over and gives her father a kiss on the cheek. She then turns and walks out of the throne room.

As the darkness of night falls across the peaceful

land, Princess Romlay sits in her room waiting for the time to make her appearance at the party. The room is a magnificent sixty by sixty foot with one window across the room from the door. The window overlooks the stables and has beautiful green and gold drapes. The floor has a huge green and gold laced rug lying across it.

There is a huge bed with white silk drapes hanging down on all sides on the east wall of the room. On the west wall is a very large dresser with a mirror. Princess Romlay sits and stares into the mirror wondering if this is the year that she will get to experience an adventure.

She breaths in the light smell of rose petals as she stands and looks at the trim fitting, green evening gown that she is wearing. At that time, there is a knock at the door.

Princess Romlay yells, "Enter!"

The door opens and a female elf walks in. She stands about 5'3" tall and weighs a trim 112 pounds. She has dark blonde hair that runs almost down to the middle of her back and incredible sky blue eyes. The elf is dressed in a light green, long sleeve top and a light green skirt that reaches down to her knees. She is also wearing brown boots that come up to the middle of her shin. She has on a brown cloak with the hood off. Like all elves, she has the distinctive pointy ears and she appears to be in her late twenties even though she is much older.

Princess Romlay smiles, "Robin, am I glad to see you."

Robin walks over to the Princess and they give each other a hug.

Robin steps back, "You look very beautiful. How old are you, 22?"

Princess Romlay grins, "Very funny. Yes I am getting older." She sighs, "And I still have not experienced an adventure."

Robin puts her supportive hand on the Princess'

shoulder, "Do not worry Alexandra, you will get your chance. Now, shall we head down to the party?"

Princess Romlay sighs sarcastically, "If we must."

Princess Romlay loves having Robin around. She can always bring things into perspective. She knows that Robin's supportiveness is one of the main reasons that she has been able to continue on each day. Princess Romlay takes Robin's hand and the two ladies walk out of the room and start for the throne room.

———————

Princess Romlay and Robin walk into the throne room where there are about a hundred men and women. The music stops as the Princess walks in. All the guests are dressed in formal tunics and dresses of many bright and lively colors. Princess Romlay nods to the band and they start playing again. It is an upbeat tune and most everyone starts dancing again.

A tall man, appearing to be in his late thirties, walks over to the Princess. He is about 6'3" tall and weighs a good 210 pounds. He has black, shoulder length hair and powerful brown eyes. The man is dressed in dark blue and gold trimmed robes.

The man speaks in a calm voice, "Happy Birthday Princess."

Princess Romlay smiles, "Thank you Gaelin. How is the King's magician tonight?"

Gaelin returns her smile, "Actually my lady, I am a wizard. I am fine." He looks at Robin, "It is good to see you again Robin. How are the cleric studies going?"

Robin replies, "Very well, thank you for asking."

At that time, another man in his early thirties walks up. He is dressed in a nice blue tunic, pants and boots. He is about 5'9" tall and weighs around 175 pounds. He has short black hair and brown eyes. He has a small scar on his left cheek, an old war wound.

The man bows, "Princess Romlay, you look beautiful tonight. Happy birthday my lady."

Princess Romlay smiles, "Thank you Captain."

The Captain smiles, "Please my lady, call me Ayron." He looks at Robin, "If no one has already asked, would you care to dance Robin?"

Robin smiles and gives a slight nod, "I would be delighted."

Ayron and Robin walk out on the dance floor while Princess Romlay and Gaelin walk over to the main table.

King Romlay, wearing his royal robes and crown, stands, "Alexandra, Gaelin, it is good to see the two of you are finally here."

Gaelin bows, "Your majesty."

Princess Romlay gives her father a kiss on the cheek, "Good evening father."

At that time, a knight dressed in full, shiny silver plate mail armor without his helmet walks up. He stands a towering 6'4" and weighs a stout 225 pounds. He has long wavy, blonde hair and deep blue eyes scanning the room in a hard gaze created by years of war. He appears to be in his mid-thirties with a battle scar on his forehead. He is carrying a medium sword with a three foot blade on his right hip.

The knight speaks, "All the men are in place your majesty."

King Romlay smiles, "Very good Sir Chaed. Now try to enjoy the party."

Sir Chaed bows, "Yes your majesty." He looks at the Princess, "Happy Birthday my lady."

Princess Romlay smiles, "Thank you Sir Chaed. How are you tonight?"

Sir Chaed replies in his business as usual tone, "Good my lady."

The tune changes to a slower beat. Everyone watches

as Ayron and Robin continue to dance. The Princess scans the room while she eats. She is happy to see all her friends, but she still longs for the wild outdoors. Her mind wanders for awhile as everyone continues to party around the throne room.

King Romlay stands and speaks in a loud, powerful voice, "Everyone, please be silent!" The music stops and the room goes quiet as the King holds up a goblet of wine, "To my daughter, who is 22 years old today. No father could be as blessed as I am to have such a wonderful daughter. Happy Birthday."

Everyone in the room replies, "Happy Birthday Princess."

Everyone with a goblet drinks to the toast and the music starts again.

King Romlay looks at his daughter, "May I have this dance?"

A huge smile comes to Princess Romlay's face, "Of course father."

They start to walk towards the dance floor and the King stops. He starts to sweat and sway back and forth.

Princess Romlay questions with some fear in her voice, "Father, are you alright?"

Suddenly, the King collapses to the floor. Chaed, Ayron, Gaelin and Robin rush over to him as the room goes quiet.

Chaed kneels next to the King and looks him over, "Something is wrong. We need to get him to his chambers."

Ayron motions for some of the guards to help carry the King. Four guards pick up the King and Chaed escorts them to the King's chambers.

Ayron, who is still in the throne room, speaks, "The party is over."

He walks out with Gaelin, Robin and the Princess to check on the King while the throne room empties.

————————

Chaed, Ayron, Gaelin and the Princess have been standing outside the royal chambers for awhile now as Robin and the royal doctor have been looking at the King. Alexandra can only think of the worse. Each of their faces carry the burden of the King's condition.

Alexandra questions nervously, "What could have happened?"

Chaed replies frustrated with himself, "No doubt foul play is at hand, and I should have seen it. I have let you down again my lady."

Alexandra knows what he is talking about and knows she must say something, "My mother's death was not your fault and neither is this. There is no way you could have seen this happening. There were no warnings."

Gaelin chimes in, "The Princess is right. You need not dwell on this. We need to focus on how to save the King now."

Chaed mutters under his breath, "There was a warning."

The others look at him as if they do not know what he is talking about. At that time, the door opens and Robin walks out.

Alexandra quickly questions, "How is my father?"

Robin sighs, obviously bewildered, "He is unconscious right now. It appears to be some kind of poison that is slowly killing him."

Ayron questions, "Can your magic help him?"

Robin shakes her head slightly, "I have tried everything and none of it has worked. All we have been able to discover is that it is undead in origin."

Chaed speaks as if he knew already, "I should have known." He sighs, "There has to be a cure."

Gaelin rubs his chin and nods, "I know of a potion

that can counter act any poison."

Everyone looks at Gaelin in disbelief and Alexandra quickly speaks, "Then we must hurry. How long will it take to prepare?"

Gaelin replies a little less enthusiastic, "Not long, however, the potion requires a root we do not have."

Robin's eyes narrow, "What root is that?"

Gaelin sighs and replies in a hollow voice, "The Dragon's Eye Root."

Robin gets a bewildered look on her face. She knows the truth about the root in which Gaelin speaks of.

Alexandra notices Robin's look and questions, "What is wrong? Let's just go get the root."

Robin looks at Alexandra, "The Dragon's Eye Root only grows on Dragon Mountain." She pauses, "On the Island of the Dead."

Everyone is quiet. The thought of the Island of the Dead runs through everyone's mind. There is an increasing unease amongst them after Robin's last statement.

Alexandra finally speaks, but a little shaky, "It does not matter where the root is, if it is what we need, then we must go after it."

Chaed speaks as if he did not want to hear what Alexandra just said, "My lady, what you're talking about is crazy. We would have to cross the vast land to the Northern Port and across the Great Sea. No one in the kingdom has ever been that far and then there is the Island of the Dead."

Ayron chimes in, "And I know of no one who has ever been to and returned from the Island of the Dead."

Alexandra stands firm, "No matter, we must try."

Robin speaks up, "I know of a ranger clan only two days ride from here and they have traveled across the lands. I am sure we can find someone there to guide us."

Ayron again points out the overlooked fact, "Even if

we make it to the Great Sea, we still have no way to get across the Island of the Dead."

Chaed speaks up, "Everyone is saying we. Why not send an army?"

Alexandra replies, "The kingdom could be in danger. We need all of our knights here to guard the castle. A small group will draw less attention than an army." She pauses, "But Ayron is right, how will we find our way across the Island of the Dead?"

Gaelin finally speaks, spreading his wisdom, "Yes, a small, loyal group is the way to go, and find the rangers, we must. The answer to the Island of the Dead lies in the prisoner in the dungeon my lady."

Chaed replies strongly, "The prisoner in the dungeon could be the cause of all this. We cannot trust it."

Alexandra looks at them, not knowing what they are talking about, "It does not matter now. We must take the chance if we are going to save my father. Chaed and Ayron will come with me. Gaelin, will you join us?"

Gaelin bows, "Of course my lady."

Robin speaks up, "I am going too."

Chaed looks at Alexandra, "Perhaps you should stay my lady. It will be very dangerous and who will run the kingdom while you are gone?"

Alexandra replies sternly, "Those are my wishes, and the Duke of Suffix will handle the kingdom. Now, everyone go and get ready, we leave at dawn. Ayron, notify the Duke of Suffix and have him come see me later." She pauses, "I am going to see what this prisoner has to offer."

Everyone bows and goes their separate ways.

Alexandra walks down the cold, dark stairway to the dungeon. The stairway is lit by only a few torches.

Alexandra shivers from the chill in the air. Her father never told her about the prisoner and that makes her wonder what is so special about this prisoner.

A knight stands at the bottom of the stairs as the Princess walks up. The knight bows to show his respect.

Alexandra speaks, trying not to show any signs of fear, "I want to see the prisoner."

The knight grabs a ring of keys off a small wooden table, "Yes my lady."

The knight takes one of the lit torches from the wall and starts walking towards the cells. The dungeon is lit only by a few torches and it has a dusky, damp smell of death in the air. They walk by three empty cells and stop in front of a large wooden door.

The knight unlocks the door, "Let me shackle the prisoner before you enter my lady."

Alexandra replies, "That will not be necessary. Give me the torch and leave us."

The knight looks at her closely, "This is a very dangerous prisoner my lady."

Alexandra repeats her command more sternly, "Give me the torch and leave us."

The knight bows, "Yes my lady. I will not be far if you need me."

The knight opens the wooden door and it lets out a deep moan from the stress. The knight hands over the torch. Alexandra walks into the cell and the knight pushes the door closed. Alexandra shivers again from a deathly chill in the air.

The prisoner stands up from his bunk. He looks to be about 5'7" tall and weighs about 135 pounds. Alexandra can tell he is wearing a thick padded cloth, long sleeve top in different shades of brown and thick padded cloth trousers also in many shades of brown. He has on brown leather boots that come up to just below his knees over his trousers. She is unable to see his face because of the shadows.

Alexandra can tell that there is something very different about this prisoner than the others.

Alexandra speaks with false confidence, "I am Princess Romlay. What is your name?"

The prisoner replies in a hauntingly hollow voice, "I am Solur." He pauses, "For what brings you down here princess?"

Alexandra questions, trying to conceal the fear in her voice, "Our wizard told me that you might have knowledge of the Island of the Dead, do you?"

Solur replies inquisitively, "Yes I do. But why would the Princess need that information?"

Alexandra decides to share a little of what is going on, "A group of us is going after the Dragon's Eye Root on Dragon Mountain. I was wondering if you could help us."

Solur replies slyly, "I know the Island of the Dead better than anyone, but I cannot help you with Dragon Mountain."

Alexandra gives a bewildered sigh, "That does not help much."

Solur quickly speaks, "I know someone on the Island of the Dead that has been up Dragon Mountain. I can take you to her."

Alexandra questions skeptically, "How would you know someone on the Island of the Dead?"

Solur steps closer, into the light. His skin is pale and his eyes are smoky green. His hair is brown, an eighth of an inch on the sides and a half inch on the top. His top row of teeth have a small set of fangs. Alexandra takes a step back in fear as she sees the prisoner's face.

Solur smiles, "Because I am from the Island of the Dead."

Alexandra replies, obviously shocked at the discovery, "You are a vampire."

Solur chuckles slightly, "No, not a vampire. I am an Undead Warrior."

Alexandra gives him a puzzled look, "Even I know there are no Undead Warriors left."

Solur slightly nods, "I am the last. Now, let us talk a deal. All I ask is that if I get you the root, you give me my freedom back."

Alexandra thinks for a second. She wonders why that is all he is asking for. She ponders whether she can trust him or not.

Solur notices the look on her face, "Your question of trust is a good one. I can make you no promises. So, what will it be?"

Alexandra replies firmly, trying to stay in control, "You do what I say, no questions."

Solur gives a slight nod, "I will need my things returned."

Alexandra lets out a sigh of relief, "Deal."

Solur holds out his left hand. Alexandra looks at his hand. Other than the pale skin it looks like a human hand. She also notices a small silver band ring on his ring finger. Alexandra finally takes his hand.

Solur shakes her hand, "Deal."

Alexandra lets go of his abnormally strong hand, "We will come and get you at dawn. Can you travel in sunlight?"

Solur smiles, "Of course. Like I said, I am not a vampire." He pauses, "Would it not be easier if I met you somewhere."

Alexandra looks Solur over and finally concedes, "Very well, I will have the guard return your things and you can meet us at the stables."

Solur bows his head and Alexandra walks out. She leaves her instructions with the guard. As she leaves the dungeon, it finally hits her that she just put her father's life in the hands of an undead, knowing it was undead poison that started all of this.

———

The sun starts to rise over the now gloomy kingdom. Alexandra is standing by a group of horses at the royal stables, ten horses in all. Each horse has a bedroll, one large pouch of food, a flask of water and a pouch of coins. Alexandra is dressed in a thick padded cloth, long sleeve top in varying shades of brown, and thick padded cloth trousers in varying shades of brown. She has on brown leather boots that come up to just below her knees over her trousers. She has a short, two foot long bladed magical sword on her left hip known as the Sword of Light. The blade is shiny silver and the handle is extravagant gold. She has a eight inch long dagger on her right hip.

Gaelin is the first to walk up. He is wearing his dark blue trimmed with gold wizard robes. He is holding an eight foot wooden staff in his right hand. Around his neck hangs an amulet shaped like a claw and it is known as the Amulet of Power.

Ayron arrives next. He is wearing light chain mail armor and leather boots. He has a short sword on his left hip and a dagger on his right. He has a quiver of 30 arrows on his back. Ayron is carrying a three foot long bow in his right hand. The bow is magical and is known as the Bow of Power. Ayron walks over to his horse where another quiver of 30 arrows hangs.

Two of the castle archers walk up with Ayron. They are dressed in light chain mail armor and leather boots as well. They each carry a short sword on their left hip and a dagger on their right. Each one has a quiver of 30 arrows and a medium bow on their back. None of their weapons are magical.

Ayron looks at Alexandra, "I have Sir Cleef and Sir

Braunt joining us my lady."

A tall red haired archer steps forward, "I am Sir Cleef my lady."

The other archer who is very stout steps forward, "I am Sir Braunt my lady."

Alexandra nods, "Very well."

Chaed is the next to walk up. He is dressed in full plate mail armor with his helmet visor up. He has a medium, three foot long sword on his right hip. He is carrying a medium three foot long shield in his right hand. The shield is magical and is known as the Shield of Deflection. Chaed walks over to his horse where there is a six foot long, two handed broadsword attached to it. The broadsword is also magical and is known as the Sword of Vulnerability.

Two castle knights walk up with Chaed. They are both dressed in full armor with their helmets off. They each carry a medium sword on their right hip and a medium shield in their left hand.

The blonde haired knight who is tall and thin walks up and bows, "I am Sir Johna my lady."

The shorter yet stouter brown haired knight bows, "I am Sir Marcus my lady."

Alexandra replies thankfully, "Welcome to the group."

Robin is the next to walk up. She is dressed in a green long sleeve top and green trousers. She has on brown leather boots that come up to just below her knees. She has on a brown cloak with the hood off. Robin is carrying a six foot wooden magical staff known as the Staff of Life.

The nine of them stand around for a couple of minutes, each thinking about the road ahead.

Robin finally questions, "What are we waiting on?"

At that moment, Solur walks up. He is dressed as he was in the dungeon, but now he is also wearing a black cloak with the hood on. He has a medium three foot long magical sword on his left hip known as the Dragon Sword. The blade is dark black and the handle is silver with a diamond on the end. He has a magical foot long dagger on his right hip known as the Dagger of the Undead. Around each lower leg he has a leather carrying pouch with five small throwing darts tipped with poison. Solur walks up and removes his hood.

Robin steps back and points her staff at Solur. If there is one thing Robin hates, it is the undead.

Robin speaks with hatred, "He is an undead."

Alexandra steps in front of the staff, "Solur knows the Island of the Dead and that is what matters. Now put your staff away."

Everyone watches Solur closely, not quite sure what to make of him. It is obvious that they each feel uncomfortable about traveling with an undead.

Alexandra notices the reservations towards Solur, "If you do not wish to travel with an undead, then you can stay behind. Now, let's go."

The ten of them get on their horses. They each keep a close eye on Solur as they start out of the castle.

As the group approaches the gate, the large wooden doors open. They exit the castle into the town. All the people on the streets notice them immediately. Whispers ripple through the crowds that gather to watch the Princess and her men leave. Sir Johna, Sir Marcus and Robin are in the lead. Behind them are Chaed, Alexandra and Solur followed by Gaelin, Ayron and Sir Cleef. Sir Braunt is behind the group.

As they start down the road, Alexandra speaks to the group, "From now on you are to address me as Alexandra or Alex, not Princess or my lady. I do not want anyone to know who I am."

Chaed speaks with some spite, "I am not sure about traveling with an undead. It is going to make us really unpopular with others."

Robin chimes in, "You cannot trust the undead. I cannot believe he is helping us out of kindness." She pauses, "And Chaed is right, not many will think highly of us."

Alexandra notices that Solur has remained extremely calm through all of this, but then she is sure that he is used to having these things said about him.

Alexandra stands firm to her position, "Solur knows the Island of the Dead and that is what matters. Besides, I promised him his freedom for helping us."

Ayron speaks a little shocked, "Why free a vampire? Nothing good can come of it."

Alexandra, noticing Solur is not going to say anything, replies, "Solur is not a vampire, he is a undead warrior and we need him."

Gaelin decides to get involved, "I would have to wonder the same thing as Robin. If Solur wanted freedom, he has it now and all he would have to do is run. So why help us?"

Alexandra looks at Solur, "Gaelin has a point. Care to explain?"

Solur, who has his hood on again, replies calmly, "I have to get back to the Island of the Dead."

Chaed speaks sarcastically, "We figured that much out ourselves, but why?"

Solur replies in an eerily calm manner, "The new Lord of the Undead decided to get rid of the undead warriors for death knights. He killed all the others except me. He sent me away on a mission and then betrayed me to ensure I was captured. I want my revenge."

Ayron can't help but question, "Why not just kill you?"

Solur continues, "He wants to take a vampire named Kyvez as his Queen. Killing me would have made that impossible."

Robin speaks in an, I told you so voice, "Revenge, I should have known. The undead only think of death and killing."

As the group rides out of town, Solur speaks, "The main reason I have to get back is because of my wife. The Lord of the Undead will destroy her when she will not give in to him."

Everyone looks at Solur with an unbelievably shocked look. None of them can believe what they just heard. An undead with a wife.

Alexandra is the first to speak, "You have a wife?"

Solur nods slightly, "Yes. Just because I am an undead, does not mean I cannot have feelings for someone. She is the most beautiful woman, so caring and loving. I have to get back to her before it is too late."

Ayron can't help but ask, "What kind of undead is she?"

Solur sighs, starting to grow tired of the questions, "She is a vampire."

Alexandra has the next question, "What is her name?"

Solur replies solemnly, "Kyvez."

Everyone looks at Solur again, recognizing that name from earlier.

Robin speaks up, "That is the one you said that the Lord of the Undead …"

Solur looks at Robin and interrupts, "Yes. That is why I must get back."

The talking dies down as everyone soaks in what they have just heard. None would have ever expected what Solur just told them. They are still unsure of him, but they can't help but feel a little different.

The group passes the last hut and starts down the dirt

road towards the dense, green forest two miles ahead.

CHAPTER 2

THE GROUP HAS BEEN RIDING through the dense forest for a few hours now. The sun has started to get low in the western sky as the trees block out most of the remaining sunlight. The trees are tall and the underbrush is thick. The path is well worn and provides plenty of room for their party to travel. There is a smell of pine in the air as the sound of wild animals stirs in the distance.

Alexandra speaks up, looking around the sky, "We are going to have to find a place to camp for the night."

Robin replies, knowing this part of the forest well, "There should be a small clearing not too far ahead. We can stop there."

As they continue to ride, Chad speaks to the group, "We will need someone awake at all times. The forest is full of bandits and thieves."

Ayron chimes in, "We are getting far enough from the castle that bandits and thieves may not be the only thing we see."

Solur speaks up, "I can watch over the camp. I do not require sleep."

Robin responds in a somewhat hateful tone, "Are we going to trust our safety to the undead?"

Gaelin, who tries not to get involved with minor problems, interjects, "Solur is the logical choice. We require sleep and he does not. There is no chance of him falling asleep in the middle of the night and we will be able to keep fresh."

Alexandra notices that the others are not too sure of the idea. She knows that it is up to her to make the decision. Whether they like the decision or not, she knows they will respect it.

Alexandra speaks decisively, "Solur will stand guard while we sleep."

The rest of the group nods at the Princess' decision. The conversation dies down and they finally arrive at the small clearing.

Robin dismounts, "This is it."

The rest of the group dismounts and ties their horse to a tree.

Alexandra speaks while removing her bedroll, "We will eat something and then get some sleep."

While everyone is getting their things, Gaelin speaks to Solur, "Gather me up ten hand sized rocks and put them in a circle in the middle of the clearing."

Solur nods slightly and walks off as the sun completely sets.

Ayron sets down his bedroll, "How is he going to find rocks in the dark."

Robin explains while putting down her bedroll next to Ayron's, "The undead's sight is not impaired by the dark."

The rest of the group sets up their bedrolls. Solur walks back up with the rocks and places them in the clearing as Gaelin has instructed. Gaelin walks over to the rocks.

Gaelin taps his staff on the ground inside the circle of rocks and speaks, "Light of the sky, rise"

Gaelin removes his staff as a small fire starts burning inside the circle of rocks.

Robin smiles. She loves magic and she always loves watching Gaelin use his magic. She admires how powerful his abilities are.

Robin lays back, "We will reach the rangers tomorrow afternoon."

Solur walks over to his horse. Everyone watches him as he moves. Solur can feel their eyes on him. He knows how they feel about him. He watches as they eat and talk. Solur tries to remember the days before he became an undead, but it has been so long that he can't remember. Once everyone finishes eating, they climb into their bedrolls.

Gaelin waves his hand and speaks in a commanding tone, "Light of the sky, set."

The fire dies out and everyone drifts off to sleep while Solur sits and watches over them.

***

The forest is pitch black with a small ray of moonlight breaking through the trees. The unknown and somewhat scary noises of the night echo in the woods around the camp. Everyone in the bedrolls shiver from the cool night air. Solur continues to sit and watch over the camp. He is unsure of how long it has been since everyone went to sleep, but he guesses that with the temperature dropping, dawn must not be too far off.

Solur continues to think about the road ahead. He knows what the group will have to face. The horrors of the wild, untamed lands, and most of all, the evil that resides on the Island of the Dead. Then, Solur's eyes catch some movement on the far side of the camp.

From the trees, a 6 foot 185 pound figure appears, dressed in a dark brown long sleeve shirt and dark brown trousers. The figure has on fancy looking brown leather boots that come up to just below the knee. The person also has on a black cloak with the hood on.

As the figure moves into the camp, he makes no noise of any kind. The person is completely quiet. The figure glances around at the sleeping party, deciding where to start his work. With so much focus on the sleeping party, the person is completely unaware of the cloaked figure moving behind him.

The figure kneels next to Alexandra. He looks her over for anything of value. He is somewhat captured by her beauty. He wonders why such a woman like this would be sleeping in such a rugged camp. As the figure looks over Alexandra, Solur moves into the camp quietly and approaches the person from behind.

As Solur draws closer, a twig snaps under his feet. The figure turns quickly, drawing a foot long dagger from his left hip and one from his right hip. Both daggers have a soft, reddish glow to their blades, obviously magical in nature. The person finishes his turn and sees a cloaked figure nearly upon him. Solur sees the face of a man. The man has shoulder length black hair and brown eyes.

The man, not knowing what he is facing, swings the dagger in his left hand at Solur. Solur steps back with uncanny reflexes and the blade misses. The man quickly reverses his swing and comes back at Solur. Solur steps in and uses his left hand to block the man's left arm. Solur brings his right knee up and slams it into the man's back. The man lets out a groan of pain from the unusually strong cloaked adversary's strike.

Before the man can recover, Solur grabs the man's left wrist with his left hand and grabs the back of the man's right shoulder with his right hand. Solur turns left and throws the man to the ground. The man hits the ground hard and makes quite a bit of noise. Hearing the noise, everyone in the camp starts to wake up. Solur draws his sword with his right hand and starts towards the man.

Gaelin grabs his staff and taps it on the ground. A bright, magical light appears from the end of the staff that lights up the entire campsite. The others now see the intruder and start to quickly gather their things.

The man scrambles to get to his left knee. The man looks up at Solur who quickly approaches. He is not sure what to make of this person coming at him. The man knows he has been discovered and that he must escape or most likely be killed.

Solur swings his sword at the man's chest from the left. The man blocks Solur's sword with the dagger in his left hand and thrusts the dagger in his right hand at Solur. Solur quickly spins left and brings his right leg around the man's right arm and kicks the man in the right side of his head. The man topples to his left, obviously dazed. Solur steps in, ready to strike the now defenseless man.

Alexandra yells quickly, "Stop!"

Solur stops the deadly strike of his sword just a hair from it piercing the man's chest. Everyone else in the camp is now on their feet, still not sure what is happening, but ready in case more trouble comes. The man looks up at Solur, and now with the light, can see Solur's face.

The man's voice is full of fear, "You are an undead."

Alexandra starts towards Solur, "Solur, back away."

Solur takes a few steps back and puts his sword away.

Alexandra looks at the man lying there on his back, "What is your name?"

The man glances around at everyone. He was expecting death, but now he realizes that this is no ordinary traveling party.

The man replies not sure what the lady is wanting, "Name is Maluc."

Solur speaks up, "You are a thief, a good one at that."

Ayron questions, "How would you know that?"

Solur points at Maluc's boots, "He moves without a sound and his daggers glow red. Both are obviously magical. Most thieves do not steal magical artifacts."

Maluc smiles as he stands, "Boots of Silence and the

Fire Daggers. I am not good, I am the best."

Chaed chuckles slightly, "He is confident, especially for someone who was nearly killed."

Maluc looks at Chaed, "I never would have expected to encounter an undead here." He pauses and looks back at Alexandra, "Speaking of which, why is there an undead with you?"

Alexandra just smiles, "That does not matter. What does is that I saved your life. Now you owe me a debt."

Maluc puts away his daggers, "What makes you think that?"

Alexandra glances at Solur, "Solur."

Solur smiles and takes a couple of steps towards Maluc. Maluc realizes he is in a no win situation and has no desire to face Solur again.

Maluc holds up his hands, "Okay, okay. What do you want from me?"

Alexandra replies, "You have skills we could use on our quest."

Maluc's eyes narrow. He knows it can't be that easy.

Maluc questions inquisitively, "And just what is this quest?"

Alexandra replies calmly, "We are going to retrieve the Dragon's Eye Root from Dragon Mountain."

Maluc laughs, "You're crazy. The Island of the Dead, no thanks."

Alexandra smiles, "You can go with us or face the undead now."

Maluc loses his smile. This is not exactly what he planned, but this lady looks like she could have wealth. He stands quietly, pondering his options. He will have to deal with the undead one way or the other.

Alexandra sighs, knowing they need a good thief with them. She just knows that they are going to need his skills at some point, plus, he doesn't seem to mind confrontation.

Alexandra knows how to bait him, "I tell you what, I will give you ten gold pieces once we have the root."

The others look at Alexandra. They each want to say something, but they do not question the Princess. Maluc can tell by everyone's reactions that the lady in front of him must be of some importance.

Maluc, being a thief, can't resist the thought of money coupled with adventure, "You have a deal."

Robin shakes her head and speaks, "Great, an undead and a thief. This just gets better and better."

Maluc notices Robin is an elf and decides to respond.

Maluc quips, "Who let the elf speak?"

Robin's eyes widen and her hand grinds on her staff. Solur can't help but smile.

Alexandra knows she better do something fast, "Enough. We must be going. The road is long."

Chaed looks at Maluc, "Do you have a horse?"

Maluc nods, "Just up the trail."

Alexandra speaks up, "Good. Gather up your things, we are leaving."

The sun starts to rise to give birth to a new day in the forest and Gaelin puts out his magical light. Everyone gets their things together and packs their horses. Once ready, they start off down the trail again.

The ride is relatively quiet. Robin, Sir Johna and Ayron are up front. Behind them is Chaed, Alexandra and Gaelin followed by Sir Marcus, Sir Cleef and Sir Braunt. Bringing up the rear is Maluc and Solur. The sun is high in the sky now with a few white clouds dotting the bright blue sky. A slight breeze blows through the tall trees. Not too far down the trail, the trees start to clear out some as everyone knows that is the sign that they are getting close to some kind of habitat.

Robin stops and dismounts, "It is just ahead. We will walk from here."

Everyone else dismounts.

Robin speaks to the group, "Remember, this is a ranger clan. They are not too fond of outsiders." She glances at Alexandra, "I'm not sure Solur should go in with us."

Alexandra replies defensively, "If they decide to help, they have the right to know what they are traveling with."

Alexandra knows that Robin is right though and she motions to Solur. Solur nods and puts his hood on to conceal his looks. They each know that the last thing they need is to provoke a fight with the rangers. They all take their horses and start walking into the clearing ahead. They pass a few men and a couple of women. All of them are dressed in padded cloth armor in varying shades of brown and green. Most of them are carrying a sword on their hip and they all are carrying a bow and arrows on their back.

The looks from the rangers is an obvious look of unwelcome. Everyone in the group keeps their eyes moving, not knowing what to expect.

Maluc whispers to the group, noticing the looks from the rangers, "This could get bad real fast."

Gaelin replies calmly, "Just stay calm and quiet."

The group enters a clearing with seven wooden and grass huts. Each one looks around at the crowd that seems to be gathering. Then, an older male ranger dressed in brown leather armor approaches the group. He is a man of tall and thick stature. He has black hair with streaks of gray and a beard and mustache to match. He has a sword on his left hip and a bow with arrows on his back. He walks towards the group with confidence.

The man stops a few feet from Robin, "What are you doing here?"

Robin glances around at all the rangers that have gathered, "We are seeking help."

The man replies in an unsure tone, "You are an elf. What help could you need from us?"

Robin replies calmly, "We are on a noble quest and need a guide to get us to the Northern Port."

The man's eyes narrow, "What quest?"

Robin knows the response that will come, "We seek the Dragon's Eye Root from Dragon Mountain."

As soon as Robin says it, mumbles and mutters start through the crowd. Alexandra looks around and knows that they have drawn too much attention now. She knows it is going to be tough to convince any of them to go.

The man smiles, "Foolishness."

Alexandra knows that she has to do something.

Alexandra steps forward, "Sir, I am Princess Romlay from Glenfin. My father, the King, has been poisoned and we need the root to save his life."

Chaed leans over and whispers to Gaelin, "So much for not being recognized."

Alexandra speaks proudly, "My father has brought prosperity to this land. All I ask is for help from those who prosper with it."

The man nods slightly. Alexandra can tell she made an impact, but is not sure if it was enough.

The man sighs, "I cannot order any of my rangers to go to the Island of the Dead."

Alexandra gets a depressed look. The rest of the group has that look as if they expected what they just heard.

The ranger continues, "However, if one volunteers, I will not stop them."

A look of hope crosses Alexandra's face. It gets completely quiet in the camp. Alexandra and the others look around to see if anyone will step forward. Of the fifteen rangers present, none step forward.

Alexandra can't believe it and lets her mind speak, "I did not take rangers for being cowards."

Chaed knows trouble is coming as soon as the words were spoken. All the rangers draw their swords. Chaed, Sir Johna, Sir Marcus and Solur draw their swords. Ayron, Sir Cleef and Sir Braunt draw their bows. Maluc draws his daggers.

Ayron glances around and whispers, "Dear God."

Both sides stand ready and stare at each other, waiting for the next move. It is obvious neither side wants to be the one to start a fight. Alexandra looks around at the rangers and her party. She did not want this, knowing someone could lose their life in an unnecessary fight.

At that time, a male and female ranger approach. The man is 6 feet tall and looks about 200 pounds. He has short black hair and brown eyes. He has a three foot long sword on his left hip and a foot long dagger on his right hip. On his back is a three foot long bow and a quiver of 30 arrows. He has a couple days growth of facial hair and looks to be in his mid twenties. He has on brown leather armor and brown leather, knee high boots.

The female is 5'11" tall and weighs a trim 125 pounds. Her beautiful blonde hair reaches just past her shoulders and she has incredible blue eyes. She has a three foot bow with a quiver of 30 arrows on her back. She has an eight inch dagger on her left hip and carries a 7 foot staff in her right hand. She too is dressed in brown leather armor with brown leather, knee high boots. She is extremely attractive and appears to be in her early twenties.

The younger male ranger speaks confidently, "We will go."

The older ranger looks at him, "Zak, are you sure about this?"

Zak nods while staring at Alexandra, "Steph and I must complete a quest. This is as good as any."

Solur gets a puzzled look at what Zak just said about needing to complete a quest. However, the words result in all the rangers putting their swords away. In turn, Chaed and the others put their weapons away as the tension settles in the camp and everyone breathes a little lighter.

Zak looks at Alexandra, "We will be your guides."

Alexandra bows her head in respect, "Thank you."

Robin speaks up, "We will wait for you just north of the camp."

Zak nods in return, "We will not be long."

Zak and Steph walk off to gather up the things that they will need.

Alexandra looks at the older ranger, "Thank you for your help. We will not forget it."

The man responds, "You have two of our best going with you. Listen to them; they know what they are talking about. I pray you all make it back safely."

Alexandra bows and everyone follows suit and does the same. They take their horses and walk north out of the ranger camp about a quarter of a mile and wait for Steph and Zak to arrive.

CHAPTER 3

THE GROUP STANDS NEXT TO A BATCH OF TREES just off the trail, waiting for the two rangers to arrive.

Chaed speaks to Alexandra, "What you did back there was very dangerous. It was trouble we did not need."

Alexandra smiles, "But it was help that we did need. I had to chance it."

Solur chimes in, "Sir Chaed is right. We should be more careful in the future."

Robin pipes up with some attitude, "What would the undead know about being careful?"

Solur looks at Robin, "I know when to fight and when not too. That knowledge is very helpful in staying alive on this adventure."

Ayron chimes in for Robin, "I would have figured that you would have wanted the fight Solur."

Solur smiles, "As much as I like to fight, sometimes, not often, I would prefer not to fight."

Alexandra, who had been staring off into space, joins in, "Leave Solur alone. He is right and so is Sir Chaed. We were very lucky."

Everyone goes quiet as the tension is obvious amongst the group. Robin just sighs at Solur and turns away in disgust. Solur knows how the elf feels and cannot blame her for it. He is sure that he would feel the same way if their positions were reversed.

Gaelin looks around at everyone. He knows that the tension and quarrels are not good for the group.

Gaelin speaks his wisdom, "What has happened is in the past and does not matter now. What is important is where we go from here. We have a quest to complete or the King dies. Bickering amongst ourselves will not accomplish anything except to push us apart. Out here, in these lands, being apart is very dangerous. We must stick together, even if we do not like each other."

Everyone looks at Gaelin. They all admire his wisdom and they each know what he said is true. If they do not work together, they will surely die.

At that time, the two rangers come walking up with their horses. Zak and Steph both have a quiver of 30 arrows on their horse, a bedroll and two pouches of food.

Alexandra nods as they walk up, "Thank you again for helping."

Zak bows his head, "Our pleasure my lady. My name is Zak, and this is my future wife, Steph."

Steph bows her head, "It is an honor to meet you my lady."

Alexandra smiles, "Please, from now on call me Alexandra or Alex." She motions to Robin, "This is my friend Robin. She is a cleric." Then she motions to Gaelin, "This is our wizard, Gaelin." Gaelin nods and she motions to Chaed, "This is Sir Chaed, Captain of our knights." She motions to the other two knights, "And this is Sir Johna and Sir Marcus." She then motions to Ayron, "This is Sir Ayron, Captain of our archers." Ayron nods and Alexandra motions to the other two archers, "And this is Sir Cleef and Sir Braunt." She finally motions to Maluc, "And this is the thief we hired, Maluc."

Maluc smiles, "How is it going?"

Alexandra notices the unease from Zak and Steph when she introduced a thief, then she motions to Solur, "This is Solur. He will be our guide once we reach the

Island of the Dead."

Steph looks at Solur, "Is there a reason you conceal your face?"

Everyone looks on, wondering what Solur is going to do. The group knows this could become a big problem. Rangers hate the undead as much as Robin does.

Solur replies calmly, "Yes. Few would understand."

Alexandra decides that it is time to expose the undead.

Alexandra speaks to Solur, "Go ahead and remove your hood Solur."

Solur removes his hood and reveals his undead face. The look on Zak and Steph's face say it all. Alexandra was afraid of this. She hopes that it will not cause the rangers to change their mind.

Zak's hand immediately grabs his sword, "An undead."

Alexandra quickly speaks, "It is alright. He is on our side. He is helping for his own personal reasons."

Steph narrows her eyes at Solur, "What personal reasons could an undead have?"

Solur smiles at Steph, "As strong a reason as I am sure yours is that you would risk traveling to the Island of the Dead."

Zak speaks spitefully, "We must complete a noble quest."

Solur glances at Zak, "We have heard that already. We just have not heard the reason why."

Everyone looks at Zak and Steph. Zak knows that he is not going to get out of this without some kind of explanation.

Robin speaks up, "Rangers are much like I am. They would never trust a thief and most definitely not the undead. So I am inclined to wonder why as well."

Steph quickly notices how close this group is, even with their differences. She admires that closeness.

Steph decides to tell, "In our clan, before two can marry, they must complete a noble quest together. It is a show of true love."

Solur nods at Steph's honesty and smiles, "I am trying to get back to my wife." Solur puts his hood back on, "Shall we go."

The two rangers are taken totally off guard by what Solur just said. Zak almost can't believe it and Steph just smiles about the idea. The rest of the group can't help but chuckle to themselves at the response from the two rangers.

Alexandra finally speaks, "If you still wish to go, we should be leaving."

Zak shakes his head back into reality, "Yes, of course. We should get about halfway to Callun before nightfall."

Everyone gets on their horse. Zak and Steph start off down the trail, followed by the rest of the group in the same order as before. Alexandra smiles to herself as she realizes they have everything they need to complete this quest and return to save her father. Then her mind wanders to her father and she loses the smile. She can't help but think that she may lose him. She looks down at the ground, then closes her eyes.

———————

Solur watches over the camp as the sun starts to rise over the land. Solur walks around the camp and wakes everyone up. He returns to the horses while the others start getting their things together. Solur watches intently, still unable to recall the days in which he was like them. He does know one thing, if he were human again, he would probably hold a dislike for the undead just like the others do.

Robin is the first to start walking towards the horses

where Solur is waiting. Robin gets about twenty feet from Solur when everyone hears movement in the forest around them.

Chaed, Sir Johna and Sir Marcus each grab their shield and draw their sword. Suddenly, 25 men in cloaks and padded cloth armor come running into the camp.

Chaed yells, "Bandits!"

Twenty of the bandits are carrying swords and five of them are carrying staffs. Alexandra, Ayron, Sir Cleef and Sir Braunt all draw their swords while Gaelin, Robin and Steph ready their staffs. Solur draws his sword with his right hand and his dagger with his left, while Zak does the same. Everyone readies for their first battle.

One sword bandit charges at Alexandra, while two bandits each charge the others. Alexandra watches as the bandits close in and she realizes that this is no longer training, this is for real.

Chaed shoulder blocks the first sword bandit charging at him with his shield and sends the bandit crashing to the ground. The second sword bandit cuts in with his sword. Chaed blocks with his sword as the first bandit starts to get back on his feet. Chaed swings his sword at the second bandit, but the bandit blocks with his sword. Chaed brings his shield across and knocks the bandit's sword away. The first bandit cuts in at Chaed.

Chaed ducks under the sword and brings his own sword across. His powerful cut hits deep across the bandit's stomach and blood flies everywhere. The bandit falls to the ground. The second bandit comes at Chaed again. Chaed spins towards the bandit and blocks the sword with his shield. Before the bandit can react, Chaed thrusts his sword into the bandit's chest. The bandit gasps his last breath as Chaed removes his sword. The bandit joins his partner lying dead on the ground.

One staff bandit and one sword bandit charges at Steph. The sword bandit cuts in at Steph. Steph blocks the sword with one end of her staff and quickly uses the other end to sweep the legs out from under the sword bandit. She turns in time to see the staff bandit swinging his staff at her head.

Steph drops to a knee and brings her staff across the front of the bandit's left knee. The bandit's knee folds back the way it was not meant to bend. As the bandit falls towards the ground, Steph brings her staff up and catches the bandit on the chin and blood flies from the bandit's mouth. As that bandit falls, the sword bandit comes at Steph again.

Steph blocks the swing and brings the end of her staff around at the bandit's head. The bandit narrowly ducks and he thrusts his sword forward. Steph spins to her left and her staff slams into the back of the bandit's head and splits his skull from the powerful blow. The bandit topples to the ground, lifeless.

Two sword bandits charge Solur. Solur smiles beneath his hood. The first bandit cuts at Solur's head. Solur ducks under the sword and brings his sword across and the bandit's right leg is removed at the knee. The second bandit is right there with his sword coming at Solur. Solur brings his sword up and stops the bandit's sword. The bandit never sees Solur's dagger as Solur drives it into the bandit's throat. Blood splatters everywhere from the deadly strike. Solur removes his dagger, turns quickly and removes the first bandit's head in one deft cut.

One sword bandit and one staff bandit charges at Sir Braunt. Sir Braunt sidesteps the sword thrust from the bandit and cuts in at the staff bandit. The staff bandit blocks the sword with his staff. The staff bandit brings the end of his staff around at Sir Braunt, but Sir Braunt ducks and the staff hits the sword bandit in the side of the head.

Sir Braunt spins around and thrusts his sword into the sword bandit's stomach as blood flows instantly. Sir

Braunt withdraws his sword just in time to block the staff coming at his head. Sir Braunt counters off the block and cuts the bandit on the left thigh. The bandit staggers from the deep cut that draws his blood. The bandit swings his staff while off balance and Sir Braunt seizes the opportunity by ducking under the staff and dealing a massive cut to the bandit's stomach. The bandit drops his staff as blood pours to the ground. Sir Braunt quickly cuts back overhead and his sword goes deep across the bandit's chest. The bloody bandit falls to the ground.

Two sword bandits rush Sir Marcus. Sir Marcus has his shield in his left hand and his sword in his right. The first sword bandit cuts in from the left. Sir Marcus brings his sword across and stops the deadly cut. The second bandit steps in and thrusts at Sir Marcus' chest. Sir Marcus spins around the sword and slams his shield into the second bandit's back, knocking him forward out of the way. Sir Marcus quickly thrusts his sword in at the first bandit. The bandit moves to block, but is just too slow.

Sir Marcus' sword pierces the bandit's chest. The power of the thrust drives through the bandit's sternum. Sir Marcus withdraws his sword as the bandit's body falls. The second bandit cuts in quick, but Sir Marcus was ready and blocks with his shield. Sir Marcus counters with his sword, but the bandit steps back to safety. The bandit shuffles forward and thrusts in his sword. This time when Sir Marcus blocks with his shield, he thrusts his sword in behind it. The bandit never sees the sword until it buries itself deep into his stomach. Blood flows from the wound as Sir Marcus pulls his sword from the bandit's stomach.

Two sword bandits charge at Zak. The first bandit thrusts in at Zak's chest. Zak brings his dagger across and blocks the sword. Zak spins off the block and brings his sword around at the second bandit. The second bandit blocks the sword, but didn't see Zak's dagger coming in behind it. Zak's dagger drives into the side of the bandit's neck and blood squirts out all over the ground.

Zak withdraws his dagger as the first bandit swings his sword at Zak's head. Zak ducks under the sword and brings his sword across and cuts the bandit across the left leg. Zak spins back to the bandit with his sword coming fast. The bandit manages to get his sword up in time to blocks Zak's sword. Zak brings his dagger in and knocks the bandit's sword out of the way. Now with a clear path to the bandit, Zak drives his sword home into the bandit's chest.

One staff bandit and one sword bandit rushes Sir Johna. Sir Johna has his shield in his left hand and his sword in his right. The staff bandit brings the end of his staff around at Sir Johna. Sir Johna blocks the staff with his sword. The sword bandit cuts in quick with his sword. Sir Johna sidesteps and blocks the sword with his sword. Sir Johna spins off and brings his sword down at the staff bandit's head. The staff bandit brings his staff up with both hands and blocks the sword.

The sword bandit steps up behind Sir Johna and thrusts in. Sir Johna, already expecting it, moves out of the way and the sword bandit's sword drives into the staff bandit's stomach, killing him. Sir Johna spins around and uses his shield to block out the bandit's sword, leaving the bandit completely open. Sir Johna's blade buries deep into the left ribcage of the bandit. Sir Johna removes his sword as the bandit falls.

One staff bandit and one sword bandit runs at Gaelin. Gaelin points the end of his staff at the sword bandit and a golden, magical arrow shoots from his staff and hits the sword bandit in the chest, knocking him off his feet.

The staff bandit hesitates as he is unsure of what he is facing. While the fighting rages on, a few more bandits come out of the forest and make their way towards the horses.

Two sword bandits rush Maluc. Maluc flips the dagger over in his left hand, taking it by the blade. He lets it fly at one of the bandits. The bandit sees the dagger at the last second, but it is too late. The dagger hits the bandit in the stomach and buries itself in the bandit's body. The second bandit continues to charge and cuts in at Maluc. Maluc dives and rolls under the sword and away from the bandit.

Two sword bandits rush Ayron. Ayron brings his sword around at the first bandit. The bandit blocks with his sword as the second bandit cuts in from Ayron's left. Ayron steps back just in time as the blade narrowly misses. The first bandit steps in and cuts down with his sword. Ayron spins left and brings his sword around at the bandit's side. The bandit steps back, but not fast enough as a shallow cut appears on his right ribs from Ayron's sword. The second bandit thrusts in at Ayron. Ayron, moving fast, brings his sword across and knocks away the bandit's sword. The first bandit cuts in at Ayron's head from the right. Ayron ducks under the sword and this time Ayron's sword cuts deep across the bandit's stomach. Ayron steps through and turns back to the other bandit.

Two sword bandits close in on Sir Cleef. The first one charges without control and swings his sword wildly at Sir Cleef's head. Sir Cleef ducks under the sword and cuts the bandit on the right leg. The second bandit comes in more controlled and thrusts at Sir Cleef. Sir Cleef brings his sword across and knocks the bandit's sword away. Sir Cleef turns right in time to see the first bandit raise his sword to strike. Sir Cleef seizes the opening and thrusts his sword into the exposed bandit's chest. The sword is true and the bandit falls.

One staff bandit and one sword bandit closes in on Robin. Robin quickly taps her staff on the ground three times and vines come out of the ground and entangle the sword bandit. The sword bandit struggles, but the vines have hold of him well. The staff bandit brings his staff around at Robin. Robin brings her staff up and blocks. The staff bandit moves back and brings his staff in at Robin again. Robin ducks under the staff this time and slams her staff into the bandit's stomach. The bandit staggers back by a tree. Robin waves her left hand at the tree while she taps her staff on the ground twice. A large tree branch comes to life and slams into the back of the bandit's head, knocking him out.

The sword bandit that was entangled has cut himself free and charges Robin. Robin turns in time to see a sword coming down at her. She brings her staff up to block at the last second. The blow from the sword knocks her to the ground. Robin hits the ground hard and loses her staff. The sword bandit readies to strike again, when a five inch poison dart hits him in the neck. The poison is instant as the bandit falls lifelessly to the ground. Robin looks to her right and sees Solur standing about ten feet away looking at her.

One sword bandit comes at Alexandra. Alexandra's heart starts to race as she prepares for her first real fight. The sword bandit cuts in from the left and Alexandra blocks out with her sword. The bandit moves quickly and cuts down at her head. Alexandra brings her sword up and blocks again. Alexandra counters off the block and cuts in at the bandit's left. The bandit blocks and counters her strike. Alexandra steps back just in time to avoid the sword. She can't believe how fast it is when it is real, nothing like practice. Alexandra shuffles back a few feet to get some distance from the bandit.

Gaelin ducks under the bandit's staff and moves back a few feet.

Gaelin raises his staff towards the sky and speaks in a commanding tone, "Enough."

A bolt of lightning comes down and hits the bandit in

the chest, blowing him away about ten feet. The impact is so loud, the remaining bandits stop. They see all the dead bandits and run for the forest.

Chaed starts to follow and Alexandra yells, "Stop! Let them go!"

Solur, having put his weapons away, walks over and holds out his hand to Robin, "Are you okay?"

Robin just looks at Solur. She can't believe that he saved her life. She can't believe she owns an undead her life.

Robin finally takes the hand, "I am fine."

Solur helps Robin to her feet and then walks over to the horses. The others put their weapons away and look around to take in what just happened. The fight started so quick and ended even quicker. Their first real test since the adventure started and they handled it well.

Sir Marcus speaks proudly, "We defeated them with ease. I expected more danger than that."

Zak chuckles lightly, "You will get it, soon enough."

Gaelin questions out loud, "Is everyone okay? Is anyone hurt?"

Maluc retrieves his second dagger and puts it away, "I am okay."

All the others nod in response.

Then they hear Solur's voice, "Only one problem. Three of our horses are missing."

Everyone walks over to where the horses are and Alexandra questions, "Whose horse is missing?"

Robin is the first to speak, "Mine is missing."

Steph is next, "So is mine."

Then they hear Maluc's voice, "Can you believe this? They stole my stolen horse. Talk about no honor among thieves."

Alexandra and the others can't help but crack a smile.

Alexandra looks at Zak, "Can we still make Callun by nightfall?"

Zak thinks for a second, "Even with three riding double, we should still make it."

Gaelin speaks up, "We should be going."

They finish putting their things away on the remaining horses. Steph climbs on with Zak, Robin climbs on with Ayron and Maluc climbs on with Gaelin. Once everyone is set, the group starts off down the trail for Callun.

The sun passes overhead as they travel through the forest most of the day. As the sun starts getting low in the sky, the forest clears out some.

Zak looks over his shoulder, "Remember, Callun is a town of wanderers. Do not let down your guard."

The forest clears into just small batches of trees and they see Callun in the distance. Callun is not quite as large as Glenfin, it only covers about five square miles. The inner part of the town is made up of forty stone buildings. The buildings vary from taverns to clothing and food shops to armory shops. The forty buildings line the six main roads made of stone.

The rest of the surrounding town is wooden buildings, mainly homes and stables. On the north side of the town is a huge church that one could see all the way from the south side of town.

All types wander the streets. Elves, dwarves and humans of all kinds. Most are adventurers, looking for fame and fortune. They are dressed in varying types of armor and clothing. It is obvious by the partying in the streets that this is a wild town.

Maluc draws in the air through his nose, "Smell that food. I love this town."

Steph pipes up, "A thief should feel at home in a town like this."

Maluc just looks at Steph and shakes his head. He is too taken by the smell of flame cooked meat and stew. It fills the air like a swarm of locusts. The group continues towards the town of drifters and dreamers. As they reach the outskirts of the town, Solur puts his hood on. The sun has almost completely set in the western sky, turning the once blue sky to shades of red and purple.

Alexandra speaks out loud, "We need to find a tavern with lodging for the night. First thing tomorrow, we will get three more horses."

The group continues down the road towards the middle of town. They have drawn looks from everyone they pass. This may be a town of adventurers, but they know there is something different about this group that just arrived. Knights, archers and rangers, humans and an elf, yes, something is different about this group.

Alexandra and the others notice the looks they are getting. They know what everyone is thinking, that they probably have wealth.

The group reaches the middle of town and the number of people in the streets has grown quite a bit. They stop in front of a three story building that has a sign saying "Noah's Tavern" hanging over the doorway. A young boy is sitting by the door on a wooden stool. The boy is dressed in not much more than rags.

Chaed speaks to the boy, "Boy, does this tavern have stables for horses?"

The boy quickly stands. The young boy seems overly excited that a knight is speaking to him.

The boy replies nervously, "Yes sir. It is just around back."

Everyone dismounts and Alexandra hands the boy a silver piece, "See that they get fed and watered."

The boy takes the coin and his eyes widen when he sees it is silver, "Thanks, I will."

Alexandra turns to Solur, "This is where we will be

staying. What will you do?"

Solur glance around, "I am just going to wander around some. I will be back at dawn."

Alexandra nods and Solur walks off down the crowded street. The others walk inside and Alexandra stops in the doorway and turns back to the street, but Solur is gone. She can't help but feel sorry for him and how lonely his life must be. She turns back to the others and follows them to an empty table.

A middle aged woman starts through the room towards their table. The tavern is full of the same kind that lined the streets and just like outside, everyone has taken notice of them. The woman, dressed in a casual brown dress with leather shoes walks up to the table.

The woman smiles, "What can I getcha?"

Alexandra licks her lips. It has been too long since she and the others had a real meal.

Alexandra sighs, "We will have eleven bowls of stew, twelve pints of ale and one meal with no meat."

The woman nods and walks off. Everyone looks at Alexandra and she smiles at them. She knows what they are thinking.

Robin speaks up, "I really should not have ale."

Ayron looks at Robin, "Come on now. It is a special occasion."

Steph gives a puzzled look, "What is so special about it?"

Maluc chimes in with his usual joking manner, "We are still alive and that is pretty special to me."

Everyone at the tables laughs. The lady brings the ale and places a pint in front of each of them.

Ayron raises his cup, "A toast." Everyone raises their cups and Ayron continues, "To new friendships."

Everyone smiles and replies, "To new friendships."

They all take a drink and think about what has happened recently. Then, the woman brings the food out.

Alexandra questions the woman before she leaves, "Do you have six rooms open for the night?"

The woman nods, "Yes, I can hold them for you for three silver pieces."

Alexandra hands her three silver pieces, "Do the rooms come with a bath?"

The woman takes the coins, "Yes madam."

Alexandra nods, "Thank you."

Chaed puts down his cup of ale, "That was some pretty fancy sword fighting this morning Zak."

Alexandra speaks up, "I was impressed with Steph's staff. To fight a sword and not get any marks on your staff is incredible."

Steph smiles, "It was not all me. My staff is the Staff of Power. It was my fathers." She pauses, "You fight pretty good for who you are."

Alexandra smiles as she pictures her father, "My father insisted that I learn. This was my first real fight."

Chaed looks at Alexandra, "You did just fine."

Maluc puts down his ale, "Did everyone see their faces when Gaelin called down that lightning bolt." Maluc lets out a laugh, "They were so scared."

Everyone else laughs picturing the faces of the remaining bandits. The laughing dies down as they continue to eat and drink. Each of them feels so much better now. This night is exactly what they needed. Not just to relax, but to help bond with each other.

Then Zak speaks, "Did any of you see how fast Solur took out those bandits? I have never seen anyone move that fast. I have heard stories about the undead warriors, but they are all gone now. I wonder if he is a death knight."

Gaelin speaks calmly, "Actually, Solur is an undead warrior. He is the last."

Robin chimes in, still not able to believe what happened, "And he saved my life. I could not believe it."

Everyone is quiet as they think about Solur and what Robin just said. None of them want to say it, but they all think the same thing. They too can't believe Solur would save the life of an elf, especially a cleric. The talking continues as they share stories and finish eating.

Once the food and ale is gone, Alexandra speaks, "Robin and I will take a room. Zak and Steph will be in one and so will Chaed and Ayron. Sir Johna and Sir Marcus will share and so will Sir Cleef and Sir Braunt. Gaelin and Maluc will take the last room. We will leave at dawn."

The lady comes over and walks them upstairs to their rooms while everyone in the tavern watches them walk off. They each walk into their rooms and get ready for the night.

Solur continues to walk the streets of Callun. He watches all the humans, elves and dwarves having fun, drinking and talking. Solur pushes his way through the crowd and he winds up at the church. Solur stands at the bottom of the steps, looking up at all the stained glass artwork. He marvels at the beauty and detail of it.

Solur hears a male voice behind him, "Good evening."

Solur turns and sees a priest standing there. The priest is a little taller than Solur and is wearing purple robes.

Solur nods, "Good evening father."

The priest speaks, not able to tell he is talking to an undead, "Are you okay my son? You seem lost."

Solur replies calmly, "I am afraid what bothers me is something you cannot help with father."

The priest replies smoothly, "Confession can help anyone my son. It is good for the soul."

Solur smiles and chuckles slightly, "My soul is

beyond saving father."

Solur bows his head, turns and walks off down the street. The priest just stands and wonders what the person he was talking to meant.

The morning sun rises over Callun where the roads show the signs of the late partying with trash and people passed out everywhere. Solur is waiting for the others at the stables.

Chaed and Ayron are the first to walk up. They appear to be moving a little slower than usual, showing the after effects of the ale.

Solur smiles at them, "A little too much ale last night?"

Chaed holds up his left hand and shakes his head, "Not another word."

Gaelin and Maluc walk up next. They too appear to be feeling the effects of the ale. Zak and Step approach next, they also appear a little shaky. Sir Johna, Sir Marcus, Sir Cleef and Sir Braunt walk up next, and they appear no better off than the others.

They are all standing there for a minute when Chaed questions, "Where is Alexandra and Robin?"

Solur replies calmly, "They are getting the three horses we need."

Ayron looks at Solur, "You let them wander out there alone. Are you mad?"

Solur chuckles slightly, "Relax. They are just across the road. I can see them from here." He pauses, "You humans worry too much."

Zak retorts, "When you are dealing with the undead, you must worry."

Solur gives an evil smile, "Compared to what is out there, I am the least of your worries."

Everyone looks at Solur, not sure to make of what he is saying. It crosses each of their minds, is there something he is not telling them. About that time, Alexandra and Robin walk up with three horses.

Robin speaks, "That cost more than we could afford. We will have to watch our money now."

Alexandra nods, "Indeed." She looks at the rangers, "What is next?"

Steph replies, "We should reach the enchanted spring in three days, then the dark forest."

Chaed speaks up, "We will have to be extra careful. The enchanted spring is the end of our kingdom."

Alexandra nods, "We should be going."

The group mounts up on their horses. They all know Chaed is right. Once they pass the enchanted spring, they will no longer be on their land.

CHAPTER 4

THE GROUP CONTINUES TO RIDE as the forest starts to thin out and an opening appears ahead of them.

Zak speaks to the group, "It should be just ahead."

The group comes out of the forest into a majestic scene. The grass is so plush and emerald green. About half a mile to their left is a huge waterfall. The water crashes down upon numerous jagged rocks. The waterfall is somewhere around two hundred feet high. The water is the purest blue ever seen by the human eye.

The water runs into a massive lake that lies almost a quarter mile in front of them. The water in the lake is just as clear as the water from the waterfall. Small waves slowly move across the lake from the slight breeze that fills the air with the fresh smell of lilac and daisies. The lake moves into a small stream about a half mile to their right.

Alexandra speaks, captured by the scenery, "It is beautiful."

Robin points to the far bank, "Look."

Everyone looks across the lake to where Robin is pointing. They all see the incredibly beautiful, snow white unicorn on the far bank. The unicorn is drinking from the lake, completely unaware it is being watched.

A mile beyond the unicorn, the scene changes drastically. Another forest, but not like the one they were just in. The trees are large, but they appear to sag a little.

Few leafs line the trees as most of them seem to be dead or dying. A dark cloud hangs over the forest giving it an ominous feeling.

The group stares at the dark forest. It sends a shiver down Alexandra's spine. The only one that doesn't appear to be bothered by the site is Solur.

Zak speaks, "The dark forest."

The unicorn's head comes up quickly as if it heard something. At that time, a pack of five wolves run towards the unicorn from its right. The unicorn turns away from the wolves and runs for the forest. The unicorn gets about a hundred yards when a large rope net comes up from the ground in front of the unicorn. Before the unicorn can change direction, the net drops over the animal. Then, as if out of thin air, ten creatures run up to the unicorn. They each stand from 5'3" to 5'8" tall and are somewhat thin in build. Their skin is dark and their hair is silver. The only distinguishing feature they have are pointy ears, like an elf. Each one carries a short sword on their hip and a bow with arrows on their back.

Steph speaks disgustedly, "Drow elves."

The wolves run up and stop next to the drow elves.

Robin speaks, "We have to do something."

Alexandra looks at Gaelin, "Can you use your magic?"

Gaelin shakes his head slightly, "I can, but I will hit the unicorn as well."

The group watches helplessly as the drow elves drag the unicorn off into the dark forest.

Ayron speaks quite heatedly, "Robin is right. We have to do something."

Chaed chimes in, equally disgusted, "We can follow them to their camp and take the unicorn away from them."

Zak sighs, "They will be well into the forest by the time we get across the spring. I am not sure we will be able to track them. Drow elves are very tricky."

Gaelin speaks up, "I will be able to find the unicorn with one of my spells."

Alexandra nods, "Good, it is settled. Let us hurry."

The group makes its way towards the spring while the drow elves disappear further into the dark forest.

The group has been riding through the dark forest for a few miles now. The sun is nearly blocked by the gray clouds that hang over the ominous forest. The trees range from ten feet to near a hundred feet tall. Most of the underbrush is wilted and dead. An eerie smell hangs in the air.

Gaelin speaks with his eyes closed and a soft glow coming from the amulet of power, "Stop. It is just ahead, about half a mile."

Alexandra looks at Maluc, "Go check while we tie up the horses."

Maluc sighs and shakes his head while he climbs off his horse, "Of course." He hands the reigns to Solur, "Send the thief."

Everyone else dismounts and ties up the horses as Maluc disappears into the forest without a sound. He moves quickly, knowing his magical boots will keep him from being heard by anything or anyone. Maluc draws closer to a group of fallen trees and sees a soft glow coming from the other side. He slows down and makes his way up to the group of fallen trees that is nearly six feet high.

Maluc peeks over the top of the trees ever so cautiously and finds what he was looking for. He sees a fifty foot by fifty foot opening. The ten drow elves are sitting across the opening from him, unaware of Maluc's existence. There is a small campfire in the middle of the opening and the five wolves are lying around it. Thirty feet to the drow elves right is the unicorn tied up by a group of twenty foot tall trees.

Once Maluc has decided he has seen enough, he turns and heads back towards the group. After a short while, Maluc reaches the others.

Robin questions, "Did you see the unicorn?"

Maluc replies a little winded, "Yes. It is tied up by a group of trees not far from here. The ten drow elves and five wolves are there."

Alexandra nods, "Okay, take us there."

The group follows Maluc through the forest, being as quiet as possible. They all finally hear the drow elves talking and laughing ahead. Maluc and the others sneak up to the group of fallen trees.

Maluc whispers, "In the clearing on the other side of these trees."

The others slowly peek over the top of the trees to get a look at what they are dealing with. After a few seconds, they duck back behind the trees.

Robin whispers, "Any ideas?"

Zak sighs, "I am not sure. They have ten bows to watch for."

Gaelin whispers, "We should come at them from two different sides."

Chaed nods in agreement, "Ayron, Sir Cleef, Sir Braunt, Zak, Steph, Gaelin and Robin will stay here and cover us. Sir Johna, Sir Marcus, Maluc, Solur and I will sneak over to the unicorn."

Gaelin continues, "Once we draw their attention, you free the unicorn."

Alexandra looks at Chaed, "I am going with you."

Chaed protests, "My lady, it is far too dangerous. You should stay here."

Alexandra glares at Chaed, "I said that I am going."

Solur whispers, "We do not have time for this. Let her go."

Chaed concedes, "Stay close to me my lady."

Chaed draws his sword with his left hand and takes his shield in his right. Sir Johna and Sir Marcus draw their swords with their right hand and take their shields with their left. Maluc draws his daggers. Solur and Alexandra draw their swords with their right hand. Gaelin and Robin ready their staves while the others draw their bows.

Chaed and the others move around the opening as quietly as possible. As Ayron and the others move into position, Sir Braunt steps on a dead branch and it snaps, breaking the silence. The drow elves and the wolves come to life.

Zak yells, "Now!"

The drow elves move for cover behind the trees. Zak fires his bow and as the arrow leaves his bow, it turns into a bolt of lightning for Zak wields the Lightning Bow. The bolt hits one drow elf and blows him off his feet. Steph's first arrow is also on target and she hit's a drow elf in the neck. The last eight drow elves aim at Zak and the others and fire. Zak, Ayron and Steph duck just in time as the arrows miss. Gaelin and Robin also manage to duck to safety. Sir Cleef is hit in his left shoulder, but not too bad. One arrow whizzes by Sir Braunt's head. The wolves charge the group hiding behind the fallen trees.

Chaed whispers to the group around him, "Okay, we sneak in, free the unicorn and get out of here."

Chaed and the others move into the group of ten, twenty foot tall trees. Maluc starts towards the unicorn.

Solur suddenly stops, "Wait, something is wrong."

At that moment, the ten trees come to life around them. Chaed and the others look around in disbelief.

Chaed speaks sarcastically, "Is this what you mean?"

Solur ducks under one of the tree branches and brings his sword across and cuts the trunk of the tree. The tree swings again, but Solur moves away. Solur moves back in with blinding fashion and his deadly sword removes one of the tree branches.

Chaed blocks one branch with his shield and brings his sword around and cuts the tree deep across the trunk. A different branch comes down and hits Chaed in the back. Chaed stumbles forward, but quickly regains his balance.

Sir Johna ducks under a limb coming at him and his sword falls just shy of the tree trunk. Another limb comes around, but Sir Johna blocks with his shield and his sword comes across and removes the limb.

Sir Marcus steps in and cuts at the tree. A tree limb comes down and stops his arm. Another limb comes around and hits him in the right shoulder before he can move to block. Sir Marcus staggers away and quickly turns back to the tree.

Alexandra ducks under one branch, but another branch sweeps her feet out from under her. She quickly rolls left as a branch hits the ground where she was just at. She rolls again as another deadly branch narrowly misses. Before the tree can strike again, Solur steps over and nearly cuts the tree in two with a massive blow from his dragon sword. The tree reels and collapses to the ground.

Ayron pops out and fires his bow. The shot is true and hits a drow elf in the heart. Ayron ducks back as an arrow narrowly misses his head. Ayron grabs another arrow as he sees a wolf about ten feet away. The wolf leaps at him and is suddenly hit with a concussive blast of air. The wolf is thrown about twenty feet and hits the ground hard. The wolf never moves again. Ayron looks over and sees Robin staring at him. He nods to say thank you.

Sir Cleef fires his arrow and it hits a drow elf in the left shoulder. Sir Braunt follows with his arrow, but it is just off target and hits the tree next to the drow elf.

Gaelin watches as two wolves charge him. Ever calm, Gaelin brings his staff up and twirls it in front of him. The wolves start to close, but Gaelin's expression never changes. He stops spinning the staff, but a circle of air continues to spin in front of him. Gaelin grabs the amulet of power with his left hand and slams his staff on the ground. The ring of air turns into a ring of fire. Gaelin points his staff and the large ring of fire launches towards the two wolves. The ring of fire hits the wolves, turns them to ash and keeps going. It finally stops when it hits a drow elf and turns it to ash as well.

Zak fires again and his shot hits a drow elf in the chest, killing it. Steph fires again, but her shot narrowly misses the target. Ayron fires again, but he too misses.

Chaed blocks the tree branch with his shield, steps in and drives his sword deep into the heart of the tree. He pulls his sword out and the tree staggers away, only to fall a few feet away. He looks right and sees a drow elf aiming at Alexandra. Chaed runs for her and brings his shield around her as the arrow flies in. The shield arrives just in time to deflect the arrow away from the Princess.

Sir Braunt fires his arrow and this time it is on target. It hits the drow elf that just fired at Alexandra in the neck.

Sir Johna steps in and knocks a limb aside with his shield and cuts across with his sword. His sword cuts the tree deep and he quickly reverses his swing and the second cut is even deeper than the first. Sir Johna steps out of the way as the tree falls.

Alexandra ducks under a branch coming at her and her sword comes across and removes the branch. She steps in and drives her sword into the trunk of the tree. She pulls her sword out and spins away from another branch. This time she cuts in and scores the killing blow to stop the tree.

Maluc cuts the ropes holding the unicorn and the unicorn runs off into the forest. Maluc turns in time to see a tree limb coming at him. He spins under the limb and drives both fire daggers into the trunk of the tree. A second limb comes down and hits him in the left shoulder, knocking him back. Maluc does a front roll at the tree, comes up to his feet and drives his magical daggers in again. This time the tree's reaction is simply to fall.

Sir Marcus ducks under one limb and blocks the follow up limb with his shield. His sword moves quickly, removing the second limb. The tree moves in again, but this time once Sir Marcus blocks with his shield, his sword cuts deep across the tree's trunk. Before the tree can react, Sir Marcus drives his sword in again and it pierces deep into the tree. When he removes his sword, the tree sways side to side and then falls.

Steph hears the ground crunching behind her. She spins quickly, catching sight of a wolf leaping in at her. She lets her arrow fly and it hits the wolf in the chest. The wolf hits the ground next to her, dead.

The last wolf leaps at Robin. Robin ducks as the wolf flies over her and lands on the ground, turning quickly for another strike. Robin turns and points her staff at a nearby tree and waves her hand. The wolf leaps again and in midair, a tree branch comes to life and drives into the side of the wolf, stopping it in the air.

Ayron pops out and lets another deadly arrow fly. It finds a drow elf not able to duck to safety and the arrow ends another life. The remaining three drow elves look around and realize that they stand no chance against whoever it is attacking them. They decide it is better to fight another day and they run off into the forest.

Zak steps out and fires at one of the trees. The lightning arrow hits the tree solid and the tree reels back. Before the tree can recover, Gaelin raises his staff towards the sky and slams it to the ground with his right hand as he points at the tree with his left. A lightning bolt comes out of the sky as if answering Gaelin's call and hits the tree. The tree explodes into pieces from the powerful magic.

Solur ducks under a limb and steps back. He hears another tree moving behind him. Solur steps forward, drawing his dagger with his left hand. His dagger comes across and blocks a tree limb as his sword cuts deep across the tree. He continues into his spin and drops to his right knee. He drops just under another branch and thrusts his sword home into a second tree. The second tree staggers away a short distance before falling. Without getting up from his knee, Solur brings his dagger up behind his head and stops a limb just inches from his head. While doing so, Solur flips his sword over in his hand, catching it blade down and thrusts it back into the tree behind him.

Solur removes his sword and slowly stands. He calmly steps to his right as the tree falls, just missing him. Solur looks back left and watches as Chaed delivers a massive blow, cutting down the last living tree.

With the battle now over, everyone makes their way into the opening. Their faces show the weary look of battle. Sweat drips from their bodies as they slowly catch their breath and take measure of what has happened.

Ayron walks over to Sir Cleef, "Are you alright?"

Sir Cleef nods with the arrow still in his shoulder, "I am okay."

Gaelin speaks up, "The arrow needs to be removed."

Chaed walks over to Sir Cleef, "Are you ready?"

Sir Cleef gives a quick nod as Chaed grabs the arrow. With a sudden yank, the arrow slides out of Sir Cleef's shoulder and blood starts to run. Sir Cleef grits his teeth as Chaed steps aside and Robin walks up to him.

Robin smiles, "Hold still."

She closes her eyes and mutters under her breath while holding her staff in her left hand. She places her right hand on the wound and a soft golden glow emanates from her hand. A couple seconds later, the glow is gone and Robin removes her hand. The wound has sealed and the blood has stopped.

Sir Cleef smiles at Robin, "Thank you."

Robin bows her head, "Anytime."

Maluc chimes in with his usual wit, "Well, that was not so bad."

The others look at him like he has lost his mind.

Maluc smiles, "What?"

Steph speaks up, "Is the unicorn safe?"

Maluc nods, "I cut it free and it ran off into the forest. I do not know if you can call anything safe in this forest though."

The others chuckle at Maluc, but deep inside, they each know that what he said is true. There are much worse creatures in the forest than drow elves.

Zak speaks, "We should get back to our horses. We still have a good three days ride in the dark forest."

Alexandra nods, "I agree."

Solur puts his hand on Maluc's shoulder, "I think I am beginning to like you."

Solur walks off and Maluc smiles, "How comforting."

The start off into the forest for their horses.

―――――――

The group continues down the narrowing trail as the sun reaches its peak in the sky. They reach a fork in the road and Zak and Steph stop. Everyone stops behind them. Everyone can tell that they are debating over which way to go.

Alexandra finally speaks, "Which way?"

Zak looks back at the group, "Both roads will lead us to Whitefeather. I say we go left because it is shorter."

Steph chimes in, "The right may be longer, but it is safer. The left takes up through the Swamp of Despair."

Alexandra questions, "How much longer is the right

road?"

Steph replies, "At least seven days."

Gaelin speaks up, "Those are extra days we cannot afford."

Zak chimes up, "We can take the left road and be in the swamp in two days. Then it is only a few days to Whitefeather."

Maluc decides to add his thoughts, "The Swamp of Despair is nothing to mess with. Bad things live in the swamp."

Alexandra sighs, "It does not matter. Gaelin is right, we cannot afford extra days, even if it means more danger."

Robin becomes the voice of reason, "Either way, it is getting late now. We need to find a place to camp."

Zak starts down the left trail and Steph reluctantly follows. Everyone else falls in behind the two rangers. They all think the same thing. It can't be good if they even considered going around the swamp. The group rides for another couple of miles as the sun gets lower in the sky.

Zak points left, "We can camp in that clearing over there."

Alexandra stops and dismounts, "It will do fine."

The others dismount and they walk their horses over to the clearing. Each person ties up their horse. Everyone except Solur grabs their bedroll and some food and walks over to the clearing. Solur stands next to the horses, watching over the camp.

Everyone lays out their bedrolls and sits down. They start eating quietly. Each one thinking of what has happened so far on the journey. Robin can tell that Alexandra is in deep thought.

Robin looks at Alexandra, "Your worried about your father."

Alexandra nods with a solemn look, "Yes. I just hope

he holds on long enough for us to return with the root." She pauses, "That is if we even make it."

Chaed speaks up, "Your father, the King, is a strong man. He will hold on as long as it takes."

Sir Braunt adds, "We have made it this far and it has not been that difficult."

Zak speaks up, "It has been easy so far, but we have yet to see the worse this land has to offer. There are creatures out there that you cannot imagine."

Sir Marcus chimes in, "It does not matter. We work well together."

Gaelin stands, "Yes, together." He holds up his staff and a soft light appears at the end, "Together is what is important. For these lands show no mercy and it devours the weak and broken. We may come from different lives, but there is a bond that holds us together. We must depend on each other if we are going to see it through."

Everyone listens intently as Gaelin continues, "Where else would you see a ranger fight along side the King's men. And a cleric stand with an undead, it is unheard of, but we must, for if this circle breaks, the land will devour us as well. Yes, together we can accomplish anything."

Gaelin puts out the light and sits back down. They are all quiet, taking in what the wizard said about staying together.

Alexandra sighs, "I cannot thank you all enough for what you have done, but I must ask one thing. Give me your word that if something happens to me, you will see this through to the end."

Chaed gets to his right knee and places his right fist to his heart, "On my life, I swear it."

Sir Johna and Sir Marcus follow suit, "We swear it my lady."

Ayron speaks next, "I swear it."

Sir Cleef and Sir Braunt chime in, "As do we, we

swear."

Gaelin is next, "I swear it."

Robin speaks up, "I swear it."

Steph is next, "I swear it as well."

Zak chimes right in, "I swear."

Maluc has grown to like those he has traveled with, "I have always been on my own because it is hard to find someone who accepts a thief. However, all of you have welcomed me as if I was one of your own." He takes a breath, "You are the only family I have ever had. I swear it."

Solur watches intently. He has grown to respect these humans and the elf. He knows the horrors that they will face on the Island of the Dead.

Everyone looks at Solur and Alexandra speaks, "What about you Solur?"

Solur takes a couple steps forward, "I have never seen a bond so strong. One thing is certain, not everyone who sits here will make it to the Island of the Dead and not everyone will leave the Island of the Dead as well. But if I am the last one, I will see this through to the end."

Solur turns and walks off as everyone remains quiet. They reflect on what Solur said and they know it is true, eventually someone will die. They each wonder who it will be.

Its mid-afternoon in the Dark Forest as the group has been riding all day. The long road has taken its toll as the faces show the signs of fatigue.

Steph speaks up, "We need to find some water for the horses."

Zak replies, "There should be a pond up around the bend."

The group rides another mile and they see a break in

the trees off to their right. About two hundred feet into the forest is a pond. Everyone stops and dismounts. They walk their horses over to the pond. The water isn't very clear and an awful odor hangs in the air. The horses don't seem to mind as they start to drink from the pond. Then, they all hear movement in the trees around them.

Chaed grabs his shield from his horse, "What was that?"

Robin walks over by Chaed, "I am not sure."

Then, more moving noises behind them and Steph grabs her staff.

Steph walks over by Gaelin, "It sounds big, whatever it is."

More sounds appear off to their right and then some off to the left. Sir Johna walks over by Sir Braunt, while Sir Marcus stands by Sir Cleef. Everyone continues to look around, trying to figure out the strange noises that are all around them.

Solur speaks up, "There is more than a few things out there."

Suddenly, a six foot long double bladed battle axe comes swinging around from behind a tree and hits Sir Braunt square in the chest. The impact is incredible as Sir Braunt is knocked to the ground and blood flies everywhere. Sir Johna moves over by Sir Braunt while everyone looks over and sees an eight foot tall minotaur step out from behind the tree. The minotaur has the legs of a goat, the body of a man and the head of a bull. It is very muscular looking with two horns extending out from it's head.

Before anyone can move, another battle axe comes around at Alexandra. Maluc pushes her to safety and dives away from the deadly axe. Another minotaur appears from behind a tree near Maluc.

Gaelin and Steph start towards Alexandra and Maluc when they stop suddenly as a large war hammer hits the ground in front of them. Ayron grabs his bow and aims at the third minotaur when he hears large footsteps coming at him. Zak pulls Ayron out of the way as another war hammer crashes in from the fourth minotaur.

Sir Marcus and Sir Cleef move towards Sir Johna when a minotaur steps out in front of them. The battle axe starts towards them. Sir Marcus brings his shield up and the battle axe knocks him back a few feet.

Solur looks over as the minotaur moves for Sir Johna who is standing alone by Sir Braunt's body. Solur moves quick to get to Sir Johna. Chaed and Robin turn around as they hear footsteps behind them from the last minotaur. The battle axe comes straight at them with incredible force. Chaed brings his shield up at the last second and blocks the axe, but the impact knocks him to the ground.

Alexandra looks up at the large creature in front of her. The minotaur swings it's axe down at Alexandra. She spins left as the axe narrowly misses. She brings her sword around, but the minotaur is too far away. Maluc quickly dives forward and his dagger cuts the minotaur on the left leg. Maluc rolls to his feet as the axe comes at him. Maluc ducks as the axe just misses taking his head off.

Chaed looks up and sees the minotaur raising his axe. Robin taps her staff on the ground and vines crawl out of the ground and start to entangle the minotaur's body. Chaed starts to scramble to his feet. The magical vines are not strong enough to hold and the minotaur rips free from them. The minotaur brings its axe down and Chaed brings his shield up and stops the deadly axe. This time Chaed holds his ground and cuts in with his sword. He manages to cut the minotaur on his stomach.

Gaelin and Steph square off with the minotaur in front of them. Gaelin points his staff at the monster and a golden arrow flies from his staff and hits the minotaur in the right shoulder. The creature takes a step back as Steph closes in. The minotaur swings his hammer at Steph, but she ducks under the hammer and her staff slams into the minotaur's ribs with a loud cracking sound. The minotaur staggers back a few feet.

Sir Cleef draws his bow quickly and lets his arrow fly. It zips in and buries itself in the minotaur's left shoulder. Sir Marcus closes in quickly and cuts in with his sword. The minotaur blocks the sword with his axe and pushes Sir Marcus away.

Sir Johna ducks as the minotaur's axe cuts at him. He tries to get his balance back, but the minotaur's size keeps the creature close. The axe comes in again and this time Sir Johna brings his shield up to block. The powerful blow knocks Sir Johna to his knee. The minotaur readies to strike again when a dagger comes flying in and hits the minotaur in the chest. Solur runs up and cuts the creature on the left side of the stomach with his sword. Sir Johna seizes the opportunity and gets back to his feet.

Maluc ducks under the axe and spins close to the minotaur. He cuts in with his fire daggers, but he is still too far away as he misses. Maluc moves away from the creature and the minotaur turns to Maluc, losing sight of Alexandra. Maluc jumps back away from the axe as Alexandra steps up and cuts the minotaur deep across the lower back. The minotaur spins with get speed and brings it's deadly axe around. Alexandra brings her sword up and manages to stop the axe, but she is knocked to the ground from the massive blow. The minotaur raises his axe when Maluc throws the fire dagger in his left hand and it hits the minotaur in the back, right between the shoulder blades. The minotaur stops and turns slowly towards Maluc. Maluc throws his second dagger and it hits the minotaur in the neck. The minotaur reels back. Then, Alexandra thrusts her sword into the minotaur's side. Once she removes her blood covered sword, the minotaur drops to it's knees and then falls face down on the ground.

Robin points her staff at the minotaur and a golden arrow flies in and hits the minotaur in the stomach. Chaed quickly follows with his sword, but the minotaur brings his axe down and stops Chaed's sword. Chaed brings his shield across and knocks away the axe. The minotaur brings his axe around, but not before Chaed thrusts in with his sword. The sword drives into the minotaur's chest. The minotaur staggers back as another golden arrow files in and hits the minotaur in the left shoulder. The minotaur brings his axe down at Chaed, but Chaed deflects the axe away and cuts in with his sword. This time his blade finds the creature's throat. Blood flies as the minotaur falls at Chaed's feet.

Steph moves in under the minotaur's hammer and jabs the creature in the stomach with her staff. The minotaur brings his hammer down at Steph, but she spins away and her staff comes around and cracks into the minotaur's right knee. Steph backs away a few feet as the minotaur staggers back. Gaelin calls forth another golden arrow and it scores a hit to the minotaur's chest. Steph runs at the minotaur and plants her staff into the ground like a pole vault. She propels herself into the air and kicks the minotaur in the chest. The blow knocks the minotaur to it's back. Steph lands on the creature's chest and brings her staff overhead and down at the minotaur. Her magical staff slams into the creature's head, splitting it's skull.

Sir Marcus charges at the minotaur and cuts in with his sword. The minotaur blocks the sword with it's axe. The minotaur brings it's axe around at Sir Marcus. Sir Marcus brings his shield up and stops the axe. Then, Sir Cleef lets another arrow fly and it hits the minotaur in the neck. The minotaur reels back and Sir Marcus seizes the opening. He cuts in with his sword again and this time draws blood across the minotaur's chest. The minotaur raises his axe up and Sir Marcus steps to the side as another arrow zips in. The arrow hits the minotaur in the right bicep. The axe comes down, but Sir Marcus is not there and before the minotaur can move again, Sir Marcus buries his sword into the minotaur's exposed lower back. Sir Marcus removes his sword and the minotaur falls to his knees. Sir Marcus cuts the creature again across the back as it falls to the ground.

Sir Johna moves in and cuts at the minotaur. The minotaur blocks with his axe, but before it can counter, Solur cuts the creature on the left ribs with his sword. Solur spins away as the minotaur turns towards him and Sir Johna steps in and cuts the minotaur's exposed back. The minotaur turns quick, but Sir Johna has moved away and Solur stabs his sword into the minotaur's lower back. He pulls his sword out and ducks under the axe as the minotaur spins around. Solur brings his magical sword across and takes the minotaur's left leg off at the knee. The minotaur starts to fall and Sir Johna catches the creature on the way down and nearly removes it's head with his sword. The minotaur falls face first.

Zak ducks away from the hammer and spins into the minotaur. His sword cuts the minotaur's left side. As the minotaur starts to turn, Ayron lets his arrow fly. The arrow zips in and hits the minotaur in the left eye. The minotaur reels back and Zak cuts the creature deep across the stomach. He quickly reverses his swing and cuts the creature across the chest. Another arrow zips over Zak's shoulder and buries itself in the minotaur's neck. The creature drops to it's knees. Zak thrusts his sword in, piercing the minotaur's heart. He withdraws his sword as the creature falls.

Maluc retrieves his daggers and Solur retrieves his. Everyone tries to catch their breath when they see that Sir Braunt is still on the ground with a pool of blood under him.

Chaed and Ayron run over to Sir Braunt. They see

the deep gash in his chest from the axe. His face already looks pale. Alexandra and Robin rush to his side as the others stand around them.

Alexandra looks at Robin, "Is there anything you can do?"

Robin kneels next to Sir Braunt. She places her right hand across his eyes and closes her eyes. She takes a deep breath. Seconds pass as everyone waits to see what will happen. Alexandra notices a tear roll down Robin's face.

Robin opens her eyes, "It is too late. He is already gone."

Alexandra closes her eyes and tries to hold back the tears. Everyone is quiet, not wanting to believe what Robin just said. Solur looks around and notices that the horses have run off into the woods a little ways.

Solur speaks calmly, "We need to get the horses and get out of here. There could be more."

Chaed speaks solemnly, "We need to bury Sir Braunt."

Solur shakes his head, "We do not have time."

Chaed looks up at Solur with anger in his eyes, "We cannot just leave him like this. If we do not bury him now, then we will take him with us."

Solur locks eyes with Chaed, "No. Pulling a horse with his body will slow us down. We must leave him."

Chaed stands and grabs the handle of his sword, "Do not test me!"

Zak stands up, "We do not have time for this. I am afraid Solur is right. We have to go."

Ayron looks at Zak, "We are not leaving him like this."

Alexandra finally speaks, fighting off the tears, "That is exactly what we must do." She looks at the others, "Get your horses. We are leaving."

Chaed looks at Alexandra, "My lady. He gave his life for the King, we cannot leave him like this."

Alexandra stands up, "We can and we must. Sir Braunt's sacrifice will not be forgotten, but we do not have the time to spare. He would understand. Now, get the horses."

Solur walks off. Maluc follows and then the others follow, one by one. They gather up their horses and get back on the trail. They mount up and look back at Sir Braunt's lifeless body.

Chaed looks back as the others ride off, "We will miss you my friend."

The group rides off into the dark forest, each thinking about the loss of Sir Braunt.

CHAPTER 5

AN OLDER WOMAN WITH GRAY RAGGED HAIR, a wrinkled and dirty face and gnarled, green and brown stained teeth sits up in an old rickety wooden bed inside her home, a large hollowed out dead tree in the swamp. The woman looks to be in her later years and wears old rags with nothing on her feet.

The woman speaks in a cackling voice, "Could it be?"

She gets out of the bed and walks over to a small wooden table with a crystal ball in the middle of the table. She pulls a small, one foot long crooked wand from her clothes and waves it over the crystal ball. The crystal ball gets smoky, but after a few seconds, Gaelin's image appears in the crystal ball.

The woman's eye widen, "It is. The amulet of power is in the swamp. I must have it."

She waves her wand over the crystal ball again and the scene gets further away to reveal the rest of the group and their surroundings.

The woman speaks again, "The southern trail."

She looks over to the door. There is a six foot tall, green scaled lizard man standing there. He has fierce yellow eyes and razor sharp teeth. The lizard man is wearing leather armor and is carrying a medium sword on his hip.

The woman continues, "Gather the others and get the

monster. We are leaving."

The Swamp of Despair, one place that is not for the weak of heart. A gloomy haze hangs over the bubbling swamp water that runs up to the weeded trail. Dead trees and weeping willow trees cover the landscape. Swamp moss hangs off everything leaving a smell of rotten death in the air.

Gaelin stops his horse and glances around. The others notice that Gaelin is on to something and they stop.

Robin looks at Gaelin, "What is it?"

Gaelin replies while looking around, "We are being watched."

The words startle the others as they start glancing around to see if they can see anything unusual. The others seem a little tense about not being able to find anything.

Ayron speaks a little apprehensive, "I do not see anything."

Gaelin replies, "Whatever it is, it is using magic to look at us."

That news makes the tension rise even more throughout the group. Dealing with something magical is not what they are wanting right now.

Steph keeps glancing around, "The Swamp Queen."

Zak shakes his head, "Those are just stories. No one has ever seen the Swamp Queen."

The news about a magical creature known as the Swamp Queen pushes the group over their limit.

Alexandra questions a little fearfully, "Who is the Swamp Queen?"

Steph replies nervously, "Legend has it that a powerful witch was banished to the Swamp of Despair. She captures and eats anyone that travels through the swamp to help her stay alive."

Maluc looks at Steph with eyes wide, "And you are just telling us this now. Good timing."

Zak speaks reassuringly, "As I said, those are just stories. No one has ever seen the Swamp Queen."

Maluc retorts, "They were probably eaten."

Chaed speaks up, "It is too late to worry about it now."

Solur decides to speak, noticing everyone's tension, "Why not stop here and rest the horses."

Alexandra shakily nods, "Good idea, we could use some food as well."

Alexandra dismounts and walks her horse over to a tree. Her eyes continue to scan the area. She ties her horse up and grabs some fruit. The others follow suit. Solur can tell the others are bothered by the Swamp Queen news.

Solur speaks to the group calmly, "Relax. If the Swamp Queen is real, she will come for us soon enough. Being nervous will not help."

Sir Johna looks at Solur, "You should have no worries. She probably does not like the taste of the undead."

Solur smiles at Sir Johna, "Not many do."

Sir Marcus looks at Steph, "So, how old is the legend?"

Steph shrugs, "I am not real sure. It is old."

Solur sheds some light on the subject, "About a hundred years ago, a powerful witch named Zeemich wandered the lands, taking any magical artifacts she could get her hands on. One day she was captured by a powerful wizard and banished."

Robin questions a little disbelieving, "How do you know that?"

Solur sighs, "I have been around awhile."

Chaed questions, "Just how old are you?"

Solur just looks at the others without saying anything. He is not ready to share that much with them.

Alexandra can't stay still, "Lets walk our horses for awhile."

Everyone retrieves their horse and they walk off down the trail. Eyes are scanning everywhere and every little sound catches everyone's attention.

———————

The group has walked a couple of miles without a word being spoken. They are all focused on the surroundings, wanting to be able to spot anything that might come for them right away, and then hoping nothing comes at all.

Zak whispers, "Listen." He stops, "Did you hear that?"

The others stop and listen intently.

Maluc whispers, "I do not hear a thing."

They continue to listen, then a feint gurgle sound comes from the swamp water.

Chaed questions, "What is that?"

Solur looks around, "It sounds like something is breathing under the water, but I cannot tell exactly where."

Then, Robin's eyes widen as she points down the trail in front of them, "Look."

The others almost try not to look. They know it can't be good. Then, one by one they look to where Robin is pointing and they see the old woman. She is about two hundred feet up the trail, just watching them with the most evil look on her face.

Steph glares at Zak, "The Swamp Queen."

Zak shrugs, "So I was wrong."

At that time, from the left side of the trail about a hundred feet ahead, lizard men start to emerge from the swamp. The group watches as one after another walks out of the swamp water, each wearing leather armor, fifty in all. Forty five of them are carrying swords while the last five are carrying a bow with arrows.

Chaed grasps his shield and draws his sword, "Good. I was getting bored."

Maluc draws his daggers, "I was just fine."

Ayron, Steph and Sir Cleef grab their bows. Sir Johna and Sir Marcus grab their shields and draw their swords. Alexandra draws her sword. Solur and Zak both draw their sword and dagger while Gaelin and Robin ready their staves.

Solur smiles under his hood, "I think I am starting to like Chaed as well."

Maluc shakes his head, "You are all crazy."

Chaed replies confidently, "This is nothing. Sir Johna, Sir Marcus, Zak, Solur and I can handle the lizard men."

Then, across the trail from the lizard men emerges a twenty foot long, green scaled lizard with a three foot horn on it's nose and razor sharp. Walking on all fours, it still stands four feet tall with foot long claws.

Maluc looks at Chaed, "You were saying."

Chaed replies a little less confidently, "Okay. I did not count that one."

Solur speaks up, "A basilisk. You must not look at it. It's gaze can kill you or at least petrify you."

Alexandra replies nervously, "Then how do we kill it?"

Solur starts towards the basilisk, "You take the lizard men. I will handle the basilisk."

Chaed, Sir Johna, Sir Cleef, Zak, Maluc and Alexandra run for the lizard men.

Robin looks at Gaelin, "I will take the Swamp Queen."

Gaelin nods, "I will help Solur with the basilisk."

Ayron draws back his bow and lets his arrow fly. It zips over Chaed's shoulder so close that Chaed hears the arrow cutting the wind as the arrow continues on to it's target. The arrow hit's a lizard man in the chest and the lizard man falls. Steph and Sir Cleef both fire an arrow at the rushing army. Both arrows find their target as two more lizard men fall.

Chaed rams his shield into a lizard man and knocks the creature down. He thrusts his sword down into the creature, killing it. He quickly withdraws his sword and uses it to block a sword coming at him. Chaed throws his left shoulder in, pushing the lizard man away. A split second later, an arrow from Ayron flies in and hits the lizard man in the neck. Chaed turns right and blocks another sword with his shield. At the same time, he brings his sword across and nearly cuts the lizard man in half as green blood flies everywhere. Chaed steps back and raises up his shield and two arrows from the lizard men bounce off it.

Gaelin calls down a bolt of lightning as Solur rushes towards the basilisk. The lightning bolt just bounces off the large creature.

Gaelin speaks to Robin, "She has protected it from magic."

Solur locks eyes with the basilisk, but nothing happens to him for the undead is immune to the creatures power. The basilisk brings it's horn around at Solur. Solur leaps over the creature and lands on the far side of it's head. He brings his sword down and cuts it on the side of the head. The basilisk's tail whips around like lightning and slams into Solur's right side sending him ten feet across the ground. Solur shakes his head as the basilisk closes in and brings it's horn at Solur again. Solur dives forward and rolls to safety.

Robin launches a magical arrow at the Swamp Queen. The Swamp Queen twirls her wand in a small circle and the arrow flies off into the swamp. The Swamp Queen points her wand at Robin and releases a small two foot bolt of ice at Robin. Robin spins her staff in front of herself very quickly. When the ice bolt reaches Robin's staff, it disappears. Robin stops spinning her staff and taps it on the ground. Vines rise up at the Swamp Queen's feet and start to entangle her body. Without panic, the Swamp Queen simply taps the vines with her wand and they shrivel up.

This time the Swamp Queen raises her wand and a ball of fire about the size of a basketball flies at Robin. Robin starts spinning her staff again, but this time the Swamp Queen was more clever. The fireball hits the ground near Robin's feet and explodes. The blast knocks Robin back and to the ground. The Swamp Queen waves her wand counter-clockwise and vines come up from under Robin and start to entangle her body.

As Zak nears the lizard men, he moves left, knowing the woman he loves all too well. Steph's arrow flies by as Zak moves and hits a lizard man in the eye. Zak blocks a sword with his own and kicks the lizard man away. He turns left and ducks under another sword. Zak brings his sword across and cuts the lizard man mortally across the chest. He spins back around and blocks out the lizard man's sword again. He brings his sword across and cuts the lizard man across the chest. Zak reverses his cut quickly and cuts the lizard man's throat.

Sir Marcus ducks under a sword and cuts the lizard man on the right leg. He brings his shield up and blocks another sword. Sir Marcus pushes the second lizard man back and turns back to the first. He brings his sword up and blocks the lizard man's sword. Sir Marcus brings his shield across into the side of the lizard man's head, gashing it open as green blood splatters all over the shield. Sir Marcus turns back just in time to block the second lizard man's sword with his own. Sir Marcus counters off the block and cuts the creature on the left arm. The lizard man thrusts in at Sir Marcus. Sir Marcus brings his shield across and knocks the sword away as he returns the thrust. Sir Marcus buries his sword into the lizard man's chest, bringing the creature to his end.

Sir Johna brings his shield up as he runs towards the lizard men. An arrow meant for his chest bounces harmlessly away. He continues his charge right into the lizard men. He knocks down one as another swings at him. Sir Johna blocks the sword with his own and pushes the creature back. As the other lizard man starts to get up, Sir Johna kicks the creature in the chest, knocking it back to the ground. Sir Johna quickly follows with a downward thrust, piercing the lizard man's heart. He withdraws his sword and turns in time to block the other sword with his shield. Sir Johna brings his sword around, but the lizard man blocks with it's sword. The lizard man counters, but Sir Johna was ready. Sir Johna brings his shield across and knocks the sword away. He continues to spin in a circle and removes the creatures head as a fountain of green blood spouts into the air.

Maluc ducks under a sword and drives his dagger into the lizard man's chest. He withdraws his dagger and turns left to see a sword cutting down at him. Maluc raises his daggers up and crosses them into an "X" above his head. He stops the sword and kicks the lizard man between the legs. He twirls both daggers in his hands and takes them blade down. Maluc drives the daggers down into each side of the lizard man's neck. He withdraws his daggers and catches another lizard man out of the corner of his eye. Maluc spins away, but the lizard man's sword cuts his right arm. Suddenly, another arrow from Ayron zings by and hits the lizard man in the heart.

Solur closes in on the basilisk again. He ducks under the tail and swings his sword, but comes up short. Then, an arrow from one of the lizard men with a bow, comes flying in. Solur brings his sword across with blinding speed, cutting the arrow out of the air, but in doing so, the basilisk brings it's horn around and drives it through Solur's left thigh. Solur yells in some pain and mostly anger. With the horn still in his leg, Solur drives his dagger into the basilisk's right eye. Before the basilisk can move, Solur withdraws the dagger, brings his sword across with incredible anger and cuts off the basilisk's horn. The basilisk reels away in pain as Solur hobbles back with the horn still in his leg. At that moment, the Swamp Queen fires an ice bolt and it hits Solur square in the chest, knocking him back ten feet to the ground.

Alexandra blocks a sword from overhead. She brings her sword down and cuts the lizard man across the chest. She follows it up by thrusting her sword into the creature's chest. Alexandra withdraws her sword and brings it around at another lizard man, but the lizard man blocks with it's sword. The lizard man pushes Alexandra back. The moment she steps back, an arrow from Sir Cleef flies in and hits the lizard man in the throat. Alexandra turns quick and ducks under another sword. She drives her sword into the lizard man's stomach. When she withdraws her sword, an arrow from a lizard man flies in and hits Alexandra in the right thigh. Alexandra cries out in pain.

Chaed looks over and screams in anger, "My lady!"

With incredible anger coursing through his blood, Chaed runs for Alexandra. He pushes his way through the battle raging on around him. Chaed reaches Alexandra in time to stop a sword coming at her with his sword. Chaed brings his sword across and the lizard man's head goes flying off into the swamp. Chaed hears something behind him and spins around. Chaed's sword cuts in with great force. The lizard man tries to block, but the impact from Chaed's sword drives the lizard man's sword into it's chest. Then Chaed turns left and brings his shield up to block another sword. Chaed cuts his sword across, but the lizard man blocks. Chaed withdraws and cuts in from another angle and again the lizard man blocks. This time Chaed brings his shield across and knocks the lizard man's sword away. Chaed steps in with his sword and drives it through the lizard man's sternum.

Gaelin turns his attention to the lizard man that fired the arrow at Alexandra. The lizard man starts to aim another arrow. Gaelin points his left hand at the lizard man and slams his staff on the ground. A bolt of lightning comes out of the sky and hits the lizard man in the chest. The lizard man flies back about six feet and crashes to the ground.

Ayron takes aim at one of the lizard men with a bow. As he aims in, a lizard man with a sword breaks free from the battle and charges at Ayron. Ayron stands firm, aims, and draws back his bow as the lizard man gets closer. The arrow is gone and it hits the lizard man with the bow in the forehead. Ayron's hand moves fast and draws another arrow out of his quiver as the lizard man closes to thirty feet. Ayron draws back the bow and brings his aim on the lizard man, now twenty feet away. Ayron lets the arrow fly. It hits the creature in the chest and the lizard man falls a mere ten feet away.

Steph takes aim at a lizard man with a bow. She lets her arrow fly. The arrow is on target and the lizard man falls. Steph reaches for another arrow as a lizard man rushes at her. Steph pulls the arrow out as the lizard man is now on top of her. The lizard man cuts at her head with his sword. Steph ducks under the sword and rams the arrow in her hand into the lizard man's neck. She removes the arrow, puts it on her bow and fires it at another lizard man. The arrow pierces the lizard man's left eye, killing it.

Sir Cleef draws back his bow and aims into the crowd of lizard men. He lets his arrow fly and it hits a lizard man in the left shoulder. The lizard man turns his attention to Sir Cleef and rushes at him. Sir Cleef calmly, but quickly draws another arrow from his quiver. He aims again as the lizard man gets even closer. He lets the arrow fly and this time it hits the lizard man in the sternum, taking the creature off it's feet.

Sir Johna and Sir Marcus move over next to Chaed and they form a triangle around Alexandra.

Zak ducks under a sword and cuts across with his sword. He draws green blood from the lizard man's stomach. Zak reverses his cut and comes back across, but the lizard man blocks with his sword. However, Zak drives his dagger in and it pierces the lizard man's throat. Zak withdraws his dagger as another lizard man thrusts in. Zak spins around the sword and thrusts his sword into a different lizard man which was standing behind the first. The other lizard man turns back to Zak when an arrow flies in from Steph, hitting the creature in the heart and killing it.

Sir Marcus blocks one sword with his shield and another with his sword. He pushes the lizard man on his left back with his shield as the other lizard man swings again. Sir Marcus brings his shield across and knocks the sword away and thrusts his sword into the lizard man's stomach. He withdraws his sword and turns, but too late. The other lizard man's sword hits Sir Marcus in the back of his left shoulder. Sir Marcus brings his sword around and the lizard man moves to block. Sir Marcus withdraws his sword before the block and thrusts in behind the lizard man's sword. The sword enters the creatures chest, killing it.

Sir Johna cuts in at a lizard man, but the creature blocks. Sir Johna sees another lizard man moving on him from the corner of his left eye. He ducks as another sword comes at his head. The sword, instead of taking Sir Johna's head off, takes off the fellow lizard man's head. Before the lizard man can recover, Sir Johna thrusts his sword into the creature's stomach. He quickly withdraws his sword and cuts the dying creature across it's chest as it falls.

Sir Cleef takes aim and lets another arrow fly. It zips in ever so close to Maluc and hits a lizard man in the cheek.

Chaed thrusts his sword into the heart of one lizard man as another approaches from behind. He withdraws his sword, flips it over in his hand taking it blade down and drives it back into the lizard man behind him. As that lizard man falls, Chaed brings his sword around and takes a third lizard man's head off.

Solur gets to his feet and limps towards the basilisk. The basilisk brings it's tail around, but Solur ducks and cuts the tail deep with his sword. Solur works his sword around with great speed and expertise and cuts the basilisk across the side. Solur continues into a quick spin and cuts the basilisk on the side of it's head. The basilisk swings it's head around, mouth open, but Solur's reflexes are too much and he drives his sword into the roof of the basilisk's mouth, piercing it's brain. As Solur withdraws his sword, an arrow flies in and hits him in the left shoulder. The mighty basilisk collapses as Solur backs away, ignoring the arrow.

Robin struggles to grab her staff as the vines start to cover her. The Swamp Queen turns her attention away from Robin and to Solur. Robin gets a hold of her staff and the vines quickly shrivel up. The Swamp Queen brings her wand up at Solur, when a large ring of ice hits at her feet and the Swamp Queen is thrown to the ground and she drops her wand. Robin starts spinning her staff in front of her. She stops her staff, but the ring of wind remains. She taps her staff on the ground and the ring turns to ice. Robin points her staff and the ice ring flies towards the Swamp Queen. The Swamp Queen grabs her wand, but is too late as the ice ring explodes into her, sending the Swamp Queen back fifteen feet and crashing to the ground. Robin points her staff at a large tree and waves her left hand. The tree moans and falls over, crushing the Swamp Queen under it's massive weight.

Maluc ducks under a sword and cuts the lizard man on the left arm. The lizard man comes back across, but Maluc blocks with the dagger in his right hand as he drives the dagger in his left hand into the lizard man's neck.

Ayron takes aim at a lizard man with a bow. He lets his arrow fly and it hits the lizard man in the head just right of the nose.

Gaelin spins his staff in front of him, creating a circle of wind. He pulls his staff back, grabs his amulet and slams his staff on the ground. The circle of wind turns into fire. Gaelin points his staff and the fire ring streaks in burning three lizard men to ashes.

The remaining lizard men, see the Swamp Queen crushed. They turn and flee into the swamp.

Everyone except for Solur rush over to Alexandra. The group puts their weapons away.

Chaed speaks as the others run up, "Robin, Alexandra is hurt."

Robin looks at the arrow in Alexandra's leg, "Zak, pull the arrow out."

Alexandra lays down and prepares herself for the pain to come. Sir Johna and Sir Marcus hold her down. Zak grabs the arrow as Alexandra closes her eyes. She tries to think of something else. Then, Zak yanks the arrow out and Alexandra cries out in pain. Robin quickly places her hands over the wound. The soft golden glow appears. After a few seconds, Robin removes her hands and the wound is gone. Alexandra continues to breath heavily, trying to hold back any tears.

Robin comforts Alexandra, "It will still hurt for a couple of days, but you will be okay."

Alexandra lets out a big sigh, "Thank you."

As they help Alexandra to her feet, Robin notices a little blood on the back of Sir Marcus' left shoulder.

Robin looks at Sir Marcus, "Sir Marcus, you are hurt as well."

Sir Marcus shakes his head, "It is just a scratch. It has already stopped bleeding."

At that time, Solur limps over with the arrow still in his shoulder and the horn still in his leg.

Everyone looks at him in disbelief. None of them can believe what they are seeing. They look at Solur, not quite sure what to say.

Alexandra finally finds the words, "My God. Are you okay?"

Solur smiles, "It looks worse than it feels."

Steph can't believe it, "How are you still standing?"

Solur shrugs, "What can I say, I can take a lot of punishment." He looks at Chaed, "Would you give me a hand?"

Chaed walks over to Solur. Chaed grabs the horn with both hands and yanks in out of Solur's leg. The wound starts to heal as soon as the horn is removed. Then, Chaed grabs the arrow and yanks it out. That wound also starts to heal.

Solur gives a nod, "Thanks."

Chaed tosses the arrow away, "No problem."

Gaelin speaks, "Given the battle, we should rest now and get a fresh start tomorrow."

Alexandra nods, stilling staring at Solur, "I agree."

They round up their horses and start setting up their camp.

Solur sits quietly and watches the sunrise. He has a medium sized bag in his left hand and two apples in his right hand. He looks over the camp as the others lay sleeping. He sits a few minutes longer, then he stands and walks over to the middle of the camp. Solur uses his right foot, and one by one, he taps each person on the bottom of the feet to wake them up. Once he is finished, Solur stands next to a tree as the rest of the group gets up and starts to roll up their bedrolls. Once they have their things together, Solur walks over to Alexandra and pulls out a good sized piece of cooked meat from the bag.

Alexandra takes the meat and looks at Solur, "Thanks."

Solur hands Steph a piece of meat and Steph questions, "What is this?"

Solur looks at her, "It is basilisk meat. I have never had it, but I have heard other humans speak of how good it is."

Maluc takes his piece, "You cooked this?"

Solur smiles, "Last night. I had nothing better to do."

He continues to pass out the meat to everyone except Robin, "I figured everyone needed a change from fruit."

Once he hands the last piece to Zak, Solur holds out the two apples to Robin, "Except for Robin. I know a cleric does not eat meat."

Robin takes the fruit and nods.

Solur then pulls out the Swamp Queen's wand, "I also thought you might want this."

Robin takes the wand and tucks it in her belt, "Thank you."

Solur nods and walks over to the horses. Robin looks at Alexandra as if to say, what is going on. Alexandra shrugs her shoulders as if to say, I don't know. The others are glancing around to see if anyone is going to eat the food Solur gave them. All eyes end up on Chaed who seems oblivious to the others.

Chaed looks up, half finished, while everyone stares at him, "What? It is really good."

Chaed digs back in as everyone else starts eating.

Alexandra looks up after a few bites, "This is good." She looks over at Solur, "I did not expect you to know how to cook."

Solur chuckles slightly, "I was human once. Besides, how hard is it. You put the meat over a fire until it is dark and is no longer bloody." Solur comically shakes his head, "Yet, I do not know why you do not like some good blood."

Everyone stops and looks at Solur. They are not quite sure what to say.

Solur finally cracks a smile, "I guess it is an acquired taste."

Solur watches as the others finish their food. Once they are done, everyone stands up and puts the rest of their things on. Alexandra picks up her bedroll and starts towards the horses. She is limping still from the wound Robin healed. Solur can tell Alexandra is still sore.

Solur walks up to Alexandra, "Let me get that for you."

Solur takes her bedroll as the others start tying their bedrolls to their horses. Solur puts the bedroll on Alexandra's horse and ties it down.

Alexandra speaks, "How are your wounds doing Solur?"

Solur turns to her, "They are already healed."

Zak climbs on his horse, "We should get started. We still have a ways to go before we get out of the swamp."

Alexandra nods, still looking at Solur. Everyone mounts up. Zak starts off down the trail and the others fall in line as before.

———————

The sun is high in the sky over the swamp. The group is walking their horses, giving them some rest. The dead trees are becoming more scarce, but the horrible odor remains.

Steph speaks a little relieved, "We should be out of the swamp by nightfall."

Maluc pipes up, "Good. I have had all the swamp I can take."

At that time, the horse in Chaed's hand rears up.

Chaed tugs at the reigns, "Steady boy."

Gaelin stops, "It is never good if the horse senses something." He glances around, "I would get your things off your horses."

Chaed takes his long sword and straps it across his back and takes his shield in his right hand. Ayron, Zak, Steph and Sir Cleef grab their extra arrows from their horses. Sir Johna and Sir Marcus grab their shields and Alexandra grabs a pouch of gold and ties it to her waist. Now, all the horses start tugging away and rearing up, sensing something very bad.

Ayron holds tight on the reigns, "What is it?"

Zak's face loses all expression as he looks at Steph, "You do not think it is ..."

Steph doesn't even let him finish, "I hope not."

Maluc looks at them, "Maybe you should tell us."

Then, the ground shakes as if something very big and heavy just fell. The horses rip themselves away from the group and run off into the swamp. Everyone starts to scramble to get their horse.

Alexandra yells, "Get the horses!"

Solur holds up his left hand, "Everyone quiet. We have bigger problems."

They can see Solur looking off to his front right. Nobody wants to look, but their eyes are drawn to what Solur is looking at. They see a huge, thirty foot tall, three serpentine headed monster emerge from the water. It is scaled like a reptile. The scales are different shades of green. The body is thick and measures twenty feet. Each head extends up from the body by a thick neck of ten feet.

The middle head has a razor sharp row of teeth with two large fangs. The right head has two rows of teeth and a small fin down the middle of it's head. The left head has four large fangs and two curled horns coming off it's head. The creature appears to walk upright on two powerful looking lizard like legs.

Zak speaks while staring, "The hydra."

The others just stare in amazement. They have never seen such a creature. Just looking at it brings shivers to their spines. Solur just licks his lips, knowing what is going to have to be done.

Solur whispers, "Move back. It has not seen us yet."

Everyone slowly moves back down the trail about fifty feet, not taking their eyes off the massive creature. The hydra steps slowly as the ground shakes under each heavy step.

Maluc whispers as the group hides by a group of dead trees, "What now?"

The hydra stops in the middle of the trail.

Zak whispers in return, "We hope it leaves."

Chaed whispers, "Great plan."

Steph whispers next, "It has not seen us yet."

Ayron looks at Zak, "Is there anything else we should know?"

Then, they hear a roar of thunder as a lightning bolt hits a tree near them and it explodes. Everyone drops to the ground as splinters of wood land all over.

Zak speaks up, "One head shoots lightning and another shoots fire."

Maluc rolls to his back, "Wonderful."

Chaed gets to a knee, "I would say it knows we are here."

Chaed, Solur, Sir Johna and Sir Marcus draw their swords. Ayron, Steph, Zak and Sir Cleef pull out their bows. Maluc draws his daggers.

Solur looks at the group, "Maluc and Alexandra will

stay here. This is far too dangerous."

Alexandra draws her sword, "We fight as a team."

Suddenly, another tree explodes from a lightning bolt.

Solur looks at Chaed and Chaed replies, "She can be stubborn." Chaed looks at Alexandra, "Stay behind me the best you can."

Solur looks over at the hydra, "Lets go."

Chaed and Alexandra rushes for the head on the left. Solur and Maluc run for the middle head as Sir Johna and Sir Marcus charge the right head. As the six of them get closer, the left head launches a lightning bolt at Chaed and Alexandra. Chaed stops and brings his shield up as Alexandra ducks behind him. The lightning bolt hits the magical shield and vanishes. The right head starts to turn red and suddenly a fireball comes at Sir Johna and Sir Marcus. The two knights duck down behind their shields. The fireball hits the shields and flows all around them, but the two knights are unharmed.

Gaelin steps out and calls down a lightning bolt. The lightning bolt hits the hydra in the chest, but appears to do no damage to the creature. Robin launches a magical arrow into the massive body, but the hydra appears to not be hurt. Ayron fires an arrow into the left neck as Steph fires an arrow into the middle neck. The hydra pays no attention to the arrows. Then Zak launches one of his lightning arrows at the creature. It hits the hydra in the right head, but again the hydra doesn't seem to be hurt. Sir Cleef follows with an arrow to the hydra's body.

The middle head comes down at Solur and Maluc. Solur rolls under the head as Maluc dives right. Solur rolls to his feet and cuts the middle neck with his sword. Before Maluc can turn on the hydra, the middle head is already gone. Maluc moves in closer to the body as the middle head comes down again. Maluc moves left at the last second and cuts the middle head with his dagger.

Solur moves in, but the head pulls away before Solur can get his sword on it.

The left head comes down at Chaed and Alexandra. Chaed brings his shield up, but the force of the impact knocks him to the ground. Alexandra jumps left to avoid the left head as it pulls back up. The left head looks down the trail and fires a lightning bolt at Zak and the others.

Zak yells, "Look out!"

The lightning bolt hits the ground next to Steph's feet and explodes. Steph is thrown back to the ground. She hits hard and drops her bow. Zak looks over as Steph stops moving. Zak turns back to the hydra and fires another lightning arrow. It hits the hydra in the middle neck and this time the hydra pulls back.

The right head comes down at Sir Johna and Sir Marcus. Sir Johna jumps back as the head narrowly misses. Sir Marcus ducks under the right head, but the middle head comes over and slams into Sir Marcus, knocking him to the ground. Sir Marcus hits hard and loses his shield and sword.

The right head stops moving and starts turning red again. Another fireball comes right at Sir Marcus. Sir Marcus sees the fireball coming, but there is nothing he can do. The fireball engulfs Sir Marcus and he is cooked alive. Sir Marcus' skin chars black and shrivels up. The smell of burnt flesh fills the air. An arrow from Ayron and one from Sir Cleef zip in and hit the hydra's right head.

Solur steps in under the middle head and cuts the middle neck deep, drawing the hydra's blood. Maluc swings at the middle head, but it has moved out of range. Then, Robin fires her magical arrow into the hydra's middle head.

The left head comes down at Chaed, but Chaed rolls away to safety. As the left head pulls back, Alexandra steps in and cuts the head. The left head moves down again. This time it just barely catches Alexandra on the left shoulder and knocks her to the ground. Chaed has made it to a knee and cuts the left head as it goes by. Then the left head reels up and launches another lightning bolt down the trail at Zak and the others. This time it hits the ground near Sir Cleef. The explosion knocks Sir Cleef down and he stops moving.

Zak yells, "Concentrate on the left head first!"

Zak fires a lightning arrow and it hits the left head in the eye. The left head reels back in pain as Gaelin calls down a lightning bolt. The lightning bolt slams into the left head. The left head sways back and forth. Chaed moves in and cuts the hydra deep across the body. Alexandra gets back to her feet as the middle head comes at her. Alexandra dives left and the middle head misses.

Solur stands his ground as the middle head comes straight at him. He allows the middle head to slam into him, but Solur drives his magical sword into the left eye of the middle head. As Solur tumbles away, Maluc quickly follows up on the stunned middle head by cutting it deep with his fire dagger in his left hand. The middle head sways around some, obviously hurt.

Sir Johna ducks under the right head and makes a deep cut across the right neck. The right head reverses its movement and slams into Sir Johna's side sending him crashing to the ground. As the right head pulls up, Sir Johna brings his shield in front of him. The fireball cooks the ground all around him, but Sir Johna is okay.

The left head opens it's mouth to launch another lightning bolt, but Zak is too fast. Zak's lightning arrow flies into the left mouth of the hydra. The arrow goes through the top of the mouth and pierces the brain in the left head. The left head flails around wildly for a few seconds, then slumps over.

Robin creates one of her ice rings and sends it in at the right head. The ice ring explodes into the right head, causing it to flail about. As the right head moves back and forth violently, Sir Johna steps in and drives his sword into the hydra's body.

The middle head comes down at Sir Johna only to be met by Solur's sword. Solur cuts through a third of the neck before the middle head pulls back. Then, Ayron fires an arrow in and hits the middle head just below the right eye. The middle head sways about as Maluc finds an opening and drives both of his daggers into the hydra's body.

Suddenly, Gaelin sends a lightning bolt crashing into the middle head. The middle head flails about and lets out a horrible groan before slumping over.

Chaed, Alexandra, Solur, Maluc and Sir Johna converge around the right head. The right head swoops down at the group, but everyone moves away to safety. Before the right head can get away, Chaed, Sir Johna and Solur each draw blood with their swords. At that moment, Zak fires another lightning arrow in and it hits square in the top of the right head. The right head lowers back down from all the punishment, right down into the awaiting swords. Alexandra, Chaed, Sir Johna and Solur swing away at the defenseless head of the hydra until it is more blood than flesh. Finally, the right head reels away and the hydra's whole body starts to sway.

Alexandra, Chaed, Sir Johna, Maluc and Solur all move away as the mighty creature finally falls. The ground shakes from the massive impact of the hydra hitting the ground. Everyone breaths a sigh of relief.

Chaed, Sir Johna, Alexandra, Maluc and Solur run over to Sir Marcus' body. The armor has turned black and the body is burnt beyond recognition. Robin starts down the trail towards Sir Marcus.

Solur looks up at Robin, "There is nothing you can do. He is already dead."

At that moment, they hear Zak's voice from behind, "Someone help! Steph is not breathing!"

Robin turns and runs for Zak and Steph. Sir Johna stays with Sir Marcus' body as the others also hurry over to Steph.

Robin kneels down at the top of Steph's head.

Zak looks at Robin, "Can you help her?"

Robin puts down her staff, "I will try." She closes her eyes and places her hands on Steph's forehead, "There is still life left in her. I need everybody to move back."

Everyone stands and moves back. Robin places a hand on each side of Steph's head. Robin closes her eyes and mutters under her breath. Zak and the others watch as Robin's hands start glowing a soft golden color. Zak holds back the tears as he watches for any signs of life from Steph. Robin starts to sweat a little as the others can only watch the battle to save Steph's life. After a minute or two, Robin inhales deeply and collapses to the ground.

The others start towards Robin and Steph. Zak kneels next to Steph and notices her chest is moving.

Zak smiles with huge relief, "She is breathing again." He looks over, "What about Robin?"

Solur is kneeling next to Robin, "She is alive, but barely."

Alexandra gives a sigh of relief, "We will camp here until they wake." Then she gets more somber as she turns to Chaed, "See to Sir Marcus' body."

Chaed bows his head and walks off. Zak picks up Steph and carries her over to the side of the trail. Solur picks up Robin and carries her over and lays her beside Steph. Solur takes off his cloak, balls it up and places it under Robin's head.

Solur looks at Alexandra, "Ayron, Maluc and I will gather some food. The rest of you watch them and start making camp."

Solur, Ayron and Maluc walk off into the swamp. Chaed and Sir Johna pick up the charred body of Sir Marcus and carry it over to the swamp water next to the trail. They lower his body into the water and it quickly disappears. As Chaed and Sir Johna are walking back over to the others, Chaed kicks the hydra's body more out of anger for the loss of Sir Marcus than anything else. Then the two knights just sit and wait.

CHAPTER 6

ALEXANDRA TOSSES AND TURNS AS SHE SLEEPS, appearing to be having a nightmare. She watches the movie in her head unable to do anything about it. She watches as the fireball kills Sir Marcus. Over and over again it plays in her dreams. Alexandra suddenly sits up, eyes wide open. She glances around and sees a figure move over by the trail. She knows it is Solur. It is still dark and Alexandra is unsure of how late it is.

Alexandra gets up and walks over to where Solur is sitting.

Solur questions as she walks up, "Having trouble sleeping?"

Alexandra sits down next to him, "Yes. All I can see is Sir Marcus and the hydra."

Solur replies calmly, "It will pass in time. There is nothing you can do about what happened."

Alexandra looks down, "Maybe not now, but I could have decided to go around the swamp or something else to avoid the hydra."

Solur looks at Alexandra, "It was Sir Marcus' time. When it is your time, nothing you do can change that. I did not want to see anyone die on this adventure, but that is what happens. People will die, but you must push on or they will have died for nothing." He takes a breath, "You are a strong person, I can see that. This might be new to you, but the others are depending on you to lead them to

Dragon Mountain and back. You must be strong for those that are still alive, or no one will make it back."

Alexandra sighs and looks at Solur with a tear in her eye, "You are right." She is quiet for a second, "I would never have imagined to be talking to an undead about something like this."

Solur wipes the tear from her eye, "I might be an undead warrior, but my wife, Kyvez, has softened me some over the years we have been together. Everything will be okay, trust in yourself and the others. Follow your feelings and instincts, they will get you home."

Alexandra smiles at Solur, unable to say anything. She is starting to admire him, and develop some feelings for him.

Solur can tell by Alexandra's look that he needs to do something, "You should try and get some more rest. It will be dawn soon."

Alexandra nods, "Your right." She stands and turns back to Solur, "Thank you."

Solur bows his head and Alexandra walks off. Solur watches as she lays back down and quickly falls asleep. Solur stands up and walks a little ways down the trail, thinking of Kyvez. He hopes that she is still alive. He knows the Lord of the Undead will kill her when she turns him down. He walks around thinking about the adventure so far and the humans he has grown to admire. They have lost two so far, and he knows that there is a good chance that more will die. He walks around some more, then returns to the camp to continue his watch.

———

Solur is unsure of how much time has passed since Alexandra was awake, but the sun has started to rise now. He watches as everyone tosses and turns, obviously still bothered by the encounter with the hydra. Solur knows that each one has been effected in their own way at the loss of Sir Braunt and now Sir Marcus. The effect will be worse if they lose Robin or Steph. Solur sees movement from Steph as the others start to wake up on their own.

Solur walks over and kneels next to Steph, "Steph, can you hear me?"

Zak sees Steph moving and he quickly crawls over to her, "Steph."

Solur decides to leave the rangers to themselves. He gets up and walks over to check on Robin.

Steph blinks a few times and starts to come to. She is still in somewhat of a daze from the incident with the hydra. She can see a blurry face looking at her, but she is still unable to make out who it is. Steph can see that the person is saying something, but she can't hear anything. She blinks some more and the image starts to come into focus. Steph sees the face of the man she loves.

Zak shows a huge smile of relief, "Welcome back my love."

Steph looks into Zak's eyes, "What happened?"

Zak replies, not really wanting to relive the incident, "You nearly died. Robin was able to bring you back." Zak can't hold back any longer and he takes Steph in a big hug, "I love you so much. I do not know what I would do without you."

Steph kisses Zak on the cheek, "I love you."

Alexandra and the others just watch and smile, each feeling better to see Steph moving again.

Steph leans back, "Is everyone else okay?"

Zak looks down, "Sir Marcus is dead and we are unsure about Robin."

At that time, everyone looks over to where Solur is kneeling next to Robin. They each hope to see the same response from Robin as from Steph.

Solur speaks, feeling the eyes on him, "She is starting to come to."

Robin eyes blink a few times as the image of Solur comes into focus. She can see a smile on Solur's face.

Robin speaks a little weak, "What a face to wake up to."

Solur chuckles lightly, "How are you feeling Robin?"

Robin sits up slowly, "I am okay. Did it work?"

Solur nods, "Yes. Steph is fine."

Robin turns and grabs Solur's cloak, "Is this yours?"

Solur replies with obvious relief to see Robin is okay, "Yes it is."

Robin hands Solur his cloak. Solur stands up and helps Robin to her feet. Alexandra is standing there with a huge look of relief on her face.

Alexandra smiles at Robin, "Good to see you up again."

Alexandra gives Robin a big hug. Solur moves away as Ayron walks up with an even bigger look of relief on his face.

Ayron gives Robin a hug, "I was so worried about you."

Robin smiles while hugging Ayron, "I am okay."

Maluc watches on as Chaed, Sir Johna and Sir Cleef each pat Robin on the shoulder to welcome her back.

Steph walks over to Robin, "Thank you. But how?"

Robin grabs her staff that is leaning against a tree, "Every full moon cycle I can cast a resurrection spell. However, if I try more than one, it will kill me."

Zak walks over and hands Steph her bow, arrows and staff. Steph takes her things.

Gaelin finally speaks, "We should be going, especially since we have no horses."

Alexandra nods, "Gaelin is right. Everyone gather your things."

Once everyone has their things together, the group starts walking off down the trail.

There is little talking as everyone watches the swamp all but disappear after a few miles.

They find themselves walking along a nice dirt road now with plush green grass and rolling hills as far as the eye can see. The musty swamp smell has given way to clean, fresh spring air. White clouds slowly move across the sky and far off to their right is smoke rising into the air from what they figure is a town.

Maluc smiles, "Now this is a wonderful sight."

Solur pipes up, "I thought you liked the swamp."

Maluc just looks at Solur. Solur smiles as the others chuckle slightly at Maluc's reaction.

The group walks a little farther and they find themselves at a three way fork in the road.

Zak speaks up, "We take the right road to Whitefeather."

Chaed nods, "Everyone keep your eyes open for any scouts from Whitefeather. They might be human, but I doubt they will like seeing people from Glenfin traveling through their land."

Everyone nods in return and they follow Zak down the road towards Whitefeather.

———

The walking has made the last two days even longer than normal. The group has seen nothing but the rolling green hills for miles on end. They have found it strange that they have not passed other travelers on the way to Whitefeather. The talking has kept to a minimum as they reach the top of the hill they were walking up. With the sun high in the sky, they see the a large castle ahead with a good sized town around it.

The castle towers above all the other buildings. It is

about three square miles in size. The walls and castle itself are made of large stones. The land inside the four castle walls is plush green grass and many flowers lining the stone walkways. Knights and archers line the walls of the castle. They are dressed much like the knights and archers of Glenfin, but instead of a blue crest on their shields, they have a green one.

The town is about eight square miles around the castle. It has numerous stone roads running both north to south and east to west. The buildings that line the roads are made of stone and wood. Most of the buildings are craft shops, taverns and supply shops. Further away from the main part of town are more huts and homes than shops. There are also numerous stables throughout the town.

People line the busy streets. Most are dressed just like the people of Glenfin. However, the town favors green vice blue.

Zak speaks, "Whitefeather."

Maluc quips, "For being named Whitefeather, they seem to like green."

Steph chimes up, "The knight who founded this kingdom named it for his owl." She looks at the others, "We are going to stand out."

Chaed nods, "And they will not be happy to see us."

Alexandra speaks up, "We get there, we get horses, food and water and we leave."

Zak nods, "Stonekeep is only a couple days ride from here. We can get more supplies there if we need to."

Sir Johna sighs, "Sounds like a good idea to me. We really do not need a whole castle after us."

The group walks on towards the town. They get a mile closer when the aroma of the food fills the air and the smell of the flowers float on the wind. Another mile passes and they find themselves at the edge of the town. They stop for a second, each thinking twice about going into Whitefeather. Finally they start down the road into town. As they pass, everyone takes notice of them, knowing they are from Glenfin and not Whitefeather.

Rumbles start through the people as the group continues down the road. Each one keeps their eyes moving, taking in everything around them. Maluc sees a young man about fourteen years old, dressed in rags, run off behind one of the buildings when he sees the group walk by.

Maluc sighs, "That boy. I bet he is heading for the castle right now."

Alexandra speaks up, "Then we must hurry. It will not be long before they come for us."

Alexandra sees the buildings open up into a stables area, "Maluc and I will pay for the horses. The rest of you round up eleven horses and saddles."

Alexandra and Maluc walk pass the three rail wooden fence towards a small one room wooden building. The rest of the group walks over to the gate and see a bunch of beautiful horses grazing. Alexandra and Maluc walk into the building while the others enter the stable and start rounding up the horses they need and putting saddles on them.

It doesn't take the group long to round up the horses and saddle them up. A short while later, Alexandra and Maluc walk out of the small building and over to the group.

Alexandra speaks, "Okay. Food and water and we are out of here."

At that moment, everyone hears the sound of armored feet coming down the stone road in their direction. Everyone turns to see four knights and seven pikemen heading their way.

The knights are in shiny plate mail armor. They each carry a medium sword on their left hip and a shield in their left hand. The shields have a green crest surrounding a silver sword on them, the symbol of Whitefeather. The pikemen are dressed in chain mail armor. They each carry an eight foot long spear.

Chaed whispers, "We have trouble."

The knights and pikemen stop about ten feet away as the road around Chaed and the others clears out. All the people move away expecting trouble.

The knight on the far left speaks, "You must hand over your weapons and come with us."

Alexandra protests, "We have done nothing wrong."

The knight replies, "Those from Glenfin are not welcome hear unless they turn over all their weapons and check in with the Captain of the Guard. So, hand over your weapons and come with us."

Chaed draws his sword, "I fear we cannot."

The four knights draw their swords and the seven pikemen ready their spears.

The knight smiles, "Have it your way."

Sir Johna draws his sword and readies his shield. Zak draws his sword and dagger as does Solur. Chaed starts for the knight on the far left as Sir Johna, Zak and Solur start for the other three knights. Alexandra, Ayron and Sir Cleef draws their swords and Maluc draws his daggers. Gaelin, Robin and Steph ready their staves as the pikemen close in.

One pikeman starts for Alexandra. He thrusts his spear, but Alexandra knocks it away with her sword. She tries to move in close, but the pikeman holds her at bay with his spear. Alexandra spins away from another thrust and then ducks away from a third.

A pikeman starts for Robin. She quickly contemplates using magic, but decides against it given the close quarters and all the innocent people around that might get hurt. He thrusts in with his spear, but Robin knocks it away with her staff. The pikeman swings his staff at Robin. Robin ducks and jabs her staff into the pikeman's stomach. The pikeman staggers back and readies himself again.

Solur blocks the sword with his dagger and cuts in with his sword. The knight blocks with his shield. Solur quickly kicks the knight in the stomach to back him away. Solur steps back in and swings his sword. As soon as his sword hits the shield, Solur spins, bringing his sword around. The knight blocks with his sword, but Solur rams his dagger into the knight's left thigh. Solur pulls out his dagger and shuffles back as the knight's sword swings by.

A pikeman starts for Gaelin. He too considers magic, but decides against it. Gaelin blocks the first thrust and swings his staff, but the pikeman ducks and thrusts again. Gaelin quickly sidesteps and scores a solid hit to the pikeman's left leg with his staff. The pikeman steps back to regain his composure.

Maluc spins away from the spear, but is unable to close in as the spear just keeps coming at him. He knocks the spear away with his dagger and tries to work in close. Then the pikeman thrusts too far and Maluc ducks under the spear and cuts the pikeman on the left arm. Maluc shuffles away as another swing misses.

Zak swings his sword, but the knight blocks with his shield. The knight brings his sword across, but Zak blocks with his dagger. The knight thrusts forward off the dagger and cuts Zak on the left arm. Zak steps back in and thrusts his sword. The knight blocks with his sword. Zak spins his sword in a small circle and knocks away the knight's sword. Zak comes in with his dagger and cuts the knight on the right arm. The knight steps back and they both get ready for more.

One pikeman comes at Ayron. Ayron blocks the spear with his sword and swings his sword at the pikeman, but the pikeman is out of reach. Ayron ducks under the spear this time and moves in. Ayron cuts the pikeman on the right arm. The pikeman hits Ayron in the side with the handle of his spear. Ayron moves away.

Sir Cleef moves in and knocks the spear away with his sword. The pikeman cuts back across and Sir Cleef blocks again. This time Sir Cleef quickly thrusts forward and cuts the pikeman on the left arm. The pikeman brings the handle of his spear around and pushes Sir Cleef away to get some distance.

Sir Johna blocks the knight's sword with his shield and counters with his own sword. The knight blocks with his shield and pushes Sir Johna away. The knight cuts in quick, but Sir Johna ducks under the sword and slams his shield into the knight's shield, knocking the knight off balance. Sir Johna cuts in and draws blood from the knight's left thigh. The knight moves away to safety and readies himself again.

Steph blocks the spear with her staff and counters. The pikeman blocks with his spear. The pikeman thrusts in again, but Steph sidesteps and pins the spear to the ground with her staff. She quickly spins, twirls her staff and slams it into the pikeman's head. The pikeman crumples to the ground and stops moving.

Alexandra ducks away from the spear again, but the pikeman brings the handle around and hits Alexandra in the shoulder. Alexandra steps back and the pikeman thrusts again. Alexandra spins in past the spearhead and brings her sword around. Her sword hits the pikeman's right wrist and cuts off his hand. The pikeman cries out and drops his spear and blood pours from his wrist. Alexandra quickly thrusts her sword into the pikeman's chest, dealing a deadly blow. She removes her sword and the pikeman falls.

Robin's staff is blocked again by the pikeman's spear. She thinks now that magic might be the only way to end this. Robin leaps back as the spear narrowly misses. Robin starts looking for her opening as she steps back in and blocks the spear with her staff. The pikeman twirls his spear around and swings at Robin again. Robin ducks under the spear and finds her opening. She points her staff at the pikeman's chest. A magical arrow launches into the pikeman and he falls quickly.

Solur swings his sword in and the knight blocks with his sword. Solur spins his sword in a small circle and knocks the knight's sword away. Solur fakes a thrust and the knight brings his shield across. Solur spins around the shield and his sword hits home in the knight's ribs. Blood flows instantly. The knight cuts across with his sword, but Solur is far too fast. Solur ducks and scores a hit to the knight's stomach as more blood flows. The knight reverses his swing and comes back at Solur. Solur blocks with his sword and rams his dagger into the knight's elbow. The knight moans in pain and drops his sword. Solur removes his dagger, steps in close and drives his sword into the knight's chest. Solur removes his sword and watches the knight fall.

Gaelin blocks the spear with his staff and brings his staff around, but the pikeman ducks to safety. Gaelin comes up with an idea to end this confrontation. The pikeman swings his spear across, but Gaelin blocks and rams his staff into the pikeman's chest. When the end of the staff hits the pikeman, lightning discharges into the pikeman's body and the pikeman is blown back to the ground. Smoke rolls off the pikeman's motionless body.

Maluc blocks the spear with his dagger and moves away. The pikeman swings again, but Maluc rolls forward under the spear. He rolls to a knee and lets the dagger in his right hand fly. The dagger hits the pikeman in the chest. Maluc is quickly up and drives his other dagger into the pikeman's neck. He pulls out both daggers as the pikeman falls.

Zak ducks under the sword and cuts the knight on the right leg with his sword. The knight brings his sword down, but Zak spins away and his sword cuts the knight across the ribs. The knight swings again, but Zak blocks with his dagger and swings his sword in. The knight blocks with his shield. Zak spins off the shield and finds himself behind the knight. Zak thrusts his sword in, killing the knight.

Sir Cleef ducks under the spear and manages to cut the pikeman on the left leg. The pikeman comes around with his spear, but Sir Cleef blocks with his sword. Sir Cleef shuffles in quick and cuts the pikeman across the stomach. The pikeman brings the handle of his spear around, but Sir Cleef sees it coming and ducks. Once the pikeman's spear passes Sir Cleef, Sir Cleef drives his sword into the pikeman's chest, just under his left arm. Sir Cleef withdraws his sword and the pikeman falls.

Sir Johna blocks the sword with his shield and counters with his sword. The knight blocks with his shield and steps in. Sir Johna moves aside as the knight pushes his shield forward intending to knock Sir Johna off balance. The knight stumbles by and Sir Johna cuts him across the ribs. The knight comes back across, but Sir Johna blocks with his shield and drives his sword in. The knight moves to block, but is too late. Sir Johna's sword buries into the knight's chest.

Ayron ducks under the spear, but is still out of range. The pikeman thrusts in and Ayron blocks with his sword. Ayron jumps in and cuts down with his sword. He cuts the pikeman's left arm. The pikeman brings his spear around, but Ayron ducks and this time he is just the right distance away. Ayron drives his sword into the pikeman's stomach, killing him.

Chaed's sword is blocked by the knight's shield. The knight cuts in with his sword. Chaed blocks with his shield and brings his sword low and across, hitting the knight in the right leg. The knight comes over the top with his sword. Chaed steps left and deflects the sword away with his shield. Chaed swings his own sword and hits the knight in the neck. The knight falls to his knees as Chaed deals the final deadly blow to the knight's chest, sending the knight all the way to the ground.

With the fight now over, they look around to see everyone watching them.

Zak speaks up, "We better leave, fast."

Alexandra nods, "Everyone get their horse."

They all climb on their horses as they hear more armored footsteps closing in.

Zak yells, "This way!"

They take off down the streets away from the army coming for them. They quickly race out of Whitefeather and don't even slow down for a few miles.

The sweltering sun is high in the sky as the temperature has risen the further north from Whitefeather they go. The group has not seen anyone follow them for the last day and a half. The road continues through the plush green, rolling hills with sparse patches of trees and a couple of ponds and meadows. The water in the ponds and meadows is clear as the sky.

The group tops the hill in front of them and they see a large town, not as large as Whitefeather, but pretty good size. It has fifteen roads both north to south and east to west. Most of the outer dwellings are homes and huts. Then as the buildings get closer to the main part of town, they start becoming stables, shops and taverns. The roads are fairly busy with people from all different status levels. Some appear to have wealth all the way down to the poor beggars. The smell of fresh cooked meat hangs in the air. The group stops are stares at the pristine view.

Steph speaks, "Stonekeep. We should not have any problems here. It is a town of travelers."

Zak speaks up, "We need supplies because the next

town is not until we reach the desert on the far side of the wastelands."

As they ride for the town, the sun gets lower in the sky as the last few miles they take their time. They find themselves on a main road leading into the heart of the town. They pass the homes and a couple of stables, yet no one has seemed to take notice of them. Alexandra glances around at the different shops.

Ayron points up ahead, "There."

The group rides up to the shop and they dismount.

Solur speaks, "I will watch the horses."

The rest of the group walks into the stone building. They see a few other people in the shop and a fairly hefty man behind a counter.

Alexandra glances around and questions, "How much will we need?"

Zak sighs and thinks for a second, "It is two more days to the wastelands and two days to cross the wastelands. The first town is a day into the desert so I would say six days to be safe."

Alexandra speaks to the group, "Everyone grab six days worth of food and water."

Everyone spends a few minutes gathering their supplies. Alexandra walks up to the shopkeeper.

The shopkeeper questions in a gruff voice, "What you got little lady?"

Alexandra replies, "I have ten of us and we each have six days worth of food and water."

The shopkeeper strokes his chin, "Two gold pieces and five silver."

Alexandra hands over the coins and everyone exits the shop to find it is now dark outside and the torch lamps are lit.

Alexandra speaks, We need to find a tavern for the night."

Solur replies, "There is a stables just ahead and a

tavern next to it."

The group walks their horses over to the stables and tie them up. A young boy walks up and Alexandra hands him a silver piece.

The boy smiles, "Thanks. I will feed and water your horses."

As the group walks towards the tavern, Robin speaks, "I hope the rooms have a bath."

Steph nods, "Indeed."

Solur speaks up, "I am going to look around and I will meet you at the horses at sunrise."

Alexandra nods and Solur walks off away from the tavern. The rest of the group walks into the busy tavern.

A middle aged woman walks up to them, "What can I get you?"

Alexandra replies, "Do your rooms come with a bath?"

The woman nods, "Yes."

Alexandra smiles, "Good. We will have ten specials, one without meat, and five rooms."

The woman holds out her hand, "One gold and three silver pieces."

Alexandra hands her the coins and the group walks over to an empty table.

Alexandra sits, "I feel kind of bad for Solur. He must spend a lot of time alone."

Steph replies, "He is an undead. He should be used to it."

Ayron speaks up, "That does not matter, he is one of us now."

The rest of the group is quiet for a second at what Ayron said. No one is really sure where his feelings changed, but they definitely wasn't expecting what Ayron said.

Then, Zak replies, "He will never be one of us. Steph is right, he is an undead. We cannot trust him completely."

The woman brings the food and ale and Gaelin speaks up, "I trust Solur."

Maluc chimes in, "So do I. We could have not made it this far without him."

It becomes obvious to Alexandra that the group is starting to change the way they feel about having an undead around. She knows what Maluc just said is true.

Robin sighs, "I am not sure. He did save my life, but will he be there when we need him the most. I am just not sure."

It gets quiet as Robin's words make them all think. What she said does make sense. Solur has been there for now, but they each wonder if his loyalties will change once they reach the Island of the Dead. It is quiet for the rest of the meal and once they are done, Alexandra and Robin walk off to their room. Gaelin and Maluc are next to go, then Zak and Steph. Next is Sir Johna and Sir Cleef and last is Chaed and Ayron.

The sun is in the afternoon sky as the group has stopped near a clear blue pond. The rolling green hills stretch on for as far as the eye can see. White clouds dot the light blue sky. A grove of trees stands only a couple hundred feet off to their left. The horses are drinking from the pond as everyone is just standing around.

Zak takes a drink of water, "We should reach the wastelands tomorrow around mid-day."

Alexandra nods, "Good. What is the desert like?"

Steph speaks up, "It will be hard. Even more than the swamp."

The others look at Steph and Zak adds, "The land will test your will. We are not as likely to encounter creatures in the desert, but if we do, they will be very dangerous."

Solur holds up his hand, "Quiet."

The talking stops and everyone hears what Solur had heard. They hear the sound of a large group of feet running across the ground.

Chaed grabs his shield and draws his sword, "It is getting closer."

Solur draws his sword and dagger, "It is just beyond the hill to our right."

Maluc draws his daggers, "I cannot wait to see what this is."

Ayron, Steph, Sir Cleef and Zak all grab their bows. Sir Johna grabs his shield and draws his sword. Alexandra draws her sword as Gaelin and Robin ready their staves.

Then, from over the hill a hundred feet away comes twenty five trolls carrying various types of clubs, some with spikes. Each troll wears old, rusted plates of armor. Their skin is various shades of green and brown with gnarled teeth showing. The smell from their bodies could turn the strongest of stomachs.

Alexandra speaks, "Trolls."

Solur, Chaed, Sir Johna, Maluc and Alexandra charge at the trolls who have caught sight of the humans and started to close in. Two magical arrows, three regular arrows and one lightning arrow flies into the charging army and six trolls fall from the deadly arrows.

Solur ducks under a club and rams his dagger into the troll's heart. He spins behind the troll, leaving his dagger in the troll's chest, and cuts the troll down with his sword as blood flies across the ground. Solur draws one of his poison darts from his left boot and lets it fly. The dart hits a troll in the neck. The undead poison works fast and the troll falls to the ground after a couple more steps. Solur rolls away from another club as an arrow from Steph flies in and catches the troll in the left shoulder.

Chaed blocks a club with his shield, steps over,

brings his sword down and cuts off the trolls right arm. Chaed brings his sword back up and across the troll's chest. As blood flies, the troll falls to the ground. Chaed turns and blocks a club with his sword. He slams his shield into the troll, knocking it off-balance. Chaed brings his sword across and cuts the troll's stomach. Chaed reverses his swing and cuts the troll across the neck, killing it. Suddenly, a lightning arrow from Zak flies in and hits a troll in the head, bringing it to the ground.

Maluc ducks under a club and kicks the troll in the stomach with his left leg. The troll comes back and elbows Maluc in the shoulder, knocking him off-balance. Then, one of Sir Cleef's arrows zip in and hits the troll in the right shoulder. Maluc seizes the opening and spins around, ramming his dagger into the troll's neck. He withdraws the dagger and blood squirts out as the troll falls. At that time, Gaelin calls down a lightning bolt and it explodes into another troll's chest, killing it.

Alexandra swings her sword, but the troll moves out of the way. The troll counters with it's club, but Alexandra blocks with her sword. The impact knocks Alexandra's sword out of the way. The troll prepares to swing again when vines come up out of the ground and entangle the troll's arms. Alexandra steps in quickly and thrusts her sword into the troll's chest. She withdraws her sword as the troll falls.

Sir Johna blocks a club with his shield as his sword cuts the troll across the ribs. The troll steps right and swings again. This time Sir Johna ducks and thrusts his sword into the troll's stomach. Blood rolls down the blade as Sir Johna removes his sword and the troll collapses to the ground. Another troll steps up behind Sir Johna and readies to strike. At that moment, Ayron releases his arrow and it hits the troll in the neck, killing it.

Solur blocks the club with his sword. Solur throws a sidekick with his right leg and it hits the troll in the chest, driving it back. Solur turns around to a troll behind him. The troll starts to swing it's club. Solur brings his right leg across and kicks the club from the troll's hand. Solur spins 180 with the kick and thrusts his sword into the first troll he kicked away. He withdraws his sword, flips it up and catches it blade down and drives it back into the troll now behind him. Solur withdraws his sword as both trolls fall dead. Then, another arrow from Steph flies in and catches a troll in the left eye, killing it.

Sir Johna blocks a club with his shield and cuts the troll across the chest with his sword. The troll steps back as a lightning arrow from Zak flies in and hits the troll in the right shoulder. Before the troll can recover, Sir Johna steps in and drops the troll with a deep cut across the chest.

Chaed swings his sword and cuts the troll across the left thigh. He blocks the club with his shield, spins around and removes the troll's head in one swift move. At that time, an arrow from Sir Cleef flies in and hits another troll in the neck, killing it.

Alexandra blocks the club with her sword. Maluc steps up behind the troll and drives his daggers down into the collarbones of the troll. The troll drops his club as Alexandra thrusts her sword into the troll's heart. Then, a magical arrow from Gaelin and one from Robin flies in and the last two trolls are killed.

Maluc puts away his daggers and catches his breath, "That was not so bad."

Solur retrieves his dagger and puts his weapons away, "We must burn their bodies."

Sir Cleef questions, "Why must we do that?"

Zak chimes in, "Some trolls can grow back even from body parts. Burning the bodies is the only way to make sure they are really dead."

Sir Johna speaks up, "That will take time."

Steph jumps in, "It is too late to get started back on the trail. We should set up camp here and burn the bodies."

Alexandra nods in agreement, "I agree."

They grab their horses and take them over to the grove of trees and tie them up.

Steph looks at Solur, "I have never seen anyone use a sword so well. You make fighting look easy."

Solur replies, "You get better when you have had a hundred years of practice."

Everyone gets quiet as they did not expect to hear that from Solur.

Robin is the first to respond, "You are a hundred years old."

Solur smiles, "No. I am one hundred and fifty years old. I was human for twenty five years before I became an undead. I spent twenty five years in training to become an undead warrior. The last hundred years I have used my skills and talents to serve the Lord of the Undead. Until I was betrayed."

Alexandra speaks up, "All I know is that you are the best warrior I have ever seen."

Chaed lets out a slight chuckle, "Maybe you have just not fought a real good knight yet."

Sir Johna adds, "I agree."

Solur lets out a sly smile, "Maybe not."

Zak speaks up, "Or a good ranger. I have beaten a death knight before. The only one to ever leave the Island of the Dead."

Solur nods, "Yes. That is the death knight who betrayed me and got me captured." Solur pauses, "Death Knights are weak. They rely on strength, power and armor. An undead warrior uses speed and skill equally with strength and power."

Robin questions, "I heard that if a death knight's sword cuts you, you will become an undead."

Solur looks at her, "That is true."

Ayron decides to ask a question, "So, how many are there on the Island of the Dead?"

Solur replies calmly, "Only ten are left."

Maluc smiles, "Could be worse."

Solur continues, "Each Death Knight has fifty skeleton warriors under his command."

Maluc loses his smile, "What?"

Steph speaks up, "That is five hundred skeleton warriors."

Solur nods and replies calmly, "Yes."

It suddenly gets quiet as everyone ponders the news about what awaits them on the Island of the Dead. That night, as the fire consuming the dead trolls burns out, each person tries to sleep. However, they find sleep a little more elusive now that Solur has shared the size of the undead army with them. None of them was expecting to hear the size of an army that Solur explained to them.

CHAPTER 7

THE GROUP CONTINUES DOWN THE DIRT ROAD in the midday sun as the rolling green hills and trees start to change. They can see the wastelands ahead. Another mile and the ground changes from green grass to charred ground that still holds an odor of death in the air. The trees that were once full of life are now dried up and dead. The ground is hard and the beauty of the grasslands has now given way to the barren and dead wastelands.

Zak speaks as the hard dirt crumbles under his horse, "The wastelands. The land where nothing grows."

Everyone looks around at the barren, dead land in awe. None of them can imagine what in the past could have caused such a disaster.

Alexandra questions, "How could something like this happen?"

Steph speaks while staring, "The Great War."

Maluc questions a little puzzled, "The Great War? I have never heard of such a thing."

Solur speaks up, "A few centuries ago, the Barbarians sought to conquer the humans and the elves."

Ayron questions, "I have heard the legends. Are they true?"

Steph chimes in, "When the Barbarians realized they could not win, they scorched the land to cover their retreat."

Solur chuckles lightly, "Is that what they teach the

humans?"

Zak quips, "You know a different story?"

Solur replies calmly, "I know the truth."

Alexandra questions, "What is it?"

Solur starts, "The Barbarians use to have a powerful army under the leadership of Boren. Once they discovered the prosperous lands south of the desert, Boren decided to lead his people out of the desert. The humans and elves, then just under the Kingdom of Glenfin, did not want to share." Solur pauses for a second, "This land is where the two armies fought. The Barbarians took the upper hand. To save their land, the humans and elves devised a plan."

Solur stops and Chaed prompts, "What plan?"

Solur sighs, "The humans invited the Barbarians to the Northern Castle to talks of peace. The Barbarians showed up and the humans lit the fields all around the castle. The Barbarians were burned alive and the humans allowed the fires to burn out."

Sir Johna speaks up, "Not a bad strategy."

Solur nods, "True. The Barbarians never expected the ambush." Solur pauses, then prompts his own question, "But do you think the Barbarians would ride into an empty castle and town?"

Alexandra looks at Solur, "What do you mean?"

Solur replies solemnly, "The King did not warn the humans in the Northern Castle or lands. He used them and let them burn with the Barbarian army."

Chaed's hand moves to his sword, "You lie! The Romlay bloodline has ruled for centuries. They would never do something like that."

Robin chimes in, "I agree. The elves would never support a plan like that."

Solur replies calmly, "Believe what you wish. Trust me when I say, every race has a little evil in them."

Gaelin finally speaks, "Whether or not it is true matters little. Both stories show one thing and that is how far someone will go when left no other choice. It is merely another lesson the land teaches us and one we must learn if we are going to survive."

Like in the past, Gaelin's wisdom prevails and the tension eases. The group continues to ride across the barren land, but not much more is said. Alexandra wonders if what Solur said is true. He is the oldest one here and he, if anyone, should know. It makes her wonder if there is evil in her bloodline that has been kept from her.

The sun starts to get low in the sky as the group sees some large ruins ahead.

Zak speaks up, "The Northern Castle, or what is left of it."

Steph chimes in, "We should stop there for the night. It is too dangerous to travel the wastelands at night."

Alexandra nods her approval and the group continues to ride towards the ruins. The Northern Castle, once a beautiful place, is now nothing but crumbling, dirty and charred stone walls that have all but fallen. The towers that once stood in the corners are nearly crumbled to the ground. Cobwebs, soot and dust cover everything. The once plush courtyard is burned up and dead. The main entrance is completely gone and all that is left is a twenty foot by twenty foot hole in the northern wall. The group rides into the empty castle.

Robin speaks while looking around, "This is an eerie place."

Steph replies, "I hear it is haunted."

Solur chuckles, "There is no such thing as ghosts here."

Maluc questions, "How do you know?"

Solur just looks at Maluc.

It finally hits Maluc, "Oh. I guess you if anyone should know."

Zak slows to a stop in the old courtyard, "We can bed down in this open area."

Everyone stops their horse and dismounts. They find some old small stones to tie their horses to. They each grab their bedrolls and some food. They set up camp and Gaelin starts a fire while Solur walks around the area to make sure they are alone.

Alexandra sits down, "I cannot believe this place. How could something like this happen?"

Gaelin speaks up, "Try not to think about it my lady."

Everyone continues to eat and Maluc finally brings up what everyone else is probably thinking, "Do you think Solur was right? I mean, it makes sense."

Chaed sighs, "I do not want to believe it, but Maluc does have a point. Solur's story makes more sense."

Zak shakes his head, "He is an undead. They are very deceitful. You cannot believe what they say. He may be helping us, but he is still an undead."

Robin nods, "Zak is right. Not everything Solur says could be the truth. He might be trying to trick us into letting our guard down."

Alexandra sighs, "I cannot believe Solur is trying to take advantage of us. Not after what we have been through."

Gaelin grabs his staff, "Everyone try and get some rest. We have a long journey ahead still."

Gaelin taps his staff on the ground and the light dies out. Everyone lays down as Solur walks up and watches over the camp as they all quickly drift off to sleep.

Alexandra wakes shortly before dawn. She looks around and sees Solur standing over by the opening leading out of the castle. Alexandra walks over to Solur.

Solur glances at her, "Not able to sleep?"

Alexandra replies, seeming distant, "No."

Solur nods slightly, "Your father will be fine. If he is anywhere as strong as you, he will be just fine."

Alexandra breaks a smile, "I am not that strong."

Solur shakes his head, "You are stronger than you think. Not many could have made it this far."

Alexandra looks at Solur, "Thanks to you."

Solur looks back out at the wastelands, "Do not thank me too soon."

Alexandra can tell Solur just hinted at something. She looks out to where Solur is looking and sees what he is talking about. In the distance is the soft glow of torches ominously lighting up the dark sky.

Alexandra questions, "What is that?"

Solur replies calmly, "A large army, and it is heading this way."

Alexandra questions again, "Can we out ride it?"

Solur shakes his head, "It is coming from the north, the direction we need to go."

Alexandra looks at Solur, "What do we do?"

Solur replies staring at the closing army, "Wake the others. We will make our stand in the castle."

Alexandra walks off. She is surprised at how Solur can remain so calm in such situations. Solur continues to watch the closing army. He wonders what the torches will bring.

———————

The rest of the group is awake as the sun has now risen. Maluc is standing atop what is left of the north wall. He watches as the army stops about a hundred yards from the castle. Maluc makes out fifteen orcs and two hundred goblins.

The orcs all stand about six feet tall and their skin is dark green and brown in color. They have gnarled teeth and sunken black eyes. They are wearing old, think plate armor and makeshift metal swords. One of the orcs has on a metal band around it's head and it is carrying a bow with arrows. That orc appears to be the one giving the orders. The goblins are smaller in stature, about four and a half feet tall. Their skin is dark green in nature and their teeth are as bad as the orc's teeth. The goblins are wearing thin, old metal plates to cover their chest, but nothing else. The goblins are carrying small, three foot long clubs.

Maluc watches a few seconds more and then climbs down from the wall. Maluc walks over to the others.

Chaed questions, "What are we looking at?"

Maluc sighs, "A couple hundred goblins and fifteen orcs. One of the orcs is wearing a band around his head. He appears to be the leader."

Ayron questions, "How far away are they?"

Maluc replies, "Maybe a hundred yards away. They appear to be making plans for an attack."

Everyone is quiet. They all have the same look on their face. Their look is a question of, can we handle an army of that size.

Solur finally breaks the silence, "We must prepare for battle."

Alexandra questions, "What should we do?"

Chaed looks around the landscape and finally speaks, "Across the courtyard is an old watchtower that still stands. Gaelin and Robin will take up positions there. Zak, Steph, Ayron and Sir Cleef will move back across the courtyard and cover the walls."

Maluc questions, "What about the rest of us?"

Chaed continues, "Solur, Sir Johna and I will meet them as they come through the gate opening. You and Alexandra will stay behind us a ways to take on those that get by us. We will fall back as needed."

Chaed looks at Solur and Solur gives a quick nod. Gaelin and Robin rush off to their position in the watchtower. Zak, Steph, Ayron and Sir Cleef grab all their weapons and rush off to the far side of the courtyard, but they stay on the ground. The four of them turn to face the wall. Alexandra and Maluc draw their weapons and walk off to halfway across the courtyard.

Chaed walks over to his horse and puts his shield on the horse. Chaed pulls out his two-handed long sword, The Sword of Vulnerability. Sir Johna takes his shield and draws his sword. Solur removes his cloak and puts it on his horse.

Solur hears the footsteps and growls getting closer, "I hope your ready."

Chaed and Sir Johna drop to a knee.

Chaed places his right hand over his heart, "Strength and honor."

The roar of the hundreds of feet continues to grow and so do the growls and howling.

Solur draws his sword and dagger, "Here they come!"

Everyone is apprehensive, waiting to see what will come through the gate opening and over the walls. Their hearts beat faster and their breathes grow shorter. Chaed and Sir Johna stand and ready themselves as goblins start into the gate opening and over the walls.

Robin launches an ice ring and Gaelin sends in a fire ring as ten goblins are killed from the powerful magic. Regular arrows and lightning arrows fly in as fast as they can be fired and goblins fall from the walls.

Chaed steps in and his first cut brings down two goblins as their blood flies everywhere from Chaed's long sword. Chaed moves quick and works his sword with great skill as the charging goblins continue to fall at his feet. Sir Johna cuts goblins down left and right as more and more surround him. A couple get shots in with their clubs, but nothing that hurts Sir Johna. His sword works fast as more goblins fall. Solur works his sword and dagger with uncanny speed as goblins fall under his deadly blades. Solur moves fast and keeps his sword and dagger going, but as every goblin falls, more appear.

Alexandra and Maluc fight back to back as the number of goblins around them continue to grow. Alexandra works her sword as fast as she can, but the number of goblins are just getting to be too much. Maluc's daggers work fast to cut down goblins, but there are just too many for him to keep up with. Arrows continue to rain down and so does lightning bolts and magical arrows.

Chaed cuts through a few more goblins as an orc approaches. The orc swings, but Chaed blocks. Chaed pushes the orc back off-balance. Chaed swings and the orc blocks. Chaed spins his sword quickly and he cuts the orc down with a deep blow to the chest. He quickly spins and cuts down a couple more goblins. A couple of clubs get in and hit Chaed, but he remains unharmed.

Sir Johna ducks under the sword of an orc as a goblin's club hits him in the leg. Sir Johna spins and cuts down the goblin as the orc swings again. This time the sword hits Sir Johna in the side. Sir Johna staggers away as the orc moves in. Then, an arrow zips in and hits the orc in the shoulder. The orc is distracted long enough for Sir Johna to kill the orc with a deadly thrust.

Solur spins in and kills another goblin and finds himself facing two orcs. The first orc swings, but Solur blocks with his dagger. The second orc swings and Solur blocks with his sword. Solur kicks away the second orc as the first orc swings again. Solur ducks and spins. He extends his leg and sweeps the orc to the ground. Solur comes around with dagger ready and drives it into the other orc's neck. Solur flips his sword, blade down and drives it down into the orc laying on the ground.

Chaed cuts down another goblin and looks around. He can tell that they are being overwhelmed.

Chaed yells, "Fall back!"

More goblins pour over the walls and more orcs come through the opening. It looks like a dark green tidal wave sweeping into the rundown castle. Then, the orc leader comes into view. He draws back his bow and lets his arrow fly. It zips in and hits Sir Johna in the back. Sir Johna drops to a knee.

Another orc closes on Sir Johna as Zak sees the orc leader aiming in on Alexandra. Zak draws back his bow as the orc leader fires his arrow. Zak turns quick and fires his lightning arrow. Zak's arrow cuts the orc's arrow in mid-air and Alexandra is safe.

Alexandra sees a sword out of the corner of her eye and she moves away. The sword cuts her on the left arm. The orc swings down again, but Solur steps over and blocks the sword with his dagger. Alexandra seizes the opening and her sword goes deep into the orc's chest. Then, the orc leader fires again and this time his arrow hits Maluc in the right thigh. Maluc drops to a knee as Chaed moves to cover him.

Sir Johna never sees the orc behind him as he cuts down a couple of goblins in front of him. The orc's sword hits Sir Johna in the back of the neck. Blood flies everywhere as Sir Johna falls to the ground. As goblins swarm his body, Sir Cleef fires an arrow into the orc's neck, killing it.

Another ice ring and fire ring sweep in and more goblins are killed.

Zak slings his bow on his back and draws his sword, "I am out of arrows!"

Zak charges into the fight and starts cutting down goblins. An orc comes at him, but Zak blocks with his sword. Zak kicks the orc in the knee, spins his sword around and cuts down the orc.

Ayron draws his last arrow from his quiver. He finds his target and lets his arrow fly. It hits the orc leader in the neck. The orc leader falls as Ayron puts his bow away and draws his sword. Sir Cleef follows suit. Steph fires her last arrow, puts her bow away and grabs her staff. The three of them rush into the massive battle.

Chaed brings his sword around, but the orc blocks. The orc cuts in at Chaed. Chaed sidesteps and removes the orc's arm with an upward cut. Chaed quickly brings his sword back down and split's the orc in two.

Steph twirls her staff and two goblins are crushed under the impact. Then, a club hits her in the left knee. Steph drops to her knee when another club hits her in the back of the neck. Then, Zak and Sir Cleef move over and cut down the goblins around Steph. Steph shakes her head and gets back to her feet.

Ayron swings at an orc, but the orc blocks. Another orc steps over and swings at Ayron. Ayron leans back, but the sword hits him in the left side of the stomach. Suddenly, Robin launches a magical arrow into the orc that cut Ayron, killing the creature. As the first orc moves in again, Steph steps over and jabs it in the gut with her staff. Then, Maluc steps up behind the orc and drives his daggers into its back.

Two orcs come at Solur. Solur spins behind the first charging orc and elbows it in the back of the head. The orc stumbles towards Chaed. Chaed takes a big swing and cuts the orc in two. Solur parries the second orc's thrust and cuts the creature on the chest. The orc swings again, but Solur blocks with his sword. Solur spins off the block behind the orc and cuts the orc's throat with his dagger.

The battle rages hard for a little longer as more goblins are killed.

Finally, one of the last two orcs growls loud. The last of the goblins stop and retreat from the humans and the last two orcs follow the goblins out of the castle opening.

The group watches as the enemy retreats. They breath heavy as they know they survived, but at a great cost as they see Sir Johna's body laying still.

Everyone rushes over to where Sir Johna's body is at. They can tell he is dead, but they wait for Robin and Gaelin to arrive. Robin runs up and kneels next to Sir Johna's body. She closes her eyes and holds her hands just above his head.

A couple of seconds pass and Robin opens her eyes, "He is gone. There is nothing I can do."

Chaed replies a little angered, "Then we help those that need it and we get on the trail."

Robin looks around, "Who first?"

Steph steps up and Robin heals her knee and neck. Alexandra is next and Robin heals her arm. Ayron steps up and Robin heals his stomach.

Robin glances around, "Anyone else?"

Solur smiles, "One second."

Solur grabs the arrow in Maluc's leg and Maluc speaks, "You are enjoying this a little too much."

Solur smiles at Maluc and yanks out the arrow. Maluc grits his teeth in pain. Solur tosses the arrow away and Robin heals the wound.

Zak speaks up, "As Chaed said, we must get on the trail. This battle took valuable time."

Alexandra nods, "Your right."

They walk off to the horses. Everyone looks back at Sir Johna's body. They each wish they could bury him, but they know that would take more time they cannot afford. They each hold a sad look as they ride out of the castle and towards the north.

The ride has been a quiet one as Sir Johna's death, added to the others has bothered everyone except for

Solur. The sun starts to set as Zak leads them over to some fallen, petrified trees. Everyone dismounts and ties up their horse. They each grab some food and their bedroll.

Everyone sets down their things as Zak speaks, "We should reach the desert tomorrow."

Solur looks at Zak, "That was some shot you made today."

Chaed sits back against a rock, "We really pulled together, but we lost another person."

Solur sighs, "It is bound to happen. Adventures are dangerous and people die, that is the facts."

Robin shakes her head, "Could you be any colder?"

Gaelin chimes in, "Solur is right. We knew when we started that not all of us would make it. We must stay focused and together because orcs and goblins are nothing compared to skeleton warriors and death knights."

It gets quiet as they all know that Gaelin speaks the truth. The Island of the Dead will test them the most and they have already lost three.

Ayron looks at Alexandra, "So, what do you think of your first adventure?"

Alexandra gives a weak smile, "It is not quite what I expected. I knew it would be dangerous, but not like this."

Steph nods in agreement, "Me too. I have traveled to the mountains, but never like this."

Zak questions, "Who else here is on their first adventure?"

Robin speaks up, "It is my first time out of Glenfin."

Maluc is next, "I have never been pass the wastelands."

Chaed speaks up, "None of us have been out of Glenfin except to Whitefeather."

Zak nods, "I have traveled all the way to the Northern Port before."

Gaelin shakes his head, "I have been as far as the

mountains."

Alexandra speaks again, "I wanted an adventure so bad. Now all I can think about is going home."

Ayron speaks supportively, "It will be over soon enough my lady."

Alexandra sighs, "I hope so. I really hope so."

Solur nods, "All of you have done well. I did not expect all of you to do as well as you have. All of you have impressed me. If you remain tight like you are now, you will make it back alive."

Everyone is surprised to hear what Solur said. They look at each other and everyone thinks the same thing, did he just compliment us. Hearing the undead speak highly of the humans and the elf shocks them all and takes their mind off of the events of the day.

The talking dies down as everyone finishes eating. Solur walks off and scouts out the surroundings while the others fall asleep.

CHAPTER 8

THE SUN IS HIGH IN THE SKY as the wastelands disappear under their feet and they find themselves in the vast, unrelenting desert. There are rolling sand dunes as far as the eye can see. The air is hot and each person starts to sweat from the increased heat of the arid desert.

Alexandra speaks while looking around, "There is nothing out here."

Zak nods, "We should reach a small trader's outpost sometime tomorrow."

Steph chimes in, "Everyone stay alert. The desert is full of danger."

Maluc chuckles slightly while looking around, "I think we will be able to see something coming."

The group continues on for about a hundred feet, then Zak stops. Everyone else stops and wonders what is happening.

Zak glances around, "Do you hear that?"

Robin questions while looking around, "Hear what?"

Steph points right, "Over there, the sand moved."

Solur speaks up, "The sand on our left moved as well."

Ayron questions, "What is it?"

Zak dismounts, "I think we rode into a nest."

Everyone else dismounts and Alexandra questions, "A nest of what?"

Maluc chimes in, "Do not hold out on us Zak."

Then from the sand about twenty feet to their left, emerges an eight foot long, giant scorpion with it's menacing pincers clacking together and it's tail poised to strike. The creature stands about three feet off the ground and the tail curls about ten feet into the air. Two more emerge from the sand in front of the group and one emerges on their right. Then another one emerges behind them.

Zak draws his sword, "Giant scorpions."

Alexandra looks around, "There are five of them."

Solur draws his weapons, "Two for each scorpion."

Chaed grabs his shield and draws his sword, "Alexandra with me."

Alexandra draws her sword and follows Chaed towards the scorpion on the left. Ayron draws his sword and Robin joins him as they move for the scorpion on the right. Gaelin follows Solur as they move for the scorpion behind them. Sir Cleef and Maluc start at the scorpion on the front right as Zak and Steph move for the last scorpion.

Chaed blocks a pincer with his shield and swings his sword, but the scorpion is out of reach. Alexandra hops back and swings, but the pincer is already gone. Chaed and Alexandra try to work in close, but the scorpion keeps them at bay with it's pincers, keeping it's tail ready to strike.

Solur ducks under one pincer and hops back from the second. Gaelin moves in and swings his staff at the scorpion, but the creature knocks the staff away with it's pincer. The pincers keep coming as Solur and Gaelin continue to duck and dodge. Finally, Solur cuts the left pincer with his dagger as the right pincer narrowly misses clamping his head.

Zak spins away from a pincer and cuts in with his sword, but the pincer is no longer there. Steph moves in with her staff, but the scorpion keeps her away with it's other pincer. Steph dives under the pincer and hits the scorpion in the body with her staff. The blow is not clean as the tail speeds down at Steph. Steph rolls away at the last second.

Sir Cleef and Maluc try everything to get in close, but the scorpion holds them off. Maluc ducks under a pincer and cuts the pincer with his dagger. Then the tail comes at him and Maluc dives away to safety. Sir Cleef moves in and cuts the pincer on the left, but the other pincer comes in and hits him in the back of the legs and Sir Cleef crashes to the ground. The scorpion readies it's tail when Maluc gets in and cuts the scorpion on it's side. Maluc tries to move away, but one pincer hits him in the back, but Sir Cleef manages to roll away.

Robin keeps moving as the pincer keeps coming at her. Ayron tries to get in close with his sword, but the other pincer and the tail keeps him from doing so. Finally, Ayron ducks and cuts the pincer as it passes over his head. Robin also hits the pincer with her staff. Then the tail comes down at Robin. Robin moves left out of the way, but a pincer comes around and slams into her back, knocking her to the ground. Ayron steps over and his sword moves the pincer away from Robin as she gets back to her feet.

Chaed and Alexandra move in on the scorpion's left. The pincer comes around at them, but Chaed blocks it with his shield. Alexandra quickly spins around Chaed's shield and removes the pincer with a cut of her sword. The tail comes down at Alexandra, but she quickly moves to the right. Chaed steps over and knocks the tail away with his shield as his sword quickly follows and removes the tail. The scorpion moves back, but Alexandra and Chaed close in. Chaed blocks the last pincer as both of them drive their swords into the scorpion's body.

Solur rolls forward under one pincer and cuts off one of the scorpion's legs. The stinger comes down at him.

Solur does a back roll out of the way as Gaelin steps in with his staff. Gaelin's staff hits the scorpion's tail and discharges lightning into the creature. The scorpion is momentarily stunned. Solur moves fast before the creature can recover and his sword removes the stinger. The last pincer comes around and Gaelin stops it with his staff. Solur steps in and drives his sword into the scorpion's head, killing it.

Robin ducks under the pincer and launches a magical arrow into the scorpion's body. The scorpion steps back and Ayron seizes the opportunity as the scorpion is distracted. Ayron's sword removes the left pincer in one quick swing. The scorpion comes across with the other pincer, but Robin blocks it with her staff. Ayron steps in and cuts the scorpion across it's side. The stinger comes down quickly, but Ayron moves out of the way. Then, Robin steps in and hits the scorpion in the head with her staff. The pincer comes around at Robin and she ducks. Ayron steps over and removes the pincer with another big cut. The scorpion moves back, but it is too late as Ayron steps in and drives his sword into the scorpion.

Zak ducks under the pincer as Steph steps over and crushes the pincer with a massive blow from her staff. The pincer goes limp as the stinger comes down at Steph. Steph moves out of the way and Zak's sword is waiting. One quick swing and the stinger is removed. Steph spins in, blocking the last pincer with her staff and then delivering a blow, breaking two of the scorpion's legs. The scorpion crumbles to the ground as Zak finishes it off with a thrust to the scorpion's head.

Sir Cleef holds the pincer at bay, but is unable to get inside. Maluc dives under the pincer coming at him. He rolls to a knee and lets the dagger in his left hand fly. It hits the scorpion in the head. The scorpion reels away for a second and when it does, Sir Cleef removes the pincer with his sword. The tail comes at Maluc, but Maluc rolls right to safety. The stinger comes down again, this time Maluc moves out of the way, but stays close enough to ram his dagger into the tail as it narrowly misses him. Sir Cleef moves in fast and cuts down the scorpion with two quick swings.

Maluc retrieves his dagger as the others come back together by the horses.

Alexandra questions, "Is everyone okay?"

Everyone gives a quick nod and Zak speaks up, "We should move, just in case there are more."

Maluc walks up, "I like that idea."

Everyone kind of chuckles as they climb back on their horses. Zak starts off again and everyone falls in behind him as the sun continues to beat down on them.

The group stops for a food break while the scorching sun is in the afternoon sky. Sweat rolls down their faces as the relentless heat pounds their bodies. The sand is vast and seems to go on forever. They dismount and grab some fruit from their saddle bags.

Sir Cleef speaks, "This cursed heat is killing me."

Zak nods, "It will get better when the sun sets. We just need to make sure we conserve our water until we reach the outpost."

Steph chimes in, "We should reach the outpost before nightfall. It is not far."

Ayron speaks up, "We are going to need more arrows as well as supplies."

Alexandra nods, "We are going to have to find more gold and silver somewhere."

Robin questions, "How much do we have left?"

Alexandra replies bewildered, "With arrows, maybe ten days of supplies."

Steph shakes her head, "That will not even get us to

the Northern Port."

Zak speaks up, "I know where we can get some more gold. It is a few days from the outpost."

Chaed questions, "Is it out of the way?"

Zak replies, "Not really. It will only add an extra day."

Maluc speaks a little cynically, "I cannot believe there is free treasure laying around."

Ayron agrees, "It does seem too easy."

Zak speaks in a not so happy tone, "It is not really free."

Maluc questions in a sarcastic tone, "Great, now what?"

Zak replies, "It is said to be guarded by a powerful creature."

Alexandra questions, almost not wanting to know the answer, "What creature?"

Zak responds, "I am not sure what it is called, but it has a large lion's body with wings and a scorpion's tail."

Gaelin looks up, recognizing what Zak is describing, "It is the scorpicore. It is very powerful and very dangerous."

Solur finally speaks, "No matter what the creature, we must try or there is no point in going any further."

Sir Cleef speaks up, "There has to be another way. Something less dangerous."

Alexandra shakes her head, "If another option comes up before the time to head for the treasure, then we will take it. If not, we will have to brave the creature." She takes her last bite, "We should get moving."

The others nod and climb back on their horses. Zak starts off again and the others fall in behind him.

The group approaches a group of thirty large, brown

tents as the sun starts to set. The torches lighting the outpost glow for miles in the expanse of the desert.

Steph smiles, "The outpost."

As they draw closer, they can make out some of the people. Most are dressed in loose robes of various colors and they are wearing sandals. However, there are other men that are dressed in brown tunics and pants with leather boots. These men also wear long brown cloaks and it is obvious that they are carrying weapons beneath the cloaks.

Zak speaks up, "It looks like some nomads are here right now."

Chaed questions, "Are they anything to worry about?"

Steph replies, "Not really. They are the thieves of the desert so we will have to watch our things closely."

Robin chimes in, "Maluc should feel right at home then."

Maluc shakes his head sarcastically, "Very funny. You should know that there is no honor among thieves."

The group stops and dismounts once they reach the first tent. They walk their horses through various tents, looking for supplies and weapons.

Ayron points left, "Over there, a weapons tent."

Alexandra looks over, "Good, those of you that need arrows, come with me."

Alexandra, Ayron, Sir Cleef, Zak and Steph hand Solur their horses and walk over to the weapons tent. There is a nomad looking at the different weapons and a male gypsy is sitting on a carpet counting some coins.

Alexandra speaks up, "Each of you grab a quiver of thirty. I will pay for them."

Alexandra walks over to the gypsy and the gypsy looks up, "What can I do for you?"

Alexandra questions, "How much is four quivers of thirty arrows?"

The gypsy replies in his gruff voice, "Three silver pieces."

Alexandra looks surprised, "What?"

The gypsy smiles, "Everything costs more in the desert."

Alexandra pulls out her pouch and takes out the coins. The nomad watches closely. He can tell that Alexandra has wealth. Once the arrows are paid for, they return to the rest of the group. The nomad walks out and off to the other end of the outpost where some of his friends are waiting.

Chaed looks at Alexandra, "We found the supply tent."

Solur watches the horses as the others walk off to the supply tent. Solur looks around and notices the nomads are keeping a close eye on the group. Solur can tell that the nomads are planning something. A short time passes and the rest of the group walks back up to Solur.

Zak speaks, "We should set up camp just outside the outpost."

Alexandra nods, "Sounds good to me."

The group walks off and the nomads continue to watch closely.

The sun starts to rise and the cool night begins to give way to the scorching hot desert days again. Solur walks around the camp and begins to wake up the others. The rest of the group sits up and begins eating their morning fruit as Solur watches over the camp. A few minutes pass when Solur notices movement amongst the tents. He glances around as if he were taking count of something.

Alexandra notices what Solur is doing and questions, "Solur, what is it?"

Solur replies in his usual calm fashion, "Nomads.

They have been watching and planning all night."

Robin quickly raises the next question, "Do you think they are trouble?"

Solur nods slightly, "They will attack soon enough. However, do nothing to let them know that we know they are there. They believe they have the element of surprise."

Chaed speaks up, "If they were going to attack, they would have done it in the dark of night."

Solur shakes his head, "They could not see what they were up against last night. Now they can see that there is only ten of us."

Steph questions, "Do you have any idea how many of them there are?"

Solur gives a reassuring smile, "I counted only fifteen last night."

Everyone stands and starts gathering their things together when they hear the sound of numerous footsteps in the sand heading their way. Everyone looks around and sees four nomads closing from the left, four from the right, two from behind and five from in front of them. All the nomads are dressed as they were the night before and each one carries a short sword.

One of the nomads yells, "Get the treasure!"

Chaed, with his sword and shield in hand, heads for the four nomads on the right with Alexandra next to him with her sword drawn. Zak, with his sword and dagger drawn, and Steph with her staff, head for the nomads on the left. Solur draws his sword and dagger and moves for the two nomads behind them. Robin, Ayron, Gaelin, Sir Cleef and Maluc ready their weapons and start at the five nomads moving in from the front.

Alexandra faces off with two of the nomads. She thrusts in at the one on the left, but the nomad parries left and counters. Alexandra blocks the sword and kicks the nomad in the right leg. The second nomad moves in at Alexandra. She ducks under the deadly sword and cuts the nomad across the stomach. She quickly comes back across at the nomad, but the nomad blocks. The first nomad comes back across at Alexandra. She deflects the sword away and spins back around to the second nomad. Alexandra catches the nomad unaware and her sword delivers a deadly cut across his throat.

Zak squares off against two nomads. The first comes at him from the left, but Zak blocks with his dagger. He spins off the block and brings his sword around at the other nomad. The nomad blocks the sword, but Zak's dagger comes in right behind the sword and buries itself into the nomad's right ribs. The first nomad comes back around at Zak. Zak removes his dagger, ducks under the sword and spins. He comes around and cuts the nomad deep across the back with his sword. The nomad is unable to recover as Zak's dagger pierces the nomad's heart from between his shoulder blades. The second nomad steps in a little unsteady and cuts at Zak's head. Zak drops to a knee and thrusts his sword into the nomad's stomach.

Robin faces against one of the nomads. The nomad cuts down at Robin, but Robin blocks with her staff. She comes around with her staff and hits the nomad in the ribs. The nomad comes back around with his sword, but Robin ducks and sweeps the legs out from under the nomad. The nomad crashes to the ground and drops his sword. Robin taps her staff in the sand and the sand reaches up as if it had arms and pulls the nomad under the sand, never to be seen again.

Sir Cleef cuts in at the one nomad he is facing. The nomad blocks and counters with his sword. Sir Cleef moves left out of the way and cuts in at the nomad again. The nomad moves quick and blocks again. This time the nomad counters low and Sir Cleef doesn't quite move back fast enough and the sword leaves a small cut across the front of his right thigh. Sir Cleef comes in at the nomad with a thrust of his sword. The nomad moves to block, but Sir Cleef withdraws his sword and comes around behind the nomad's sword. He cuts the nomad across the left arm. The nomad comes back across with his sword. Sir Cleef ducks under the blade and delivers the final blow to the nomad's ribs.

Gaelin squares off with one nomad. The nomad brings his sword around at Gaelin, but Gaelin blocks with his staff. Gaelin brings his staff in at the nomad, but the nomad spins away and brings his sword around at Gaelin's head. Gaelin moves quick to block the sword. Gaelin brings the end of his staff up at the nomad, but the nomad hops back out of the way. Gaelin gets a look on his face like he has had enough. This time when the nomad steps in with his sword, Gaelin brings his staff around to block. However, when the sword touches the staff, lightning shoots through the sword into the nomad's body. The nomad jerks around a little and then falls to the ground with no life left in his body.

Steph faces two nomads with her staff ready. The first nomad cuts in at her right. Steph comes across and blocks with her staff. She sees the second nomad moving in on her left and she brings her staff across at the nomad. The nomad blocks the staff with his sword. The first nomad moves in again, but Steph moves fast and brings her staff across and jabs the nomad in the right side, cracking a couple of the nomad's ribs. The second nomad swings at Steph's head. Steph ducks under the sword and her staff crushes the nomad's right knee. As the nomad starts to fall, Steph comes up and breaks the nomad's neck with an upward swing. The other nomad steps in and swings his sword at Steph. Steph brings her staff around and breaks the sword blade off, just above the handle. She reverses her swing and crushes the side of the nomad's head.

Ayron cuts in at the nomad he is facing, but the nomad blocks the sword. The nomad counters off the block, but Ayron steps back and the sword misses him. Ayron thrusts back in, but the nomad spins right and brings his sword around at Ayron. Ayron ducks under the sword and cuts the nomad across the front of his left leg. The nomad comes down at Ayron, but Ayron steps left and cuts the nomad across the ribs. Before the nomad can recover, Ayron cuts him down with another swing.

Solur squares off with the two nomads from behind the group. The first nomad cuts in from the left, but Solur blocks with his dagger. The second nomad cuts in at Solur, but Solur spins away behind the first nomad. Solur's left hand moves like lightning and he cuts the nomad's throat. The second nomad thrusts in at Solur. Solur brings his dagger across and knocks the sword away. Solur continues into a spin and brings his sword up. Solur removes the nomad's head in one quick stroke.

Maluc faces off with one of the nomads. Maluc comes in from the left with his dagger. The nomad blocks with his sword, but Maluc's other dagger cuts in and draws blood on the nomad's right arm. The nomad brings his sword around at Maluc's right. Maluc uses his right dagger to deflect the sword up and drives his left dagger into the nomad's gut. Maluc removes the dagger and brings his other dagger across and slices the nomad's throat.

Chaed faces the two nomads in front of him. The first nomad cuts in from the left. Chaed brings his shield across and blocks the sword. Turning his back to the nomad, Chaed brings his sword around at the second nomad. The second nomad blocks with his sword as the first nomad cuts in again. Chaed spins around the sword and cuts down the nomad with a powerful blow to the nomad's exposed ribs. The second nomad moves in and thrusts his sword at Chaed. Chaed brings his shield across and knocks the sword away and thrusts his sword in behind the nomad's sword. Chaed's sword pierces the nomad's heart and lungs.

Alexandra faces the last nomad. The nomad comes in at Alexandra from her left. Alexandra brings her sword across and blocks. Alexandra counters off the block, but the nomad moves back to safety. The nomad moves back in and Alexandra cuts in at him from the right. The nomad blocks with his sword. Alexandra spins her sword in a small circle and knocks the nomad's sword away. She cuts in behind the sword and draws blood across the nomad's chest. The nomad comes back across at Alexandra, but she drops under the sword and delivers the final cut to the nomad's gut.

The last nomad falls and the group moves back to the campsite.

Robin slows down her breathing, "We should leave. They may not like us killing their friends."

Chaed nods, "I agree."

Alexandra looks at Zak, "Okay, take us to this treasure."

The group gathers up their things and put them back on their horses. They can hear some of the gypsies and other people from the outpost starting their way. Zak and the others mount up on their horses and quickly start off into the vast sand dunes.

———

The mid-day sun beats down on the traveling group as they stop for a minute. Sweat rolls down their faces as the relentless heat pounds their bodies. Each one carries the look of being exhausted.

Chaed speaks up, "Cursed heat."

Zak swallows some water, "Tomorrow we will reach the Valley of the Damned."

Maluc looks at Zak, "The Valley of the Damned. Is it not possible for people to use happy names, but no, we have the Dark Forrest, Swamp of Despair, Island of the Dead and Dragon Mountain. Did I forget anything?"

Steph pipes up just to egg on Maluc, "You forgot the Cave of the Lost Souls. It is in the mountains we must pass through."

Maluc shakes his head, "I did not need to know, really."

Alexandra questions, "Why is the cave called that?"

Zak replies, putting away his water flask, "It is said that the cave system is so confusing that a person could get lost forever and perish, thus, a lost soul."

Ayron questions, "Do we have to go through the caves or is there another way around?"

Steph responds, "We will have to go through the caves only if the weather has made the trail impassable."

Zak adds, "Not to mention, the dwarf kingdom is hidden amongst the caves."

Sir Cleef speaks up, "We have never had a problem with the dwarves in the past."

Robin speaks up, "But you never had an undead and a thief with you. That could prove a problem."

Chaed nods, "True."

Zak nods also, "The dwarves are very protective of their kingdom and the magical items they make."

Gaelin puts his water away, "Before we can worry about all of that, we must make it through the desert."

Solur finally speaks, "We should get going."

The others put away their water as they think about the caves that lie beyond the desert. Zak starts off again and the others fall in behind him.

The group reaches the top of a large sand dune and they see two ten foot tall stone pillars about eight feet apart and thirty feet in front of them. The desert sun beats down on all of them as each person narrows their eyes and sees a large stone pyramid in the distance.

The pyramid is about two hundred feet tall, made out of large stones, rectangular in shape and each about three feet tall by six feet wide. The stones are worn and are obviously very old.

Zak speaks up as they slowly ride towards the pyramid, "The treasure is inside the pyramid."

Chaed questions, "Where is the scorpicore?"

Zak replies with his eyes scanning the surroundings, "It is around."

Gaelin questions, "Is there anything inside the pyramid that we will have to face."

Zak shrugs, "I do not know. I have heard stories of mummies and other creatures, but I have never heard of anyone getting past the scorpicore."

Robin speaks up, "It is going to be dark inside the pyramid."

As the group gets closer, they see skeletons of humans and other creatures laying in the sand. Everyone just looks at the skeletons and thinks the same thing. They start scanning around with their eyes, even more alert than before.

The pyramid gets closer and closer as Ayron brings up a suggestion, "Perhaps we can sneak a small group into the pyramid while everyone else keeps the scorpicore busy."

Alexandra nods, "Good idea Ayron, but who can we send into the pyramid?"

Solur speaks up, "I can go into the pyramid since I can see in the dark. All I need is Maluc. A thief's skills might come in handy."

Sir Cleef protests a little, "Solur is our best warrior, we will need him to fight the scorpicore."

Gaelin speaks up, "Solur must go into the pyramid for he is the only one that can see in the dark without assistance. He is also probably the only one that can handle what might be inside on his own."

Zak nods, "It sounds like a good plan to me. I say we give it a try."

Steph points up at the side of the pyramid as the group stops, "It looks like the entrance is about halfway up."

Solur looks up and sees the six foot by six foot opening Steph is pointing at. The group dismounts and each person grabs their weapons, readying themselves for the scorpicore. At that moment, they hear a deafening growl. Ayron, Sir Cleef, Zak and Steph ready their bows. Chaed grabs his shield and sword as Alexandra draws her sword. Robin and Gaelin ready their staves.

Solur looks at Maluc, "We must hurry."

Maluc and Solur quickly start climbing up the side of the pyramid. They get about fifty feet up the side when the fabled creature comes flying over the top of the pyramid. The massively powerful looking lion's body is twenty feet long. The wings extend out from the sides of the body about twenty five feet on each side. The large scorpion's tail curls ten feet about the creature's back. The four legs are ten feet long with long, sharp claws.

Everyone except for Solur just looks at the creature in disbelief. The scorpicore starts down at Maluc and Solur. At the last second, Solur pulls Maluc out of the way as the scorpicore's razor sharp claws scratch the stones where Solur and Maluc were standing.

Ayron, Sir Cleef, Zak and Steph fire their arrows at the scorpicore, but the creature veers away and all four arrows miss. Solur and Maluc are back up and moving quickly.

Chaed brings his shield up at the last second as the scorpicore slams into it. The impact is incredible and Chaed is knocked to the sand. Robin launches a magical arrow at the creature. The scorpicore, with it's cat-like reflexes, leaps away as the magical arrow misses. Then the scorpicore moves as if it has a sixth sense and it takes to flight as a lightning bolt from Gaelin hits the ground, sending sand into the air, where the scorpicore was at. The scorpicore comes swooping down at Alexandra. Alexandra dives left as one claw barely scratches her on the back.

Solur and Maluc run into the entrance and find themselves in a long, black passageway. The smell of dust and death fills the old air inside the pyramid.

Solur speaks, "Stay close to me."

Maluc replies, "You do not need to worry about that."

Solur and Maluc start down the passageway, moving slowly. The dirt and sand crumbles under their feet. They walk about a hundred feet when Solur sees a large hole in the floor and a stone wall behind the hole. A rope hangs down from the ceiling and it goes into the hole in the floor. Solur gets on his stomach and looks into the hole.

Solur speaks, "A large chamber of some kind." He stands back up and grabs the rope, "Down we go."

Solur slides down the twenty foot long, frayed rope. Once he reaches the floor of the chamber, he moves out of the way and Maluc slides down.

The scorpicore veers away from another one of Sir Cleef's arrows and the left wing slams into Steph, knocking her to the ground as she drops her bow. Zak fires again and the scorpicore veers right, but the lightning arrow scratches down the creatures left side.

Chaed is back on his feet and he runs at the scorpicore as it lands near Robin. The scorpicore rears up away from Chaed's sword. The scorpicore comes back down at Chaed. The right leg crashes into Chaed's shield, pinning Chaed to the ground. The tail readies to strike, but Alexandra cuts the scorpicore on the left front leg. The scorpicore turns and knocks Alexandra away with it's wing. Gaelin fires a magical arrow into the massive body of the scorpicore and the creature takes to flight again as Robin's magical arrow narrowly misses.

The scorpicore turns at Sir Cleef. Sir Cleef fires his arrow at the scorpicore as it draws closer. The arrow is on target and hits the scorpicore in the neck. However, the scorpicore is too close for Sir Cleef to get out of the way and the right front claws slams into his chest and rip through his flesh. Sir Cleef flies back and crashes into the sand as blood pours out of his chest.

Solur and Maluc start across the fifty foot by fifty foot chamber. Stone pillars stand along each side of the dark and musky chamber. As they walk, Maluc kicks something on the ground and he looks down. They both see a human skull on the ground.

Maluc's eyes widen, "I did not need to see that."

Solur nods, "Lets go. I do not know how long the others will hold out."

They continue across the chamber and pass ten mummy caskets. Once they reach the far side of the chamber, they come to a ten foot by ten foot stone door with many pictures scratched on it. Solur pushes on the door, but even his great strength can't move the door.

Solur steps back, "It must have a lock on it." Solur looks at Maluc, "This is where you come in."

Maluc steps over to the door as Solur watches out into the chamber. Maluc slowly runs his hands over the different pictures on the door, feeling for anything to give away the hidden lock. Solur keeps glancing back at Maluc, silently urging him to hurry. Then, Maluc's right hand stops. He pulls out a dagger with his left hand.

Maluc slips his dagger into a hole on the door that was disguised as a picture, "I will have it in a second."

Maluc works his dagger around for a few seconds when they finally hear a dull thump sound on the other side of the door.

Maluc puts his dagger away, "Give me a hand."

Solur walks over and they both push on the door. The heavy door starts to give as dust falls on them from overhead. The door slowly slides open to revel a small room with a small golden chest in the middle of the room.

Solur looks at Maluc, "You get the chest, I will wait here in case."

Maluc nods and steps into the room. His steps are slow and calculated, expecting any traps that might be waiting for him.

Zak dives left, twists his body around and fires his arrow as the scorpicore flies by. The lightning arrow hits the scorpicore in the underbelly. Steph rolls to her bow, grabs an arrow, turns and fires. Her arrow hits the scorpicore in the right front leg. Steph drops to the ground as the left rear claws slightly rake down her back.

The creature lands in front of Robin and swings at her. Robin moves to get out of the way, but a couple of claws cut across her legs. Robin falls to the sand. Suddenly, a bolt of lightning slams into the scorpicore. The scorpicore steps back and takes to flight again.

Maluc picks up the small, yet fairly heavy chest and turns around. Then, Solur and Maluc hear some creaking noises from out in the chamber.

Maluc retraces his steps back over to Solur, "I do not like that sound."

Solur nods, "Lets get out of here."

The two of them start back across the chamber when they see the ten mummy caskets starting to open. They take only another step when the caskets spring open and ten mummies step out into the chamber. The mummies are old and smell of death. Their bandages are starting to deteriorate.

Solur draws his sword with angry determination, "You stay here. I will deal with this."

Maluc nods and smiles, "They are all yours."

Solur starts walking towards the ten mummies. Solur's face is that of hatred and disgust as if there was some bad history between his kind and the mummies in which he figures to rectify at this time.

Chaed ducks as the scorpicore flies over his head and goes straight at Ayron. Ayron fires his arrow and the creature catches it in it's teeth. The scorpicore veers left and it's right wing slams into Ayron and he crashes to the ground. The scorpicore lands in front of Alexandra and swings at her. Alexandra ducks under the claws, but her sword is too slow and misses. Zak fires another lightning arrow into the scorpicore's body, just under the right wing. Chaed runs over and his sword cuts the scorpicore deep across the left rear leg. The tail comes down, but Chaed blocks it away with his shield. Then, the left wing comes around and knocks Chaed to the ground again. As the tail readies to strike again, an ice ring from Robin slams into the creature. Obviously starting to hurt, the scorpicore leaps into flight once again.

Solur moves quick on the first mummy and his deadly sword cuts the mummy in half from it's left shoulder to it's right hip. He turns quick and removes the second mummy's head in one smooth motion. Solur flips his sword, blade down and rams it back into the third mummy that is behind him while he kicks the fourth mummy standing in front of him away. He removes the sword and brings it around, still blade down, and removes the fourth mummy's legs, just above the knees.

Solur sees an arm reaching for him out of the corner of his left eye. He brings his left arm around with great speed and catches the outside of the mummy's wrist. Solur quickly flips his sword back around to blade up and cuts the fifth mummy in half at the waist. Solur reverses his swing and buries his sword into the sixth mummy's chest.

Solur withdraws his sword, turns left and thrusts

across his body. His sword goes through the seventh mummy's head. Moving fast, Solur removes his sword, spins right 180 degrees and cuts down. His sword removes the eighth mummy's outstretched arms at the elbows. Solur brings his sword back up and takes the eighth mummy's head off from the nose to the back crown of the skull.

Solur does a back kick to knock the ninth mummy away. The tenth mummy comes at Solur from the front as the ninth mummy comes at him from behind. Solur takes a couple steps back, ducks under the ninth mummy's arms and spins right. He elbows the ninth mummy in the back, knocking the ninth mummy forward into the tenth mummy. Solur thrusts his sword forward into the back of the ninth mummy's head, out the front of the head and through the tenth mummy's head.

Solur withdraws his sword and puts it away. He has a look a satisfaction on his face as he walks back over to Maluc.

Maluc has a look of disbelief on his face, "I take it you do not like mummies."

Solur just smiles, "Lets go."

Maluc and Solur run over to the rope and start climbing out of the chamber, each one hoping that nothing has happened to the others who are still battling outside.

Steph lets her arrow fly and it hits the scorpicore in the left wing. Zak fires another lightning arrow and it hits the creature in the chest area. Ayron lets his arrow fly and it hits the scorpicore in the neck. The scorpicore starts down at Alexandra. Alexandra dives out of the way as Chaed steps over and cuts the scorpicore along it's underbelly. Then, another lightning bolt hits the creature. The scorpicore lets out a painful howl and flies off back over the top of the pyramid.

Alexandra yells to the others as she sees Solur and

Maluc come out of the pyramid, "Get the horses!"

Solur and Maluc nearly fall numerous times coming down the side of the pyramid as fast as they can. Ayron rushes over to check on Sir Cleef. He rolls the body over and can tell right away that Sir Cleef is dead.

Maluc speaks with a grin as he runs up to the others, "We got the treasure."

Zak replies nearly out of breath, "The scorpicore is still alive."

Maluc loses his smile, "What?"

Alexandra yells, "We need to get out of here, now!"

Robin speaks up, "What about Sir Cleef?"

Ayron runs over to his horse next to the others, "He is dead."

Chaed speaks up, "Then we leave him here."

Solur gets on his horse, "Lets go."

The rest of the group gets on their horses as they hear the scorpicore off in the distance.

Zak yells, "This way!"

Zak takes off on his horse and the others are close behind as they leave Sir Cleef's body and the wounded creature behind.

It has been two days since the scorpicore encounter. As the sun gets low in the desert sky, causing a magnificent red and purplish effect, the group sets up camp for the night. Gaelin starts his magical fire in the middle of the camp as everyone sits down to eat some fruit.

Alexandra speaks up, "With the treasure, we have more than enough to make it to the Island of the Dead and back."

Chaed sighs, "This has been an expensive trip, not just in gold either."

Everyone knows what Chaed is talking about now that they have lost the fourth member of the original group.

Solur speaks up, "The lands are dangerous and people die. That is just how it is. We cannot think about the past or we will never make it to the end of this quest."

Zak nods, "As much as I hate to, I would have to agree with Solur. We have far too much to worry about ahead of us to think about what has happened in the past." He pauses, "And we may not have enough gold still."

Robin questions, "What do you mean?"

Zak looks at her, "The pass through the mountains."

Steph chimes in, knowing what Zak is going to say next, "If the weather is bad, we will have to go through the caves."

Ayron looks puzzled, "How is that a problem other than we might get lost?"

Zak replies, "We cannot take the horses through the caves. We will have to leave them behind."

Steph continues, "That means we will have to cross the snow lands on foot and buy more horses in the Northern Port. And horses are not cheap."

Solur shakes his head, "We do not need to worry about buying more horses. We can get them once we get to the Island of the Dead. The problem will be affording the price of a ship to take us there and wait for our return."

Gaelin finally speaks, "Then we must conserve our gold. Especially for the trip back to Glenfin."

Chaed speaks up, "We are also running low on supplies."

Zak nods, "We should reach a trader's outpost tomorrow, we can get more supplies there."

Maluc smiles, "It is funny how things seem to work out for us. As long as our luck holds out, we should be fine."

Alexandra nods in agreement, "Maluc is right. We have managed so far." She slides down into her bedroll, "But now it is time to sleep."

Everyone else except for Solur crawls into their bedrolls. Gaelin lowers the fire and everyone is soon asleep. Solur watches over the camp. He is amazed at how positive everyone still is given the loss of four of their comrades. He smiles and thinks to himself that there might be hope for the humans yet.

———

Robin wakes a little before sunrise. She blinks a few times and looks around. She sees Solur standing about twenty feet away and Ayron is standing next to him. They appear to be talking. Robin climbs out of her bedroll. She walks over to Solur and Ayron.

Solur speaks as Robin walks up behind him, "Having trouble sleeping as well Robin?"

Robin gets a puzzled look, "How did you know it was me?"

Solur smiles, "I can tell by your scent and the sound of your footsteps."

Robin looks at Ayron, "I see I am not the only one having trouble sleeping."

Ayron nods, "I was just doing some thinking."

Solur can tell by how Robin and Ayron are looking at each other that it is time for him to make an exit.

Solur turns to leave, "I am going to check on the horses."

Solur walks off and leaves Robin alone with Ayron.

Robin questions intently, "What are you thinking about?"

Ayron stares off into the darkness, "I was thinking about how things might change when we get back to Glenfin."

Robin looks at him, "What kind of change?"

Ayron sighs, "Our lives. And maybe the relationship between the humans and the elves."

Robin pushes a little, "Between the races, or between us?"

Ayron looks at Robin, "We have waited for years to be together, hoping that the two races would embrace us being together. This quest might make that possible."

Robin smiles, "I really hope so. But even if our races do not embrace our feelings for each other, my feelings for you will never change."

Ayron smiles in return, "I know Robin. I was just hoping that we could show our feelings for each other and even one day get married."

Robin gets a tear in her eye, "I would like that very much."

The sun starts to rise as the sky starts to change from clear black and stars to a reddish blue color.

Solur walks back up, "I am going to wake the others. You two should get your things together so we can get an early start."

Solur walks off and starts to wake the others as Ayron and Robin gather up their things. Once everyone is awake, they eat a quick piece of fruit and gather up their things. Once the horses are packed up again, the group starts out across the desert.

The sun is in the late morning sky and the heat is already pounding the group as they get closer to the outpost of tents. Off in the distance they can see a huge range of snow capped mountains.

Zak speaks up, "We will reach the mountains in two days."

The group continues to ride until they reach the first

tent. The group stops and gets off their horses.

Steph speaks up, "We should need seven days of food and water to get to the Northern Port."

The group walks up to a supply tent. Each person gathers up the food and water they need. Alexandra pays the gypsy woman for the supplies and they walk back out to their horses. Everyone puts their supplies on their horses when they hear screaming from some of the other tents. People are running pass them in fear.

Chaed stops an older man, "What is it sir?"

The elderly man replies out of breath, "A barbarian raiding party."

The elderly man runs off and Alexandra speaks up, "We need to get out of here."

Gaelin points at the tents off to the north, "It is too late."

The group looks north to see twenty barbarians on horseback riding into the outpost. Each barbarian is large in build and is wearing animal skins. Ten of the barbarians are carrying swords, eight are carrying battle axes and two are carrying war hammers. Chaed draws his long sword from his horse while Solur, Zak and Alexandra draw their swords. Gaelin, Robin and Steph ready their staves as Maluc draws his daggers.

Ayron grabs his bow, draws an arrow and fires. The arrow zips in and hits one of the sword barbarians in the chest, taking him off his horse. Solur draws one of his poisonous darts as the barbarians get closer. Solur throws the dart and hits one of the sword barbarians in the left eye.

Chaed ducks under a war hammer and swings his sword at another sword barbarian. Chaed's sword slams into the barbarian's chest and blood flies everywhere as the massive blow takes the barbarian clean off his horse.

Gaelin ducks under a battle axe and fires a magical arrow into the chest of another axe barbarian. Robin steps across in front of a horse and lowers her staff in front of the horse's legs. She takes the horse's legs out and the war hammer barbarian crashes to the ground as sand flies everywhere. Before the barbarian can recover, Alexandra steps in and thrusts her sword into the barbarian's back, killing him.

Maluc ducks under a battle axe and turns quick as the barbarian passes by him. Maluc throws the dagger in his right hand and it hits the barbarian in the back, right between the shoulder blades. Zak draws his dagger as a sword barbarian closes in on him. The barbarian swings his sword at Zak. Zak blocks the sword with his sword and rams his dagger into the barbarian's right forearm. Zak steps back and drags the barbarian from his horse. When the barbarian hits the ground, Zak finishes him off with a thrust of his sword. A battle axe comes in at Steph. Steph brings the left end of her staff around and knocks the axe away. As the barbarian passes her, Steph brings the right end of her staff around and hits the barbarian in the back of the neck, crushing all the bones. The barbarian slumps forward and falls from his horse.

Chaed sidesteps and cuts the legs out from under the horse of the sword barbarian charging at him. As the sword barbarian goes over the front of the horse, Zak spins in and takes the barbarian's head off with his sword. A sword barbarian rides up to Solur and swings. Solur ducks and spins under the horse's head to the other side of the barbarian. Solur quickly thrusts his sword up into the left side of the barbarian's chest.

Ayron takes aim with another arrow and lets it fly. The arrow hits the war hammer barbarian in the neck. Gaelin calls down a lightning bolt and a barbarian carrying a battle axe is blown from his horse.

One of the remaining sword barbarians can tell they are up against powerful opponents and he yells, "Retreat!"

The remaining barbarians turn their horses to the east

and ride out of the outpost. Maluc retrieves his dagger as everyone comes together again and they put away their weapons.

Chaed speaks up, "If that was a raiding party, then the army is not far behind."

Solur nods, "Chaed is right. We should get moving."

Ayron agrees, "I really do not think we need to try and fight a whole barbarian army. That might be more than we can handle."

Gaelin questions, "Does everyone still have their supplies?"

The others check their horses and give a quick nod.

Alexandra speaks up, "Good, then lets go."

Zak climbs on his horse, "This way."

The rest of the group mounts up and follow Zak off towards the mountains to the north.

CHAPTER 9

THE DESERT FADES BEHIND THE GROUP as grass and pine trees become more abundant around them. The pounding desert heat has dropped and the cooler temperatures have moved in. The mountains rise up into the sky higher than any of them can see. The dirt and rock trail disappears into the mountains ahead. A cleaner more crisp smell fills the air. Patches of moisture start to form on the ground. At first it is just water, but as the group continues to ride up into the mountains, the ground starts to show signs of snow and frozen water.

The trail goes up for a ways when they pass a ten foot by ten foot cave entrance off on their right. The snow starts to fall harder and harder as the wind picks up.

Zak speaks, squinting his eyes, "That is the entrance to the dwarf kingdom, the Cave of the Lost Souls."

The wind is blowing even harder now as the snow makes the trail disappear in front of them. The group pushes on, but only makes it another couple hundred feet before the trail disappears completely.

Steph yells, shielding her face, "We have to turn back! We will never make it through the pass!"

Alexandra is also covering her face, "Where can we go?!"

Zak yells, looking back at the group, "We will have to try the caves!"

Alexandra nods and the group turns their horses

around and starts back towards the cave entrance. Then, the ground shakes as if a small bomb landed nearby.

Maluc questions, "What was that?"

They see the cave entrance through the heavy snow as the ground shakes again.

Ayron looks back over his shoulder and his eyes can't believe what he sees, "A giant!"

The giant, a human that stands nearly sixty feet tall, starts up behind them. The giant is dressed in a tunic and trousers with brown leather boots. He is carrying a large wooden club in his right hand.

Chaed yells, "Get to the cave!"

The group rides hard for the cave as the giant catches sight of them. The ground shakes more as the giant steps closer towards the group. The group stops just outside the cave entrance. They grab their weapons, food and water as the ground shakes even harder now that the giant is nearly upon them.

They all run into the cave entrance which opens into a smooth rock cavern about thirty foot by thirty foot round. In front of them are three tunnels each about ten foot high by eight foot wide. Suddenly, the giants club smashes into the side of the mountain just above the cave entrance. The massive blow causes the cavern to shake and the ceiling starts to collapse.

Solur yells as rocks start to fall, "Watch out!"

The nine of them scramble to get out of the way of the large falling rocks. The rocks pile up on the floor of the cavern and dust and dirt fills the air. The last rock finally falls and the dust settles.

Chaed stands up, having run into the right tunnel, "Is everyone okay?"

He hears movement to his right and turns. Chaed sees Steph stand up.

Steph stands up, "I am okay."

They hear Gaelin's voice behind them, "I too am

fine."

Chaed glances around, "Where are the others?"

Steph yells, "Zak!"

They hear Zak's voice a bit muffled, "Steph!"

Steph yells again, "Where are you?"

Zak's voice again, "I am in the left tunnel!"

Chaed yells, "Who else is with you?!"

Zak's voice, "Maluc and Ayron!"

Chaed yells, "Princess, where are you?!"

They hear Solur's voice, also muffled, "Alexandra and Robin are with me!"

Chaed yells, "Where are you?!"

Solur's voice, "We are in the right tunnel!"

Steph looks at Chaed, "What now?"

Chaed replies, "We have to find a way to the others."

Gaelin taps his staff on the ground and his magical light appears. The three of them look at all the rocks blocking the tunnel entrance.

Gaelin shakes his head, "We will never get through all that rock."

Zak's voice, "We need to get moving!"

Steph yells, "We need to find a way to each other!"

Solur's voice echoes, "We do not have time for that!"

Gaelin speaks, "They are right. We must trust that the tunnels will meet up later in the dwarf kingdom."

Chaed nods unwillingly, "Very well." He yells, "We are moving out! Maybe the tunnels meet up later!"

Zak's voice, "We are moving out!"

Solur's voice, "We are moving too!"

Chaed, Steph and Gaelin start down the middle tunnel with Gaelin's staff providing light.

Robin taps her staff on the ground and a magical light appears. Alexandra, Solur and Robin start off down the right tunnel.

Maluc pulls out his left dagger, "Light burning bright to light up the night."

His dagger that is usually glowing a dull red catches fire to light up the tunnel. Zak, Ayron and Maluc start down the right tunnel.

———————

After walking down the dusty, musty smelling passageway for awhile, Chaed, Steph and Gaelin stop to rest and eat. At first it is quiet, everyone is thinking about the other two groups and how they are doing.

Gaelin decides to bring up something happier, "How long have you and Zak known each other?"

Steph breaks a smile, "I have known him since I was five."

Chaed joins in, "So the deal is that the two of you must complete a noble quest together before you can get married?"

Steph nods while eating, "That is the law of the clan. They believe that if two people complete a noble quest together, then it must be true love."

Gaelin questions, "Do you have any plans for the wedding yet?"

Steph smiles thinking about the wedding day, "Oh yes. I have this beautiful dress that I have been working on for months. We have this beautiful place picked out. It is a small waterfall by this flower grove and clear spring. It is not far from our village."

Chaed smiles, "It sounds nice. I wish the two of you the best."

Steph loses her smile, "All that will happen if we make it back. We have been lucky so far, but the Island of the Dead scares me. If the other undead is anything like Solur, we do not have a chance."

Gaelin responds in a reassuring manner, "Solur is the last of his kind and he is on our side. The Island of the Dead will be the hardest test, but I think we will be okay."

Steph questions, "Are you not scared?"

Gaelin smiles, "Of course I am, especially after seeing how powerful Solur is. It makes me wonder about how powerful the other undead will be, but I have faith in the group. If we stay together, we will make it back."

Chaed speaks up, "I think the two of you are giving Solur too much credit. He is good, but I doubt he is that good."

Gaelin smiles at Steph, "Do not worry too much." He looks around, "We should try and get some rest."

Chaed nods, "Good idea."

The three of them get as comfortable as they can on the rock floor. It doesn't take long for them to fall asleep.

———

Zak, Maluc and Ayron have been walking down their passageway for some time now. Zak stops and so do the others.

Zak speaks, "We should take a break."

Maluc sits down and pulls out some food, "I wonder how the others are doing."

Zak replies while sitting down, "Chaed, Gaelin and Steph should be okay. I am not sure about Solur, Alexandra and Robin."

Ayron pulls out some food, "I doubt that they will encounter anything that Solur cannot handle."

Maluc nods in agreement, "Solur is good. You guys should have seen how fast he killed ten mummies in the pyramid." He pauses, "But I guess I would be that good to if I was a hundred and fifty years old."

Ayron speaks up, "Speaking of time." He looks at Zak, "How long have you and Steph known each other?"

Zak smiles, "I have known her since I was seven. What about you Ayron? Is there something going on between you and Robin?"

Maluc jumps in, "Yea, you two seem kind of close."

Ayron smiles, "We really like each other, but the elves do not approve of elves being with humans."

Zak shakes his head, "If you two are in love, it should not matter. What is the worst that can happen?"

Ayron sighs, "Robin would be banished from the elf kingdom and it might cause a problem between the humans and the elves. We are not ready to take that chance."

Maluc speaks up, "I am sure it will all work out once the quest is over."

Ayron replies unenthusiastically, "If we make it back."

Zak looks at Ayron, "Why would you think that? We have made it this far."

Ayron gazes at them, "The Island of the Dead."

Maluc nods slightly to agree, "I have been worrying about that also since Solur told us what we might encounter there. We cannot beat an army of that size, especially when it is an undead army."

Zak nods, "I know. Only a fool would not be worried, but let us hope that we do not have to face that army."

The talking dies down as they each think of the undead army and what might happen on the Island of the Dead.

Finally, Zak breaks the silence, "We should get some rest."

Ayron and Maluc nod as the three of them lay down and get as comfortable as they can on the rock ground. Maluc puts out the flame on his dagger and the three of them quickly fall asleep.

———————

Alexandra, Robin and Solur have been walking for quite some time now and the passageway seems to have no end.

Alexandra speaks up, "I can see why this place is called the Cave of the Lost Souls."

Solur speaks up, "We should stop and rest some."

Robin nods, "That is a good idea."

Alexandra sits down, "I wonder how the others are doing."

Solur sits down, "I am sure they are fine."

Robin sits, "I just hope that none of them get lost."

Solur leans back against the wall, "I am more worried about one of them doing something to turn the dwarves against us. Not to mention, there is a powerful wizard that travels these mountains."

Alexandra looks at Solur, "I did not figure you to be afraid of anything."

Solur smiles, "It is not fear. It is more of a concern."

Robin sighs, "I wish I could say that."

Solur looks at Robin, "You seem brave enough to me. In fact, all of you have earned my respect. This journey has been hard, but you have met every challenge head on."

Alexandra speaks up, "But we have not reached the Island of the Dead yet. And that place scares me."

Robin nods in agreement, "Me too."

It is quiet for a second, then Solur speaks up, "The Island of the Dead will be the most difficult task and I am sure not everyone will return from it, but I do believe this quest will be completed and the king will be saved. I have never seen a group so closely bonded."

Alexandra questions, "What is the Island of the Dead like?"

Solur sits up, "It is a charred, desolate land covered with the ashes and bones of those that have dared to travel there. A dark cloud hangs over the entire island, making it a constant night. The undead roam the land looking for anything to feed on."

Robin looks at Solur, "Why would anyone ever travel there?"

Solur smiles, "There are riches there beyond your wildest dreams and that draws enough people." He sits back, "But enough talk for now. The two of you should get some rest. No telling how long this passageway is."

Alexandra and Robin both nod and Robin puts out the light from her staff. The two ladies lay down on the uncomfortable rock ground and quickly fall asleep as Solur sits and watches over them.

———————

The dark, dank, musty passageway is lit up by Maluc's fire dagger. Zak, Ayron and Maluc have followed the twisting and turning passageway for what seems like an eternity. They have talked very little since they awoke.

Then, the first decision arises. The three of them walk into a small cavern and see two tunnels in front of them.

Maluc sighs, "Any ideas?"

Zak shakes his head, "Your guess is as good as mine. Lets just hope we pick the tunnel that leads us to the others."

Maluc chuckles, "The others. I want the tunnel that leads out of here."

Ayron lightly chuckles, "I say we try the left tunnel."

Zak shrugs, "Sounds good to me."

They look at Maluc and Maluc smiles, "I am just providing the light."

The three of them walk off into the left tunnel. It too is dark and musty smelling. The three of them continue to walk for about two hundred yards through the twisting and turning passageway when they find themselves standing in another cavern and facing another decision. This time they see three tunnels in front of them.

Maluc shakes his head, "I am really starting to dislike this place."

Ayron looks at Zak, "Your turn."

Zak smiles, "The right tunnel is as good as any."

The three of them start off into the dark and dingy right tunnel. Each one is thinking the same thing, they are lost.

———

Chaed, Gaelin and Steph are standing in a cavern looking at the three tunnels in front of them.

Steph shakes her head, "I have no idea."

Gaelin shrugs, "How about the right tunnel?"

Chaed nods, "I like it."

The three of them start into the right tunnel with Gaelin's staff lighting up the dark and dirty passageway. The passageway bends left and back right. It slopes up and bends right again. After about three hundred yards, the three of them walk into another cavern and see two tunnels in front of them.

Steph sighs, "We are lost. And we have no chance of finding the others."

Gaelin smiles, "Keep up the faith. We will find our way out."

Chaed motions with his head, "Lets try the left tunnel."

The other two nod and the three of them walk off into the left tunnel. It bends right and left as well as sloping up and down. The three of them are quiet, but they know that they are all thinking the same thing, Steph was right, they are lost.

———

Robin's staff lights up the dark and dank cavern that

she, Alexandra and Solur just walked into. The three of them look at the two tunnels in front of them.

Alexandra looks at Solur, "What do you think?"

Solur shrugs, "I am thinking that it does not matter."

Robin looks at Solur, "What do you mean?"

Solur smiles at the two ladies, "They both lead away from here."

It takes a second when Robin and Alexandra realize that Solur is joking with them. They both chuckle and shake their heads.

Solur nods, "Felt good to laugh, did it not?"

Alexandra nods, "It did."

Robin shakes her head, "I did not know the undead had a sense of humor."

Solur smiles and teases, "At times." He pauses, "I think we should try the left tunnel."

Alexandra nods in agreement, "Sounds good to me."

The three of them start off down the winding, dark passageway. It bends to the left quite a bit and then comes back to the right. The three of them walk for about four hundred yards to find themselves in another cavern, looking at two more tunnels.

Robin shakes her head, "I really do not like this place. How could anyone find their way through?"

Solur says just one word, "Luck."

Alexandra motions towards the right tunnel, "Lets try that tunnel."

Robin and Solur nods in agreement and the three of them start off down the right tunnel. It, like all the others, holds a musty odor that the three of them are getting tired of smelling. They walk for a ways and the thought crosses their minds, that they might be lost.

———

Zak, Maluc and Ayron stop in the next large cavern

as they stare at another choice of three tunnels.

Zak sighs, "I do not know about you two, but I am getting tired. I think we should rest before we get too far into the caverns that we fail to catch something that might give us a clue to which is the right way to go."

Maluc nods in agreement, "I could use a bite to eat too."

Ayron looks around, "This is as good a place as any to stop and rest."

Zak walks over to one of the cavern walls and sits down, "I really hope that we have not gone in a circle."

Maluc sits next to Zak, "I do not even want to think about that."

Ayron sits down by the other two, "How could someone tell. All the caverns and tunnels look the same."

Zak pulls out a piece of fruit, "I will be so happy to see the sunlight again."

Ayron nods, "I am never going into a cave after this, if we get out."

Maluc sighs, "If we do not get out, I am going to haunt the dwarves for the rest of eternity for creating such a stupid maze of caves."

Zak and Ayron laugh at Maluc. It breaks the tension some. The three of them finish their fruit and slide down to the cavern floor to go to sleep.

Zak speaks, "I hope the others are having better luck than us."

Ayron sighs, "I am sure they are."

Maluc puts out the fire on his dagger and the three of them get some sleep.

Chaed, Gaelin and Steph are walking down a tunnel that continues on a downward slope for awhile. Then the three of them stop when they see that the tunnel is half full of water in front of them.

Chaed sighs, "Well, this is just what we needed."

Steph just stares at the water that goes about twenty feet down the tunnel, "I wonder how deep it is."

Gaelin speaks up, "We have to try and cross it. It will take too long to go back and try a different tunnel."

The three of them are quiet for a few seconds, then Steph speaks up, "I will cross first. Chaed's armor will weigh him down and Gaelin can use his magic if something goes wrong."

Chaed looks at Steph, "Be careful. If it starts getting too deep, turn back. Do not take any chances."

Steph nods and starts into the water. She shivers from the cool, chilly water. Her steps are slow and calculated. Steph feels for the ground in front of her before each step. The water gets to her knees and she keeps going. About ten feet into the water, it reaches up to her waist.

Steph calls back to the others, "I think this is as deep as it gets."

Chaed replies, "Just be careful."

Steph continues across and the water starts going back down until she reaches the other side. She shakes from the cold water. Chaed starts across, followed by Gaelin. The two of them take it slow, just to make sure that they do not take a wrong step.

Chaed and Gaelin make it across and Steph looks at them, "Well, that was refreshing."

The three of them walk for another hundred yards and enter a cavern with a choice of two tunnels.

Gaelin sighs, "I think we should stop here, dry off and get some rest."

Chaed nods in agreement, "That sounds good to me."

Steph walks over and sits against a cavern wall, "I really hope the others are doing better than we are."

Chaed sits down, "I wonder if any of them have already found the way out."

Steph questions, "What are we going to do if we find the way out or one of them do?"

Gaelin sits, "We will wait and if they do not show up after a time, we continue on without them. I am sure that is what they will do."

The three of them eat some food and lie down on the cold cavern floor. It doesn't take them long to fall asleep.

———————

Robin's staff provides enough light in the dark and damp tunnel for the three of them to see the upcoming down slope ahead. Solur gets closer to the slope and realizes that it is very steep.

Solur stops when he sees a rope anchored in the wall by an iron ring. The rope is fairly old and somewhat frayed.

Alexandra questions from behind Solur, "What is the matter?"

Solur looks down the tunnel, "The tunnel slopes down at a very steep angle. We will have to use the rope to help climb down."

Robin looks over at the rope, "Will that thing hold all three of us?"

Solur grabs the rope and tugs on it. The rope gives a little, but stays together.

Solur shakes his head, "We will have to go down one at a time. I will go first since I do not need the light. I will yell back when I reach the bottom."

Alexandra nods and Solur takes hold of the rope. He backs down the slope at a slow pace, making sure his footing is good before taking the next step. Robin and Alexandra watch as Solur slowly goes down the tunnel until they can no longer see him.

Solur continues down into the darkness, keeping a close eye on the rope to make sure it doesn't start to give.

Robin and Alexandra stand at the top of the slope, waiting to hear from Solur.

Robin looks around, "I hate to admit this, but I do not like being here without Solur around."

Alexandra nods, staring into the darkness, "Me too."

The two ladies continue to wait, hoping to hear from Solur soon. After a short time and a two hundred foot climb down, Solur reaches the bottom where the tunnel levels out.

Solur looks around and then yells back up, "Okay!"

Alexandra and Robin breath a sigh of relief when they hear Solur's voice. Alexandra starts down next, leaving Robin alone at the top of the slope. Alexandra quickly disappears into the cold, darkness of the tunnel. The rope creeks, but holds up and after a short while, Alexandra reaches the bottom.

Alexandra stands next to Solur and Solur yells again, "Okay Robin!"

Robin hears the signal and she starts down the slope, clinging tightly to the rope. Robin disappears into the darkness as Solur and Alexandra wait at the bottom. After a short while, Solur sees Robin coming down the rope.

Robin reaches the bottom and turns to the others, "That was fun."

Robin taps her staff of the ground and her light appears again. The three of them walk a little longer and then they reach another cavern.

Robin sighs, "This is getting old."

Solur chuckles slightly, "I say we stop and rest here. We can continue after the two of you get some food and sleep. We have been walking for a long time."

Alexandra nods, "That is a good idea."

Alexandra and Robin walk over by one of the cavern walls and sit down. Solur walks around the cavern, looking down the two tunnels that they will have to soon choose from. Robin and Alexandra eat a piece of fruit and lay down on the cold cavern floor. The two of them quickly fall asleep as Solur sits quietly in the dark and watches over them.

Zak, Ayron and Maluc are walking down one of the many tunnels they have been in, using Maluc's dagger for light. They walk a little while longer when they start hearing the faint sounds of banging metal echoing in the tunnel.

Maluc stops, "What is that noise?"

Zak listens intently, "It sounds like metalworking."

Ayron chimes in, "Maybe it is the dwarves."

Zak shrugs, "Only one way to find out."

The three of them walk on and the echoing gets louder and louder. They start to see the glow of light in the tunnel ahead of them. After another hundred or so feet, the three of them enter a huge cavern.

The cavern is four hundred feet by four hundred feet. It rises up just over ten stories high. The three of them look up and see ten rope bridges spanning the cavern from one tunnel on their side to a tunnel on the far side. The rope bridges are one on top of the next with about fifteen feet of clearance between them.

Zak and the others stop and take in the magnificent sight. Dwarves of all kinds are moving about the cavern. Large metal bowls filled with liquid metal dot the massive cavern. Fires burn in numerous stone fire pits where dwarves are heating up rudimentary swords and then hammer them into shape. The noise is very loud and echoes throughout the entire cavern.

Zak looks around, "This is incredible."

Ayron nods in agreement, "I have never seen a sight such as this."

Maluc stares at the bridges, "No wonder people get

lost. Look at all those tunnels."

They hear a gruff older voice behind them, "And only a few of them lead out. Most tunnels circle around back to here."

The three of them turn quick to see who is behind them. They see a four and a half foot tall dwarf. He has long black hair and beard, both of which has some gray in them. He is wearing some lightweight armor and is carrying a four foot long battleaxe.

The dwarf speaks again, "The name is Hericlat. What brings the three of you to the dwarf kingdom?"

Ayron replies, not wanting to say too much, "We are on a quest for King Romlay. We must make it through to the northern lands."

Maluc puts the flame out on his dagger, "Can you tell us which tunnel leads out?"

At that time, another gruff old dwarf yells, "Valfor, is that you?!"

Maluc looks at the others, "This could get bad."

The four foot tall dwarf with long red hair and beard walks up, "Hey, you are not Valfor."

Maluc gives a big smile, "The name is Maluc."

The dwarf eyes him closely, "Is Valfor dead?"

Maluc loses his smile, "No."

Zak questions, "Who is Valfor?"

The dwarf replies, "He is the one I made the fire daggers for." He looks at Maluc, "And if he is not dead, you must have stole them."

Hericlat draws back quick at the sound of a thief, "We do not like thieves here."

The other dwarf chimes in, "Even worse when they steal from our friends."

Ayron glances at the others, "I think we should be leaving now."

Hericlat speaks boldly, "Give us back the fire daggers and you can leave."

Maluc retorts, "I do not think so."

Hericlat readies his battleaxe, "Then you cannot leave."

Zak moves so slow to Hericlat's left that the dwarf doesn't see him moving.

Ayron takes a step back, "We do not want any trouble."

Hericlat steps closer, losing sight of Zak, "Too late for that."

Zak steps over quickly and kicks Hericlat in the side of the head, "Run!"

Hericlat hits the ground hard as the three of them take off running across the cavern at a tunnel off to their front right.

Hericlat scrambles back to his feet, "Intruders! Get them!"

Suddenly, the cavern is echoing with the sound of banging gongs as dwarves in armor, carrying axes start running everywhere. Zak, Ayron and Maluc disappear into the tunnel quickly. Maluc lights up his fire dagger again as the dwarves start into the tunnel after them.

Solur, Alexandra and Robin are walking down one of the many tunnels when they start hearing the faint echo of the gongs.

Alexandra questions, "What is that noise?"

Solur shakes his head, "It sounds like banging metal."

Robin chimes in, "It could be one of the other groups trying to signal us."

Alexandra nods, "They could be in trouble."

The three of them speed up down the tunnel as the noise gets louder. Another two hundred feet and they see the glow of the main cavern ahead of them. They speed up some when they see the glow of fire. As the tunnel opens into the main cavern, Solur suddenly stops. A rope bridge hangs a few feet in front of him and the ledge is not very wide.

Robin looks around, "This place is amazing."

Solur looks over the ledge, "We are fairly high so watch your step."

Solur steps onto the bridge first, followed by Alexandra and then Robin. They look down and see dwarves running everywhere.

Alexandra speaks, "Something must be wrong."

They hear a voice from below, "Up there on the sixth bridge! Get them!"

Robin questions, "Are they talking about us?"

Solur quickly counts the bridges, "Yes they are."

Alexandra gets a puzzled look, "Why would they be after us?"

Solur responds, "I do not plan on finding out. Lets go."

The three of them hurry across the rope bridge and disappear into the tunnel on the far side.

———

Chaed, Gaelin and Steph have been walking for some time when they start to hear the banging noises echo down their tunnel.

Steph questions as the noise gets louder, "What could that be?"

Gaelin replies, "It could be one of the others trying to signal us."

Chaed chimes in, "Only one way to find out."

The three of them continue down the tunnel for a couple hundred yards and then they enter a cavern with three tunnels in front of them. They stop and stare at their choices.

Chaed speaks up, listening to the echo intently, "I

cannot tell where it is coming from."

Steph shakes her head, "I cannot tell either."

Gaelin speaks up, "All we can do is pick one and hope it is the right one."

It is quiet for a couple of seconds as everyone waits to see who will make the first suggestion.

Chaed finally speaks, "I say we take the middle tunnel."

Steph pipes up, "The middle is the most obvious choice and usually the worst. Everyone picks the middle." She pauses, "I think we should go right."

Chaed speaks sarcastically, "What kind of thinking is that?"

Steph retorts, "Everyone knows that you never pick the middle."

Gaelin finally speaks, "I believe the best choice is the left tunnel."

Steph and Chaed just look at each other and they speak at the same time, "Sounds good to me."

Gaelin nods, "Then it is settled."

The three of them hurry off down the left tunnel.

Zak, Maluc and Ayron are running down the tunnel with the dwarves not too far behind. The tunnel bends right and slopes gradually up. After a few hundred feet, they enter a small cavern with two tunnels in front of them. The three of them stop.

Ayron speaks a little winded, "Well, which way?"

They hear the dwarves getting closer.

Zak speaks up, "This way."

They start down the left tunnel and about fifty feet into the tunnel, they turn around and head back to the cavern.

Maluc speaks as they enter the cavern they just left,

"Good choice."

Zak retorts as they run into the right tunnel, "Shut up."

A few seconds later, ten dwarves come out of the left tunnel into the cavern. They stop for a second and then run off into the right tunnel.

Zak and the others put some distance between them and the dwarves as the tunnel bends right and slopes up some. After a couple hundred yards of running, they enter the main cavern again and quickly stop. The three of them are standing on a ledge looking at a rope bridge.

Ayron speaks up, "This is the wrong place to be."

They look down and find themselves on the third bridge. They hear the dwarves getting closer.

Zak speaks up, "Lets go."

The three of them race across the bridge as voices below yell at them. Once across the bridge, they disappear into the far tunnel.

———

Solur, Alexandra and Robin continue down the tunnel as it bends left and slopes up. They reach another cavern with two tunnels in front of them.

Alexandra speaks a little winded, "It is like a maze in here."

Robin catches her breath, "I think we should try the left tunnel." She looks at Solur, "What do you think?"

Solur shrugs, "Left is as good as any."

The three of them run off down the left tunnel. It continues to bend left and slope up. It finally straightens out and after two hundred yards, the three of them run up to the main cavern again as they look at another rope bridge in front of them.

Alexandra sighs, "Not here again."

They start across the bridge when they hear screams

from below them.

Solur looks down from the seventh bridge and sees Zak, Ayron and Maluc on the bridge below them, "Hey!"

Zak looks up, "There you are! Have you seen the others?!"

Solur yells, "No!"

At that moment, a small throwing axe flies pass Zak.

Zak yells, "Have to go! Wait at the exit if you find the way out before us!"

Solur nods, "Okay!"

The two groups rush across their bridges and into the far tunnels.

Zak and the others run down the all too familiar tunnels. The tunnel bends left and slopes down. The three of them run for awhile, but they eventually find themselves back at the main cavern, looking at the second rope bridge.

Maluc can't help but yell, "I hate this place!"

They hear Robin's voice from below on the surface level, "Down here! I think we figured the way out!"

Ayron yells, "Wait there! We will try to find our way down!"

Zak and the others race across the bridge and into the far tunnel. Solur, Alexandra and Robin move off to the side of the main cavern and hide behind one of the large metal bowls. They watch intently for Zak, Ayron and Maluc.

After a few minutes, Zak, Ayron and Maluc enter the main cavern on the surface level. Three dwarves see them immediately and run at them. Solur, Alexandra and Robin come out of their hiding place and rush over to the others. The three dwarves stop as they realize they are out numbered.

Zak nods, "Good to see you three."

Solur sees the dwarves, "We need to get out of here."

Maluc chimes in, "We have been trying, trust me."

Ayron speaks up, "You said you figured the way out."

The dwarves slowly move closer and Robin nods, "I think so. It is this way."

Alexandra speaks, "Lets go."

The six of them rush off and leave the dwarves standing there. They run into a tunnel on the far side of the main cavern.

———

Gaelin, Chaed and Steph continue down the winding tunnel. After a short time, the banging noise fades away. The three of them stop for a minute to rest.

Chaed speaks a little concerned, "I really hope that was not the others in trouble."

Gaelin speaks up, "All we can do is push on and if we find the exit, we will wait for the others."

Steph nods, "Then lets get going and hope they find the way out."

The three of them start off again. They get about four hundred more yards through the winding tunnel when they see a light in the distance.

Chaed speaks jubilantly, "Sunlight."

The three of them continue towards the light and it gets brighter with each step they take. The three of them start to squint their eyes as they try to adjust back to the sunlight from the dark caves.

Finally, the tunnel opens up into the outside. They find themselves on a ten foot by ten foot ledge about twenty feet in the air. They continue to squint as their vision adjusts to the bright sunlight. The three of them glance around at their surroundings. Pine trees dot the landscape and tundra lines the ground. There are small patches of snow on the ground and a fresh smell in the air.

They hear an older male voice from below, "You dare trespass on the lands of Balumat."

The three of them look down and their vision has adjusted enough for them to see a ball of fire about the size of a basketball heading at them. The fireball hits the ledge and it explodes. The ledge crumbles and Chaed, Gaelin and Steph crash to the ground below as their things fly everywhere.

Balumat, an elderly man in silver and black robes with long white hair and beard, speaks, "Deal with your own."

He raises his eight foot staff in his right hand and a red ball of light flies at Chaed. The magical ball hits Chaed in the chest and knocks him to his back. Gaelin scrambles to his staff. Steph crawls over to her staff as Chaed grabs his shield and draws his medium sword, leaving his long sword on the ground.

Chaed shakes his head, unable to figure out what is wrong with himself.

Then Chaed sees Steph and an uncontrollable anger comes over him, "You must die."

Chaed rushes at Steph and swings his sword at her. Steph blocks with her staff and backs off a few steps.

Steph looks at Chaed a little confused, "What is wrong with you?"

Gaelin yells, "He is under a spell." He turns to Balumat, "We meet again."

Balumat smiles, "You could not defeat me before."

Gaelin replies confidently, "I was younger then. Things are different now."

Gaelin taps his staff on the ground twice and a see-through shield appears in front of him. Balumat raises his staff and a see-through veil falls over him. Gaelin steps back into a fighting stance and launches a lightning bolt at

Balumat. The lightning bolt hits the veil and the veil absorbs the lightning bolt as Balumat is unharmed.

Balumat chuckles, "Still playing with lightning I see."

Balumat launches a fireball at Gaelin. The fireball hits the shield in front of Gaelin and explodes, however, Gaelin is unharmed.

Balumat nods, "Your powers have grown."

Chaed swings at Steph. Steph blocks with her staff and counters. Chaed blocks with his shield and thrusts his sword in. Steph steps left and brings her staff around. Chaed moves in quick and blocks the staff with his sword as he slams his shield into Steph, knocking her to the ground. Chaed brings his sword down, but Steph rolls out of the way. Steph rolls to a knee as Chaed steps in and delivers another blow. Steph blocks with her staff, but the impact knocks her back to the ground. Chaed raises his sword to strike when a lightning arrow comes flying at him. Chaed brings his shield around to block the lightning arrow, but Steph rolls away to safety.

The other six come running up to Steph and Ayron questions, "What is going on?"

Steph replies a little winded, "Chaed is under a spell."

Robin points her staff at Chaed, "I will handle this."

A golden ball of light flies at Chaed. Chaed raises his magical shield and the magical ball of light disappears into the shield.

Robin sighs, "I forgot that his shield protects him from magic."

At that time, they hear Balumat's voice, "I see that your friends want to join in." He twirls his staff around and slams it on the ground, "I will give them something to play with."

The ground starts to shake all around the group.

Maluc steadies himself, "This cannot be good."

As the ground shakes, the earth splits open into a crevice about twenty feet long and ten feet wide. They see a pair of rock, three finger hands reach up out of the crevice. The group just stares as a humanoid creature made of rock climbs out of the crevice. The creature stands up next to the crevice. It stands fifteen feet tall. It looks at the group with it's hollow eyes. The crevice seals back up and the shaking stops.

Ayron stares at the creature, "What is that?"

Robin replies while staring, "It is a rock golem."

Solur looks at the others, "Robin and I will handle Chaed. The rest of you deal with the golem."

Solur and Robin move away from the others towards Chaed.

Robin questions, "What is the plan?"

Solur draws his sword, "I will take his shield from him. When I do, you cure the spell."

Zak pulls out his bow and fires a lightning arrow at the stone golem. The arrow hits the golem in the chest and explodes. The stone golem reels back as Ayron launches his magical arrow in and it sticks in the stone golem's body. Steph, Maluc and Alexandra charge at the stone golem with their weapons ready.

The stone golem swings his right hand at Maluc. Maluc dives under the slow moving arm and cuts the golem on the right leg with his fire dagger. Steph swings her staff and hits the stone golem in the left leg with a crushing blow. The golem staggers away as another lightning arrow flies in and explodes into the stone golem's head.

Chaed swings his sword at Solur, but Solur blocks with his sword. Chaed brings his shield across and knocks Solur's sword away. Chaed thrusts in behind his shield. Solur spins away from the sword and brings his sword around. Solur moves slow enough that Chaed is able to bring his shield back across and block Solur's sword.

Chaed cuts across with his sword. This time Solur ducks and moves back a couple of steps.

The stone golem swings wildly and hits Maluc in the back, sending him flying to the ground. Alexandra cuts the golem on the arm as it passes by. Another arrow flies in from Ayron and sticks in the golem's left eye. The stone golem reverses his arm and sends Alexandra to the ground with a heavy blow. Zak fires another lightning arrow and it slams into the stone golem's chest. This time the stone golem crashes to it's back and the ground shakes from the impact. Steph runs at the golem and does a front flip, landing on the stone golem's chest. As she lands, Steph brings her staff over the top and splits the stone golem's head with a massive blow.

Solur swings in at Chaed, but slower than normal like he is setting Chaed up. Chaed brings his shield across and knocks Solur's sword away. Chaed thrusts in behind his shield just like before. Solur spins away from the sword. Chaed brings his shield up, expecting the same move from Solur as before. This time Solur drops down and sweeps Chaed's feet out from under him with his right leg.

Chaed crashes to his back. Chaed swings his sword at Solur from his back. Solur stops Chaed's sword with his own. Solur puts his right foot on Chaed's left wrist and pins his arm to the ground. Chaed brings his shield up to knock Solur off of him. Solur grabs the shield with his empty hand. With a powerful tug, Solur takes Chaed's shield.

Solur yells, "Now Robin!"

Solur dives away as a golden ball of light from Robin's staff comes flying in. Chaed starts to stand when he is hit in the chest by the golden light. Chaed falls back to the ground and stops moving.

The ground at Gaelin's feet explodes. Gaelin flies back and crashes to the ground, hanging onto his staff.

Balumat sighs, "Pity. I guess you are not ready yet."

Gaelin smiles, "Keep thinking that Balumat."

Gaelin slams his staff on the ground. This time, Gaelin's lightning shoots through the ground at Balumat. It goes under Balumat's veil and explodes. Balumat flies back and hits the ground hard, dropping his staff. Gaelin stands and places his staff vertically on the ground in front of him. Gaelin spins his staff on it's end. Dark clouds start to form in the sky. Balumat shakes his head as Gaelin throws his hands into the air. Gaelin's staff launches into the sky as the menacing black clouds start to swirl in a circle.

Balumat looks at Gaelin and Gaelin speaks, "It ends now."

Gaelin brings his hands down to chest level, crossing them at the wrists with his fingers spread out like claws. A huge tornado vortex comes down from the blackened sky. The winds pick up as everyone is nearly blown to the ground. The vortex hit's Balumat and the ground around him and retracts into the sky. In a few seconds, the black clouds disappear. Gaelin's staff falls from the sky and Gaelin catches it in his right hand. Balumat and most of the ground where he was standing is gone.

Robin and Solur walk over to Chaed as he shakes his head like he is having a very bad hang over from too much ale. Chaed stands up and looks at Robin and Solur.

Chaed blinks a few times, "What happened?"

Robin replies, "You were under a spell. You nearly killed Steph."

The rest of the group walks up by Chaed and Chaed looks at Steph, "Sorry."

Steph smiles, "No harm done."

Solur holds out Chaed's shield, "Here is your shield."

Chaed just shakes his head, "I do not even want to know how you got this."

Alexandra looks at Gaelin, "Is the wizard gone?"

Maluc pipes up, "Gone. Are you kidding? Did you see that spell?"

Gaelin smiles, "Yes, he is gone."

Robin speaks up, "You are going to have to teach me that spell."

Gaelin nods, "I can, but it takes a lot out of me so I cannot use it often."

Ayron questions, "What now?"

Zak looks around, "I think we should gather up all our things and rest some before we start across the snow lands."

Maluc questions, "How far until the Northern Port?"

Zak replies, "A few days."

Steph chimes in, "Zak is right, we should get some rest."

Alexandra puts the approval in, "We will camp here tonight and start off at first sunlight."

Everyone else nods and gathers up all their belongings. They start to set up camp for the night. Once they get some food in them, they lay down to rest.

CHAPTER 10

THE SNOW LANDS COMPLETELY surround the group as they walk on through the ankle deep snow. The land is fairly flat with some small hills and is pure white. Snow covered pine trees dot the landscape as a soft snow fall starts coming down. The temperature has dropped vastly and everyone except Solur feels the effects of the frozen land.

Robin speaks while shaking, "I do not like the cold. I would definitely prefer the warmth."

Alexandra agrees with a little shiver, "Indeed. How long to the Northern Port?"

Zak replies, fighting back the cold as best he can, "Three days walk."

They continue to walk as the sun moves into the afternoon sky. A few darker clouds move in and the snowfall picks up some more as it gets closer to the sunset. Then, they hear a deep howl in the distance.

Maluc stops, "What was that?"

Ayron looks at Maluc, "It was probably a wolf."

Maluc shakes his head, "I have heard wolves before and that was no wolf."

Zak speaks up, not wanting to alarm the others, "We should keep moving."

Chaed questions, "Is there something you are not telling us?"

They feel the ground shake as if something big was

walking towards them. The shaking is followed by another howl.

Solur glances around, "I think it is coming from over the hill to our right."

Alexandra questions, "What is it?"

Her question is answered when a huge, long white haired creature comes over the hill to their right. It stands upright on two legs about fifteen feet. It looks like a bear with some human features. It has razor sharp claws on it's hands and razor sharp teeth. The creature is very thick and bulky looking with it's shaggy hair.

Steph just stares, "The Yeti."

Maluc questions quickly, "Should we run?"

Zak gives an even quicker answer, "It would catch us."

Chaed draws his medium sword and readies his shield, "Then we fight."

The Yeti slouches over and charges at the group. Solur and Zak quickly draw their swords and daggers. Alexandra and Ayron draw their swords. Maluc draws his daggers as Robin, Gaelin and Steph ready their staves. The Yeti closes quickly for it's size.

The Yeti brings his right arm around in an underhand motion, scooping up a large chunk of frozen snow and throws it at the group. Everyone dives to get out of the way, but the full impact slams into Gaelin and he crashes to the ground. Alexandra scrambles to her feet and turns to see the back of the Yeti's left hand coming at her. She tries to move, but it is too late. The powerful blow from the creature sends Alexandra flying ten feet back and crashing into the frozen snow. Alexandra does not get up.

Robin stands and launches an ice ring at the creature. Everyone watches as the ice ring hits the creature, but appears to have no effect. The Yeti turns and charges Robin. As the Yeti is nearly upon her, Solur leaps by, hooking Robin with his left arm and pulls her out of the way as the Yeti rushes by. Chaed moves in quick and cuts the Yeti across the left leg. The yeti moves with amazing quickness, bringing it's right arm around. Chaed gets his shield up in time as the powerful hand slams into it, sending Chaed to the ground.

Steph steps in behind the creature and delivers a blow to it's lower back. The Yeti lets out a howl and turns quickly, scooping up another chunk of frozen snow. Steph dives left as the chunk of frozen snow narrowly misses. However, Ayron, who was closing behind Steph, is hit by the full force of the snow and he goes down hard.

Maluc flips over the dagger in his left hand, taking it by the blade. He throws it at the Yeti. The fire dagger hits the Yeti in the left shoulder. The Yeti takes a step back and lets out a howl, obviously bothered by the fire dagger. Zak steps in and drives his sword through the Yeti's right thigh. Solur is right behind him and Solur's sword takes off the Yeti's left arm just below the elbow. The Yeti howls again and swings it's other arm wildly, but Zak and Solur have already moved to safety.

Then, a very upset Gaelin stands and turns to the Yeti.

Gaelin starts to twirl his staff in front of him, "Let us see how it likes fire."

A second later, Gaelin launches a ring of fire at the Yeti. The ring of fire explodes into the creature. The Yeti staggers for a few steps and finally falls to the ground. The impact shakes the ground, but the fight is over.

Steph and Zak rush to check on Ayron as Robin and Chaed rush over to Alexandra. Maluc walks over to the creature and retrieves his dagger. Solur walks over and helps Chaed back to his feet.

Ayron comes to after a couple of taps on the face, shortly followed by Alexandra. The group moves over by the Yeti's body as the snow still falls and the sun is nearly set.

Maluc questions, "Is this the only one?"

Zak nods, not overly convincing, "I have heard of only one Yeti, but just to be safe, we should push on some more before setting up camp."

Solur gives a quick nod, "I like that idea."

The group puts away their weapons and gathers up their things. Then they set back off on the trail for the Northern Port.

———

That night, as the cold winter air blows through the camp, the group gathers around the magical fire Gaelin has summoned. They each still shiver from the cold, but the fire has made the cold bearable.

Zak sits, embracing Steph to help keep warm and share some fruit, "Two more days and we will be in the Northern Port."

Chaed nods, "Then we must find transport across the great sea."

Maluc chimes in, "To the Island of the Dead."

Solur notices everyone's reaction of unease at the mention of the island, "How do we look as far as gold?"

Alexandra shakes her head, "We still have a lot, but I doubt we have enough for supplies and transport. Not to mention horses."

Solur nods, "We can get horses from my home once we get to the island. It is not far from the shore."

Maluc looks puzzled, "You have horses?"

Solur replies with a slight smile, "They are one of the animals we breed, mainly for food. Not all undead eat humans."

Maluc gives a sarcastic smile, "That makes me feel better."

Steph speaks up, "So all we need is supplies and transport."

Chaed chimes in, "I am sure it will cost a lot to find someone to take us to the island and wait for our return."

Solur speaks up, "No ship will go all the way to the island. There is a wooden platform with two small skiffs about a mile out from the island. That is how we will get there."

Ayron smiles, "That makes me feel even better."

Gaelin questions, "Is there any chance that we can get the root and escape the island without the Lord of the Undead knowing we are there?"

Everyone hangs on Solur's response, wanting to hear something good, but almost expecting the worse. Solur is quiet for a few seconds.

Solur draws a breath, "No. There are beholders everywhere, and what they see, the Lord of the Undead knows."

That news quiets everyone. Solur can tell that the group is nervous, even though they try not to show it. He looks at their faces and each face says the same thing, who will make it and who will not. Everyone finishes eating without another spoken word. Once finished, they each find sleep is hard to come by.

The group has been walking for the better part of the day through the ankle deep frozen snow. The air is crisp and fresh, but very cold. Each one tries to block out the cold in their own way. As they continue to walk, the group approaches a grove of pine trees, about twenty five in all. The smell of fresh meat fills the air the closer they get to the pine trees.

Alexandra questions, "What do you think that smell is?"

Solur replies, "A dead animal of some sort."

The group walks into the grove of pine trees and sees

a large piece of raw meat hanging from one of the trees.

Robin questions, "What do you make of that?"

Zak replies, eyeing the surroundings, "It looks like an animal trap of some kind."

Ayron speaks up, "What is it doing out in the middle of nowhere?"

Solur's head jerks right, "We are not alone."

Chaed lowers his hand to his sword, "Can you tell what it is?"

They hear a slight movement amongst the trees around them. Suddenly, as if out of thin air, twelve Neanderthals rush the group from out of the trees. They are fairly large and stout, dressed in various animal skins. Each one carries a spear.

Solur draws his sword and dagger as he starts for two Neanderthals on the left of the group. The first Neanderthal thrusts his spear. Solur spins pass the spear and rams his dagger into the Neanderthal's throat. The blood pours out instantly, staining the crystal white snow. Solur brings his right leg up and kicks away the second spear. He thrusts his sword forward into the second Neanderthal's chest. Solur withdraws both his weapons and the two Neanderthals fall into the frozen snow.

Zak draws his sword and dagger and moves for two Neanderthal's on the right of the group. Zak blocks the first spear with his dagger. The second spear comes at him, but Zak brings his sword around and knocks the spear away. He reverses his swing and cuts the Neanderthal across the chest. The first Neanderthal thrusts in again. Zak uses his dagger to redirect the spear into the other Neanderthal's stomach. Before the first Neanderthal can withdraw his spear from his friend, Zak drives his sword into the Neanderthal's chest. Both Neanderthals collapse into the snow.

Alexandra draws her sword as one Neanderthal charges her. She sidesteps the spear and cuts the

Neanderthal across the right ribs. The Neanderthal brings his spear around, but Alexandra ducks under it and draws blood from the Neanderthal's stomach. She reverses her cut and delivers a killing blow to the Neanderthal's chest.

Robin taps her staff on the frozen snow as a Neanderthal rushes her. Vines come up out of the snow and entangle the Neanderthal, stopping him in his tracks. Robin steps in and her staff slams into the side of the Neanderthal's head. The Neanderthal drops quickly.

Ayron draws his bow with great speed as a Neanderthal approaches. Ayron grabs an arrow as the Neanderthal is only ten feet away and closing. Ayron, staying calm, lets the arrow fly. The arrow zips in and hits the Neanderthal in the sternum, sending it into the snow.

Gaelin blocks the thrusting spear with his staff. He spins in and hits the Neanderthal in the chest, discharging lightning into the Neanderthal. The Neanderthal is blown off it's feet and stops moving after it hits the ground.

Steph spins pass the Neanderthal's spear and crushes it's knee with a quick blow from her staff. As the Neanderthal falls, Steph twirls her staff around and hits the Neanderthal in the back of the neck, crushing the vertebra. The Neanderthal falls to the snow, twitches a little and then stops moving.

Chaed moves at two Neanderthals behind the group. He knocks away the first spear with his shield and the second spear with his sword. Chaed brings his shield across as the first spear comes back at him. He knocks the spear away, but this time he drives his sword in behind it and into the Neanderthal's chest. Chaed withdraws his sword and spins around the second spear. His sword comes around fast and removes the Neanderthal's head.

Maluc reaches down and grabs the dagger on his right hip with his right hand and the dagger on his left hip with his left hand. In one quick move, he draws the daggers and lets them fly. Both daggers hit the charging

Neanderthal in the chest. The Neanderthal's feet come out from under him and he crashes to the frozen snow.

With the last Neanderthal down, Maluc retrieves his daggers and everyone puts their weapons away.

Zak speaks up, "This was no doubt a hunting party."

Steph shakes her head, "Why would they attack us? I thought they were a peaceful people."

Solur replies, "They are."

Chaed chimes in, "Something must have scared them."

Alexandra speaks up, "No time to worry about that now. We should be going, in case others are around."

The others nod and the group starts off across the frozen, white land again. However, they each wonder what spurred the attack.

The group has stopped for the night. The full moon shines bright in the clear night sky with plenty of stars. The temperature has dropped, but the magical fire rages in the middle of the camp to make the cold bearable. Everyone has a piece of fruit and their bedrolls out. Zak and Steph sit, embracing each other for comfort and warmth. Ayron and Robin are also sitting in an embrace.

The talking starts as everyone eats their meal for the night.

Maluc speaks, holding off the cold night air, "I think when this adventure is over, I will settle down and give up the traveling."

Ayron chimes in, "Glenfin does sound good right about now."

Robin nods, "We will be back there soon enough."

Steph speaks up, "Zak and I will have to come and see all of you from time to time when all this is over."

Chaed nods, "The two of you are definitely welcome

in Glenfin."

Zak smiles, "And all of you are definitely invited to our wedding." He looks over at Solur, "Even you can come. Just make sure none of the other rangers find out what you are."

Everyone is kind of surprised at what Zak just said. It kind of takes Solur off guard.

Solur slightly bows his head, "I would be honored. As I am sure my wife will be."

Maluc can't keep from saying something, "I still do not see how an undead has a wife and what would seem like a normal kind of life."

Solur smiles, "Not all undead are like the stories you hear. Most are, but not all. I cannot wait until all of you get to meet Kyvez."

Alexandra questions, "What is she like?"

Solur replies, "She is very sweet and kind of quiet. She is very beautiful. She is very caring and her sense of humor is what really hooked me."

Gaelin smiles, "It sounds like she is a wonderful woman."

Solur stares off into the darkness, "She is."

The others can tell that even though Solur is an undead warrior and seems to be very deadly, that the thoughts of his wife make him somewhat saddened. They notice that Solur changes some when he talks of the one he loves.

Alexandra slides down into her bedroll, "We should get some rest. It will probably be a long day tomorrow."

The others nod and one by one they slide into their bedrolls. Solur stands and walks over to where the horses are tied. He watches over the camp as everyone falls asleep. He hopes that all will turn out well for them, but he knows the truth. The truth that some of them will not make it back.

Chapter 11

THE GROUP CONTINUES TO WALK as the snow starts to get less and less and the pine trees become few and far between. They finally catch sight of a large town in the distance.

Zak speaks up, "The Northern Port."

Alexandra speaks, "It looks big."

Zak nods, "It is as big as Glenfin. Only, the people are not so cultured."

Chaed chimes in, "First thing we need to do is get supplies."

As they get closer, Solur speaks up, "Everyone keep your eyes open. There are a lot of bad people in the Northern Port."

They start to hear all the noise the closer they get. The town is huge. About twenty north to south streets by twenty east to west streets. Most of the old stone buildings are taverns and pubs where adventures go to drink. There is an open town square in the middle of the town, about two square blocks. The streets are lined with adventurers and pirates of all races. Some are dressed in wizard robes, some in armor and some are in tunics and cloaks. Most of the pirates stand out because they are wearing different colored sashes to distinguish which ship they are from. Everyone has a weapon of some kind on their person, even the females.

The group starts down one of the crowded streets as it

always seems to be party time in the Northern Port. Drunk adventurers line the roads, sharing tales of their last adventures. The group makes it's way through all the people.

Steph speaks up, "Up on the left. A supply shop."

The smell of fresh cooked meat fills the air as they walk pass a tavern on the way to the supply shop. They walk into the supply shop and everyone starts to gather the food and water that they will need for the trip.

The shop owner, an older, heavier man watches as the nine of them walk around his shop. He is dressed in nice clothes and is obviously not hurting for wealth.

Steph walks up to the shop owner, "Where can we find a ship to take us to the Island of the Dead?"

The shopkeeper looks at her closely, "The only ship captains that I know of that are that crazy are at Deadman's Tavern."

Steph nods and Alexandra walks up, "How much for a week of food and water for eight people?"

The shopkeeper rubs his chin, "Hmm, I will give you a deal, only three gold coins."

Alexandra pulls out the coins and gives them to the shopkeeper. The group walks out of the shop back into the busy street.

Chaed questions, "How are we looking for gold?"

Alexandra replies, "We have two gold coins and five silver pieces."

Solur shakes his head, "That will not even come close to getting us a ship."

Robin sighs, "We need to find a way to get some gold, without fighting a scorpicore for it."

Zak looks at Maluc, "Do not even think about it."

Maluc replies, acting surprised, "I said nothing."

At that time, they hear a man yelling, "That is right, twenty gold pieces to anyone who can defeat Sir Robert in a duel!"

Ayron smiles, "I think we found our gold."

Zak sighs, "I know this Sir Robert. He has never lost a duel."

Maluc speaks up, "Like that matters. Nobody can beat Solur."

Solur replies, "I do not think they would allow an undead to fight in a duel. However, I am sure Chaed can beat him."

Chaed nods and smiles at Solur, "No problem."

Alexandra pulls out the pouch of coins, "Take these. I am sure there will be an entry fee." She hands the pouch to Chaed, "Ayron and Robin will go with Chaed. Zak, Steph and Gaelin will try and find us a tavern with some open rooms."

Ayron questions, "What about you my lady?"

Alexandra looks at Ayron, "Solur, Maluc and I will go to Deadman's Tavern to find a ship. We will all meet back here at the supply shop by sunset."

Maluc shakes his head, "Why me? We will just add Deadman's Tavern to the list of other names."

Everyone chuckles at Maluc. Then, Alexandra, Solur and Maluc head off and leave the others by the supply shop.

Ayron, Robin, Chaed, Zak, Steph and Gaelin walk over to the man who announced the duel with Sir Robert. The man is younger and dressed in a nice green and brown tunic and trousers with nice leather boots.

Ayron asks the man, "How much to challenge Sir Robert?"

The man smiles, "Just two gold pieces."

Zak looks puzzled, "And the prize is twenty gold pieces?"

The man chuckles, "In the five years since we started,

Sir Robert has never lost." The man pauses, "The duels are being held in the square."

Ayron bows his head, "Thank you."

The man nods and walks off.

Chaed opens the pouch of coins, "We have two gold and five silver. We will take the gold for the duel. Zak, Steph and Gaelin will take the silver and try to find us rooms."

Chaed takes out the gold coins and hands the pouch to Zak, "We will meet back like the Princess said."

Everyone gives a nod of understanding and the two groups go their separate ways.

———————

Zak, Steph and Gaelin make their way through the busy streets for a couple blocks when they see a tavern ahead. The three of them walk into the tavern. The tavern is full of adventurers and pirates of all ages and races. Most are drunk and the noise is incredible. The three of them push their way through the tavern towards the beer barrels.

An older pirate grabs Steph's backside as she walks past him. The man lets out a laugh, but Steph turns quick and drops the pirate with a right hook. The four pirates laugh at their friend for getting knocked down by a female. The three of them finally reach the beer barrels.

A middle aged lady dressed in a nice brown dress looks at them, "You three must be new around here. What can I do for ya?"

Zak replies, trying to talk over the noise, "Do you have any open rooms?"

The lady shakes her head, "Nope, full up. You might try Willy's Tavern. Not much room left since the last ship came in."

Steph questions, "Where is the tavern?"

The lady replies, "Just go straight towards the pier, you cannot miss it."

Zak nods, "Thank you."

The three of them push their way back to the door and out into the street which seems to get more crowded by the minute.

Steph speaks, "There are a lot of people here."

Gaelin nods, "I just hope that no one recognizes the Princess."

Zak smiles, "She is about as safe as she can be with Solur."

The three of them weave their way through the masses and they catch sight of Willy's Tavern. They fight their way inside and it looks just like the last place they were in.

An older man dressed in ragged clothes walks up, "Strangers, what can I do for ya?"

Gaelin replies, "Do you have any open rooms?"

The man nods, "Sure do. How many you need?"

Steph questions, "How much for the rooms?"

The man replies, "Each room is one silver piece."

Zak questions, "Do you have four rooms?"

The man smiles, "I do, if you have four silver pieces."

Zak pulls out the coins and hands them to the man.

The man nods, "Up the stairs, to the end of the hall, turn right. There are four open rooms on the left."

Zak nods, "Thank you."

The man walks off and Gaelin speaks up, "Well, we should make our way back to the supply shop and wait."

The three of them make their way out of the tavern and start weaving their way through the busy streets back to the supply shop.

Solur, Maluc and Alexandra fight their way through the crowded streets of the Northern Port. The three of them get closer to the pier and the number of people increase and the crowds get more unruly.

Maluc points up ahead, "There it is."

The three of them weave their way over to the entrance of the Deadman's Tavern. They walk inside and Solur scans the room from under the hood of his cloak. The tavern is full of drunk and unsavory pirates. The noise is incredibly loud. All the pirates look like they have been in the business awhile. They all carry swords and daggers. Their dress is mostly trousers and tunics with coats and boots. Some are wearing extravagant hats and they all are wearing sashes with different colors to denote which ship they belong to.

Alexandra speaks up, "I guess we will start with the first table."

The three of them work their way through the room over to a table where four older pirates and enjoying drinks and sharing stories.

Alexandra lays it out, "I am looking for a ship to go to the Island of the Dead."

The four pirates continue without even noticing Alexandra.

Maluc looks at her, "Maybe we need to be more direct and forceful."

Alexandra shrugs and slams her hand on the table, "I am in need of some help!"

The four pirates look at Alexandra and the others, not looking pleased to be interrupted.

Maluc whispers, "I was not serious."

The pirate on the far left, next to Alexandra and Solur replies, "If you help me, I might be able to help you."

The four pirates let out a hearty laugh and the pirate reaches for Alexandra's arm, "Come over here wench."

Solur's left hand shoots out and grabs the pirate's

wrist, "The lady asked you about a ship."

The pirate tries to pull his arm away, but Solur's undead strength is way too much for the pirate, "Let go of my arm."

Solur squeezes harder, "A ship to go to the Island of the Dead?"

Maluc notices the other three pirates slowly moving their hands for their weapons and he whispers to Alexandra, "This is not good."

The pirate's free hand moves for his dagger, but Solur is much too fast. Solur's right hand draws his dagger with amazing speed and he holds it to the pirate's throat.

The pirate and his friends move their hands away from their weapons. Maluc glances around and sees that no one has taken notice of them.

The pirate replies with a little more fear now, "I was just playing." He swallows hard, "The only ship that I know of that is leaving soon is the Turesk."

Alexandra questions, "Who can I talk to about the Turesk?"

The pirate replies, "The table in the far back corner."

Alexandra nods, "Thank you."

Solur lets go of the pirate's arm and the three of them start for the back of the tavern.

Maluc speaks as they weave through the crowd, "Do you think we can avoid attention? I really do not feel like getting in a fight with a tavern full of pirates."

Solur gives a slight nod, "I will be more subtle next time."

Maluc smiles, "Thanks."

Alexandra chuckles at Maluc as they get to the far table where three more pirates are sitting. All three show the scars of battle. The one in the middle is wearing a leather hat. The three of them are drinking and no doubt sharing stories of past glories.

Alexandra stands across the table from the pirates, "Do any of you know the Turesk?"

The pirate with the hat replies, "I am Captain Jake Morrison, Captain of the Turesk."

Alexandra looks at him, "I am looking for passage to the Island of the Dead."

The three pirates chuckle and the Captain replies, "The Island of the Dead is no place for a lady. What business do you have there?"

Alexandra replies coldly, "Personal. How much?"

The Captain sits back, "What is the cargo?"

Alexandra responds, "Just nine people."

The Captain rubs his chin, "Are you looking for us to wait so you can come back?"

Alexandra nods, "Yes. It will take about three to four days."

The Captain sits forward, "Fifteen gold pieces then."

Alexandra replies, "When can we leave?"

The Captain smiles, "The gold first."

Alexandra returns his smile, "When we are on the ship, then you will get your gold."

The pirate to the left of the Captain speaks up, "The Captain said now."

Alexandra looks at the man, "I do not trust pirates."

Maluc rolls his eyes at the comment from Alexandra, knowing trouble is surely coming.

The two pirates next to the Captain stand and reach for their swords. Before their hands touch their swords, Solur draws his sword and the tip stops just shy of the Captain's throat. The tavern gets quiet as everyone sees what is going on, but the two pirates stop moving.

Maluc glances around to see every pirate in the tavern looking at them, "This is bad."

It is quiet for a few seconds, then the Captain responds, not really showing any kind of fear in his voice, "The ship sails tomorrow at sunrise. Be there with the gold."

Alexandra bows her head slightly, "I will. Thank you."

Alexandra taps on Solur's arm. Solur puts his sword away and every pirate watches them as they walk for the door. Once the three of them are outside, the partying continues.

Maluc lets out a sigh, "I thought you were going to be subtle?"

Solur looks at him, "I was. If I was not, I would have killed him."

Maluc gets a look of confusion on his face and Alexandra tries not to laugh.

Solur looks at Alexandra, "We should get back to the supply shop."

Alexandra nods and the three of them start working their way through the busy streets, back towards the supply shop.

———————

Ayron, Robin and Chaed walk into the crowded town square. They hear cheering and clapping. People of all kinds are in the town square, awaiting the next duel of Sir Robert.

Then, they hear the announcer from before, "Are there any brave warriors out there? For only two gold pieces, a chance at Sir Robert and twenty gold pieces."

The three of them push their way through the crowd and see the announcer standing next to a knight. The knight is in full, shiny plate mail armor without his helmet on. The knight is about six feet tall with black hair and looking of Hispanic origin. The knight holds a shield in his left hand and a sword on his left hip.

Chaed yells, "I will challenge!"

The announcer looks over, "Step up brave warrior."

Chaed walks over to the announcer and Sir Robert. Sir Robert notices the emblem on Chaed's shield immediately.

Sir Robert speaks, "You are from Glenfin."

Chaed bows his head, "I am Sir Chaed."

Chaed hands the announcer the two gold coins.

The announcer smiles, "Three good strikes to the winner!"

Chaed walks over to Robin and Ayron. The announcer puts on Sir Robert's helmet. Sir Robert puts down his visor and draws his sword. Chaed removes his long sword from his back and hands his stuff to Ayron. Chaed turns back to Sir Robert and puts down his visor and draws his sword. At the same time, the two knights tap their shields with their swords and raise their swords to the sky. The crowd erupts into a cheering frenzy as they prepare for the duel.

Sir Robert moves in fast and cuts in with his sword. Chaed comes across quick and blocks the sword with his shield. Sir Robert spins off the block and slams his shield into Chaed, knocking him off-balance. Another quick swing and Sir Robert scores a hit to Chaed's back. The crowd goes wild as Chaed stumbles away and Sir Robert holds up his sword.

Chaed steps in and thrusts. Sir Robert parries with his sword and brings his shield across again. Chaed brings his shield up and stops Sir Robert's shield. Chaed pushes Sir Robert back and cuts in with his sword. Sir Robert brings his shield across and blocks. Sir Robert spins off the block and brings his sword around. This time Chaed was ready and he ducks under Sir Robert's sword. Chaed brings his sword across and scores a heavy blow to Sir Robert's stomach. The crowd gasps as they have never seen Sir Robert hit. Sir Robert steps back and Chaed holds up his sword.

Sir Robert moves in with his sword cutting in fast.

Chaed steps back and brings his shield up and blocks the sword. Chaed thrusts in behind his shield. Sir Robert brings his shield across and blocks the sword. Chaed spins off the block. Sir Robert brings his shield around, expecting Chaed's sword. Chaed uses his momentum and slams his shield into Sir Robert's shield, knocking him off-balance. Chaed quickly follows with his sword and scores a hit to Sir Robert's ribs. Sir Robert staggers away and Chaed holds up his sword again. The crowd is silent for they cannot believe what they are seeing. Robin and Ayron just stand there smiling.

Sir Robert yells out from under his helmet, "You are quite skilled Sir Chaed!"

Sir Robert flips his sword over in his hand a couple of times and charges Chaed. Sir Robert thrusts his sword in at Chaed. Chaed parries with his sword. Sir Robert retracts his sword with great speed and cuts in from the side. Chaed brings his shield across to block, but Sir Robert has already withdrawn his sword and cuts in behind Chaed's shield. Sir Robert scores a hit to Chaed's ribs. The crowd comes back to life as Chaed steps back. Sir Robert raises his sword.

Sir Robert yells again, "However, not quite skilled enough!"

Chaed yells back, "We shall see Sir Robert!"

Chaed charges and thrusts in his sword. Sir Robert brings his shield across to block, but Chaed set him up. Chaed has already withdrawn his sword. Chaed spins around Sir Robert's shield and cuts in with his sword. Chaed's sword slams into Sir Robert's back, knocking Sir Robert to a knee. The crowd is instantly quiet, knowing Sir Robert just lost.

Ayron breaks the silence, "Yes!"

Everyone looks at Ayron and Ayron lets out a slight smile. Chaed puts his sword away and raises his visor as Robin and Ayron walk over to him. The three of them walk over to the announcer.

Chaed speaks, "I believe that is twenty gold pieces."

The announcer hands Ayron the pouch of gold, "I cannot believe Sir Robert lost."

Chaed smiles, "We must all face defeat some day."

Chaed turns to Sir Robert and places his left hand to his chest. Sir Robert puts away his sword and returns the motion.

Robin speaks up, "We should get back to the supply shop."

Chaed and Ayron nod and the three of them start back through the busy streets to the supply shop.

Zak, Steph and Gaelin are standing outside the supply shop as the sun starts to get low in the sky and the party starts to pick up in the streets. Alexandra, Solur and Maluc walk up a few minutes later.

Alexandra questions, "Did you have any luck finding rooms?"

Zak replies, "We have four rooms?"

Steph questions, "Did you find a ship?"

Alexandra replies, "Yes, the Turesk. It sails at dawn, but it is fifteen gold pieces."

Solur speaks up, "If the others did their part, we are set."

At that time, Chaed, Robin and Ayron walk up.

Chaed hands the pouch of gold to Alexandra, "We have twenty gold pieces now."

Alexandra smiles, "Great. We will go to the tavern and get some food and rest. Tomorrow at sunrise, we will set sail for the Island of the Dead."

Alexandra motions to Zak.

Zak nods, "This way."

The group follows Zak through the streets that get

more crowded by the minute. Before long, the group arrives at Willy's Tavern. They walk in to see that the party is still going on.

Alexandra speaks over the noise, "Lets find a table so we can eat."

Solur speaks up, "I will be back at dawn."

Robin speaks up, "Why not stay and join us Solur?"

Solur looks at Robin, surprised by her response.

Maluc chimes in, "Join us at the table. We can share some stories."

Solur looks at the others and they are all giving him the look as if they want him to stay.

Solur nods, "Very well."

The group pushes their way through the crowd and they find an empty table in the back. Once the food and drinks are ordered, the conversation begins.

Ayron questions, "Solur, is there any chance that we can get off the Island of the Dead without facing the undead army?"

Solur replies, "Like I said before, there are beholders everywhere, and what they see, the Lord of the Undead knows."

Maluc speaks up, "But it should take them time to gather the army and come after us."

Solur nods, "Yes it will, but there is always two death knights and one hundred skeleton warriors roaming the island at all times."

Chaed speaks up, "So we will have to face that army, if not the rest of the undead army."

Solur nods slightly, "Yes."

The mood does not get any better and Steph changes the subject, "How long have you been married Solur?"

The group watches as Solur breaks a smile at the thought of his wife, "This will be our one hundredth year."

Zak nods, "Now that is dedication."

Solur replies, "Kyvez is so wonderful and loving. I could not imagine a life without her."

Alexandra speaks up, "Maybe someday I will find love like that."

Solur looks at her, "I am sure you will."

Chaed chimes in, "I am not so sure, with as stubborn as she can be."

The group looks at Chaed like they can't believe he just said that. Chaed tries to keep from smiling, but he can't hold it back when he sees Alexandra's expression.

Chaed starts to laugh and Alexandra throws a piece of bread at him, "You are teasing me. Chaed, are you starting to lighten up?"

Gaelin chimes in, "I think Maluc is rubbing off on him."

The others laugh as they each remember some of Maluc's comments along the way.

Maluc smiles, "Whatever I can do to help."

Everyone continues to eat and share stories of their past. Solur gets many more questions and the night passes quickly. Once the food and drinks are done, everyone except for Solur heads off to their room. Solur walks out into the street and walks around the rest of the night, thinking and hoping that all his new friends will make it back alive.

Alexandra and the others start down the pier as the sun starts to rise in the morning sky. The smell of salt water fills the fresh morning air. The pier is somewhat busy with pirates and other people doing business.

The pier is full of ships. Large ships, most with four large masts and nearly a hundred pirates each. The large wooden ships are each carved in a unique pattern around the front with the large letters spelling out each ships name.

Alexandra speaks up, "Has anyone seen the Turesk yet?"

Before anyone can answer, an arm comes around Alexandra from behind and a dagger is held at her throat. Solur, standing only a couple feet from Alexandra, turns first. The others quickly turn around as well to see what is happening. Solur recognizes the man from the night before. It is the pirate whose arm he grabbed. The pirate's three friends are standing close by.

The pirate speaks, "Raise your hands away from your weapons. Do not try anything or I will slit her throat."

The others do as they are told. Solur eyes the man closely from under the hood of his cloak, judging how far away the man's arm is.

The pirate speaks, "Now you will pay for last night. Hand over any kind of gold or silver you have."

Alexandra replies, "It is in the pouch tied around my waist."

The pirate takes his eyes off the others for a second to look around in front of Alexandra. Solur seizes the chance. Solur brings his right foot behind his left leg and kicks the bottom of his sword scabbard really hard. The impact launches Solur's sword up out of the scabbard. Solur catches the handle, blade down as the tip clears the scabbard. In a quick motion, Solur's sword comes up and removes the pirate's arm at the elbow. The forearm and dagger fall to the pier. The pirate screams in pain.

Alexandra, sensing Solur's next move, drops to her knee. Solur's sword comes back around and removes the pirate's head. Blood flies everywhere as the pirate's head lands at the other three pirate's feet. The three pirates look at each other and decide it best to not face this group. The three pirate's turn and run off down the pier.

Alexandra stands back up, "That was a nice move Solur. You are going to have to teach me that."

Solur puts his sword away, "It would be my pleasure."

Maluc chuckles and turns to Solur, "Is there anything you cannot do?"

Solur nods, "Yes. I just have not discovered what it is yet."

Everyone lets out a light laugh at Solur's attempt at a joke. The group starts off down the pier and the next ship is the Turesk.

The Captain is standing at the gangplank on the pier as they walk up.

The Captain looks at Alexandra, "What was that all about?"

Alexandra shakes her head, "Nothing. We had a difference of opinions."

The Captain replies, "Remind me not to have any differences with you."

Alexandra pulls out the pouch of gold. She counts out fifteen pieces and places them in the Captain's hand.

The Captain smiles, "Shall we go."

Alexandra and the others follow the Captain up the gangplank onto the huge and well built ship. The wood is darker brown with four large mast poles spread out across the deck. About a hundred pirates are running around, getting the ship ready to sail.

Once on the ship, the Captain yells, "Cabin boy!"

A young teenage boy dressed in rags comes running up, "Yes Captain."

The Captain speaks, "Show our guests to their quarters."

The boy replies, "Yes Captain."

Alexandra and the others follow the boy to their quarters as the Turesk drops it's sails and pulls out of the Northern Port.

The group has been sitting below most of the day in a large open room that has ten beds in it. They have been resting when they all hear a bell ringing from up on the deck of the ship. They look at each other, wondering what the bell might mean.

Alexandra speaks up, "Maybe we should go up to the main deck to see what is going on."

The others nod at the idea and the nine of them walk up to the main deck. As soon as they walk out of the door, they see pirates running everywhere as if in a controlled state of panic.

Chaed stops one of the pirates running by, "What is going on?"

The pirate replies, "It is Captain Dracu's ship, closing on us."

Alexandra questions, "Who is Captain Dracu?"

The pirate replies, obviously scared, "He is the most deadly pirate on the Great Sea. He looks to board us."

The nine of them rush over to the side of the ship where most of the pirates are gathering. They see a large four mast ship closing in with the skull and crossed swords flying high. As the ship gets closer, they can see that the side of the ship is lined with pirates holding grappling hooks. All the pirates look battle tested and they wear red bandanas to signify what ship they belong to.

Once the ship is right next to the Turesk, grappling hooks come flying over to the Turesk, pulling the two ships closer together. All the pirates from the other ship start swinging across to the Turesk.

Solur draws one of his poison darts and tosses it at one of the pirates swinging across. The dart hits the pirate in the neck. The pirate lets go of the rope and slams into the side of the Turesk and falls into the water. More pirates land on the Turesk and Solur faces off with two of them. One pirate thrusts in with his cutlass. Solur parries with his sword, spins and kicks the pirate in the chest. The second pirate steps in and cuts across at Solur. Solur blocks with his sword, draws his dagger with uncanny speed and cuts the pirate's throat. The first pirate steps back up and swings his sword. Solur blocks with his dagger and drives his sword into the pirate's chest. Solur withdraws his sword.

Zak squares off against two pirates. Zak thrusts his sword at the first pirate. The pirate parries with his sword. The second pirate steps in and swings at Zak. Zak blocks with his dagger and brings his sword across. The pirate ducks, but Zak continues to spin all the way around and comes back around to the first pirate. The pirate blocks with his sword, but Zak rams his dagger into the pirate's ribs. The second pirate thrusts in with his sword. Zak blocks the sword with his dagger and kills the pirate with a deep cut across the chest with his sword.

Gaelin launches a magical arrow into one of the pirates as they swing across. The magical arrow hits the pirate in the stomach and the pirate falls into the water between the ships. Gaelin steps back and calls down a lightning bolt. The lightning bolt explodes into the deck of Captain Dracu's ship. Wood pieces fly everywhere as a fairly large hole appears in the deck of Captain Dracu's ship.

Robin catches one of the pirates in mid-swing with a magical arrow. The magical arrow hits the pirate in the chest. The pirate lets go of the rope and falls into the clear blue water of the Great Sea. Robin creates an ice ring and launches it at Captain Dracu's ship. The ice ring hits the side of the ship, sending pieces of wood everywhere, creating a sizable hole.

Chaed, having left his shield below deck, faces off with two pirates and only his medium sword. The first pirate swings in with his sword. Chaed parries with his sword and counters. The pirate leaps back to safety. The second pirate thrusts in. Chaed sidesteps and cuts the pirate on the arm. The first pirate thrusts his sword back in. This time Chaed moves to the side and cuts the pirate deep across the stomach. As the pirate falls, Chaed spins around to the second pirate. The pirate blocks with his sword. The pirate counters, but Chaed parries and thrusts in at the pirate's open chest. Chaed's sword hits home and the second pirate falls.

Ayron quickly draws an arrow and lets it fly. The arrow catches a pirate in mid-swing. The arrow hits the pirate in the left eye. The pirate falls into the water between the two ships. Ayron draws another arrow and turns right. He sees one of Captain Dracu's pirates raise his sword at the cabin boy that showed them to their quarters. Ayron lets his arrow fly. As the sword starts down at the cabin boy, the arrow hits the pirate in the back, right between the shoulder blades. The pirate falls next to the cabin boy.

As a pirate lands on the rail of the Turesk, Steph steps up and jabs him in the chest with her staff. The pirate falls backwards off the Turesk and into the water. Steph sees a sword out of the corner of her left eye and moves back. The sword hits the rail where Steph had just been. The pirate thrusts in with his sword. Steph knocks the sword away and brings the other end of her staff around at the pirate. The pirate ducks under the staff, but before the pirate can react, Steph brings the original end around again and sweeps the legs from under the pirate. The pirate crashes to his back. Steph brings her staff straight down into the pirate's sternum.

Maluc draws both of his daggers as a pirate charges him. The pirate swings at Maluc's head. Maluc ducks and brings his left dagger across, but the pirate steps back out of the way. The pirate thrusts in with his sword. Maluc blocks the sword up with the dagger in his right hand and cuts the pirate's arm with the dagger in his left hand. The pirate spins and brings his sword around at Maluc's head. Maluc drops to a knee and drives the left dagger home between the pirate's legs. Maluc quickly comes up with his other dagger and finishes the pirate off.

Alexandra faces off against one pirate. Alexandra thrusts in with her sword. The pirate parries left and counter swings. Alexandra blocks and cuts back across with her sword. The pirate steps back and the sword misses. The pirate thrusts in, but Alexandra parries right and counters. The pirate blocks and comes around at her head. Alexandra drops to a knee and thrusts. Her sword pierces the pirates stomach.

Captain Dracu, a massive pirate, stands on the deck of his ship by the wheel and watches the battle. He does not recognize the nine strangers, but he knows his men cannot handle them and definitely not the magic they have.

Captain Dracu yells in a powerful voice, "Cut the lines!"

The remaining pirates on Captain Dracu's ship cuts the ropes holding the two ships together. Once free, the two ships head their separate ways. The remaining pirates from Captain Dracu's ship are finished off quickly. All across the deck of the Turesk, pirates are cheering their great victory over the feared Captain Dracu.

The Captain of the Turesk walks over to Alexandra, "The nine of you come in handy. Who did you say you were?"

Alexandra replies, "I did not say, nor will I. You have your gold and we have our transport. That is all you must know."

The Captain bows his head, "As you wish. However, do me the honor of the nine of you dining with me tonight."

Alexandra replies, "Of course."

The Captain smiles, "I will send my cabin boy to get

you when the food is ready."

Alexandra nods and she and the rest of the group put their weapons away and return to their quarters.

The sun is about mid-sky as everyone is out on the bow of the ship getting some fresh air. The white clouds move slowly across the clear blue sky. The sun sparkles off the serene, crystal clear water. The smell of salt water fills the air and for a moment, everyone has forgotten about where they are heading.

Maluc points out away from the bow, "Look."

Everyone looks ahead of the ship and they all see it. Off in the distance lies a dark cloud that appears to come up out of the water. The cloud looks black and gray and is impossible to see into from where they are at.

Solur speaks, "The Island of the Dead."

Chaed stares at the deathly cloud, "So, that is it."

The group just sits quietly and stares at the menacing dark cloud. Solur can feel the worries of everyone.

Solur speaks, "My wife is so incredible. Her hair is shoulder length. It is black with some blonde streaks in it. She has deep brown eyes that you can get lost in. She is a few inches shorter than I am. She sure is beautiful, and loving." He pauses and notices everyone is looking at him now, "I remember when we first met. She had not been a vampire very long. It was love at first sight. I had just became an undead warrior and the old Lord of the Undead was holding a ball in our honor. We danced and talked all night long."

Solur looks at Alexandra, "I cannot wait for all of you to meet her. I know you will like her." He sighs, "It has been too long since I have seen her beautiful smile which reveals the cutest set of fangs you have ever seen."

The others smile and chuckle listening to Solur talk

about his wife. Solur continues with his stories and knows that at least for the moment, he has taken their minds off what lies ahead.

Chapter 12

AS THE TURESK GETS CLOSER TO THE DARK CLOUD that engulfs the Island of the Dead, a hundred foot by hundred foot wooden platform rises out of the water about ten feet. The Turesk slows down as it nears the wooden platform. Alexandra and the others are waiting on the deck with all of their belongings. The Turesk slowly moves up next to the platform. Once the ship is tied up to the platform, the gangplank is lowered from the ship down to the platform.

Alexandra looks at the Captain, "We should be back in a few days."

The Captain nods, "We will be here."

Before they walk off, Alexandra turns back to the Captain, "If we are not back in five days, you can leave."

The Captain responds, "How will you get back if we leave?"

Solur speaks up, "If we are not back in five days, then we are dead."

The rest of the group just sighs and starts down the gangplank to the wooden platform. The wood is old and creaks under their weight. They follow Solur across the platform to a set of steps that leads down to the water. At the bottom of the steps is two small, flat bottom canoes with two paddles in each, tied to the platform.

Alexandra questions, "How many can fit in a skiff?"

Solur replies, "Five. Six and the skiff might sink."

Alexandra nods, "Solur, Gaelin and Steph with me.

The rest of you in the other."

Chaed, Ayron, Robin, Zak and Maluc climb into their skiff. Chaed grabs one paddle and Zak grabs the other. Solur unties their skiff from the platform. Alexandra, Gaelin and Steph climb into their skiff. Gaelin grabs one of the paddles. Solur unties the skiff and hops in. He grabs the other paddle.

The two skiffs get closer to the dark cloud and no one says a word. The tension rises as no one knows what to expect when they enter the ominous cloud. Then, the two skiffs cross into the dark cloud. The fresh salt water smell is gone. It is replaced by an odor of rotten fish. Everyone is surprised that they can still see some.

The water is a dark color now and the sky looks like a constant dusk. The dark haze has impaired their vision some, but before too long, they all see land ahead. That is when the odor of death hits them. It is old death and the smell is so thick you could cut it with a knife. Once they get a few feet from the land, Solur hops out of the skiff and drags both skiffs onto the land. Everyone else climbs out. The ground crumbles under their feet as if it were hardened ash being crushed.

Robin questions, "What is wrong with the ground?"

Solur replies, "Centuries ago, a powerful dragon swept through the flourishing land and turned it into a charred wasteland."

Maluc questions while looking around, "Is the dragon still here?"

Solur smiles, "No. It was killed a long time ago." He points off to the right, "This way. We have a long walk ahead of us."

The group follows Solur. Everyone looks around, taking in the Island of the Dead.

The group has been following Solur for quite some time now, unable to tell what time of day it is given the eternal dark cloud hanging over the island. They walk over small hills and pass some burnt, dead trees that still manage to stand. The odor of death is strong and none of them has become accustomed to it yet. They look around and are able to only see a mile or so. Then, a small hut comes into view. As the group gets closer they can see a wooden fence with about twenty horses. They also see a figure moving around the outside of the hut.

Solur smiles, "Home."

The group continues towards the hut and as they get closer, they can make out the figure more clearly. It appears to be a female that stands about 5'4" tall and weighs about 115 pounds. She has shoulder length black hair with some blonde streaks in it. She is wearing a skin tight, white long sleeve top with a dark brown, tight fitting dress over it that hangs down to just past her knees. She also has on brown boots that come up to her mid-calf.

Solur stops the group about a hundred feet away, "You should wait here."

Everyone stops and Solur walks towards the lady. Solur's steps are light, making hardly a noise. The lady appears to be patching a hole in the hut. Solur stops about ten feet behind the lady.

Solur speaks, a little nervous, "Kyvez."

The lady stops immediately, recognizing the voice.

Kyvez turns to face Solur who has his hood off, "Solur, is it really you?"

Solur smiles, losing himself in Kyvez's deep brown eyes, "Yes my love."

Kyvez smiles as a tear rolls down her cheek. She runs to Solur and they embrace, sharing a long, passionate kiss.

The group watches the reunion from where they stand.

Maluc speaks to the others, "This kind of touches the

heart, in a weird, creepy sort of way."

Kyvez finally lets go and steps back, "I thought I lost you forever."

Solur wipes the tear from her cheek, "That will never happen."

Kyvez catches sight of the others over Solur's shoulder, "Who is that?"

Solur motions for the group to come over, "My new friends."

Alexandra and the others walk up. They see Kyvez up close and realize Solur wasn't lying, she is very beautiful and has a natural tan complexion.

Kyvez gives Solur a puzzled look, "They are human."

Robin speaks up, "Actually, I am an elf."

Solur smiles, "A long story. Perhaps we should go inside."

Everyone follows Kyvez inside. They find whatever they can to sit down on.

Solur sits next to Kyvez, "I was betrayed and captured. Alexandra freed me in exchange for my help."

Kyvez questions, "Help with what?"

Alexandra speaks up, "I am Alexandra, Princess Romlay. My father has been poisoned and we need the Dragon's Eye Root to save him. Solur told us that you might know where it is."

Kyvez nods slightly, "I do."

Robin speaks up, "Time is running short. Will you help us?"

Kyvez is quiet for a minute. Solur can tell she is unsure about the humans.

Solur leans over to Kyvez, "They are good people. You can trust them, they are my friends."

The others are surprised at what Solur just said. He considers them his friends.

Kyvez looks at Alexandra, "If Solur and I can return with you and be given a safe home in your land, then I will help you."

Gaelin looks puzzled, "But this is your home."

Solur speaks solemnly, "The Lord of the Undead."

Kyvez nods, "He will certainly kill us when he discovers you have returned. Our only hope to be together is to leave this place."

Alexandra doesn't even hesitate, "If you help us, you will have your wish."

Kyvez nods, "Dragon Mountain is a full days ride from here."

Solur speaks up, "I will get ten horses ready, the rest of you get something to eat. We can leave as soon as all of you are finished."

Alexandra nods, "Very well."

Solur walks out of the hut to prepare the horses while the others sit and eat some fruit. Kyvez walks over to a chest and opens it. She pulls out a short sword attached to a leather belt. Kyvez ties it around her waist and then walks out to help Solur with the horses.

———

After riding for quite a few miles, the group stops to rest. The horses are tied up to some of the burnt trees and everyone is sitting in a small circle.

Ayron speaks up, "I have been wondering. How are we going to get Kyvez off the island if it is daylight. She is a vampire, right."

Kyvez smiles, "Solur's cloak will protect me from the sunlight."

Steph questions, "How is that?"

Kyvez replies, "It is magical. It protects the undead from sunlight. As long as I have the hood on."

Everyone looks at Solur.

Solur smiles, "I am fine in the sunlight. I was going to use my cloak to get Kyvez off the island anyway."

Alexandra looks at Solur, "You planned this from the very beginning."

Solur nods, "Yes. I knew that the Lord of the Undead would eventually return for her."

Robin speaks up, "I knew there had to be a reason you were helping us."

Solur smiles, "Just as Maluc has his reasons, I have mine."

Maluc, who is just staring at Kyvez in awe of her beauty, blinks a few times then looks at the others, "Gold is always a good reason to do something, or if magical artifacts are involved, that too is a good reason."

Zak speaks up, "Like stealing the fire daggers from a friend of the dwarves. That nearly got us killed."

Maluc replies defensively, "I merely stole from their friend. You are the one who kicked the dwarf in the side of the head, not me."

Ayron smiles, "Maluc is right. You did kick the dwarf."

Zak shrugs, "I got caught up in the moment."

Everyone chuckles at Zak's response. Kyvez can tell why her husband has taken a liking to this group of humans and the elf. She can tell that they are good people, just like Solur said. She is surprised at how close they are given their diverse backgrounds.

Solur speaks up, "Kyvez, Zak and Steph are going to be getting married once this quest is over."

Kyvez looks at Steph, "Congratulations. I can still remember my wedding day. Solur was so nervous, he nearly fainted."

Everyone looks at Solur and Maluc speaks up, "Big, bad Solur nearly fainted at getting married."

Solur stares at Maluc coldly and Maluc continues, "Which I can understand. I mean, Kyvez is very beautiful. Not that I was thinking anything. I mean…" He smiles, "I will just be quiet now."

Solur can't hold back the smile and the others get a good laugh.

Alexandra looks at Kyvez, "When we get more time, I would be interested in hearing more of Solur's secrets."

Steph chimes in, "Me too."

Solur lowers his head, "Wonderful."

Chaed smiles, "You are in trouble now."

Kyvez glances at Solur, "It would be my pleasure."

Gaelin speaks up, "We better get moving again."

Alexandra nods, "Gaelin is right."

Everyone gets up and walks over to the horses. They climb on their horses and fall in behind Kyvez. After a few more miles, the see an enormous mountain off in the distance. It reaches up so high that they cannot see the top as it disappears into the black cloud.

The group has gotten a ways up the side of Dragon Mountain, when it starts to get really steep.

Kyvez stops and gets off her horse, "We must go on foot from here."

Everyone dismounts and ties their horse to one of the burnt trees.

Kyvez speaks, "We must be careful. The root is guarded by a very powerful creature."

Ayron smiles, "We have seen our share of those on this trip."

Kyvez looks at Ayron, "I doubt you have seen any like this."

Everyone looks at Kyvez, not seeming too happy about the news. They start up the side a little further, then they see a cave entrance ahead.

Robin sighs, "More caves."

Kyvez takes them into the cave entrance which is about twenty feet high. The tunnel goes into the mountain for about five hundred yards. Kyvez stops the group behind some large rocks at the entrance to a massive cavern. The cavern is every bit of five hundred feet high and at least a half mile wide by a half mile long. Large rocks dot the inside of the cavern. In the very middle of the cavern is a lake of boiling lava. The lake of lava is about two hundred feet around. Everyone looks around and they see a green patch of roots about a quarter of the way into the cavern.

Kyvez speaks, "This is the only place the Dragon's Eye Root grows." She pauses, "We need one person to go inside and get the root."

Maluc smiles, "No problem. I will grab two, just in case."

At that time, they hear the most horrifying sound any of them have ever heard before, echoing from inside the cavern. Everyone watches as a creature, human in shape, emerges from the lake of lava. The creatures skin is deep red. It has the horns of a ram, with black eyes and razor sharp teeth. It's fingernails are black and razor sharp. The creature rises up to a full one hundred feet high, then steps out of the lake. The ground shakes from the heavy footsteps.

Maluc loses his smile, "What is that?"

Kyvez replies in a whisper, "A demon, born of fire."

Zak pats Maluc on the shoulder, "Times like this makes me glad that I am not a thief."

Maluc gives a sarcastic smile and nod, "Very funny."

Maluc puts his hood on and slowly moves around the rocks the group is behind. His boots make his movement completely silent as he swiftly moves to another rock about ten feet away.

Alexandra whispers to the others, "Stay ready, in case he is spotted."

Everyone looks at her as if to say, just what are we suppose to do if he is spotted. The nine of them watch as

Maluc moves fast to another rock as the demon walks around the cavern.

Maluc peeks around the side of the rock and ducks back quick as the demon turns it's head his way. Maluc holds his breath, as if it mattered. He closes his eyes and prays that the demon did not see him. A few seconds pass and he peeks out again. He sees the demon's back, so he moves fast for another rock, just about fifty feet from the patch of roots. Another quick move to the next rock and Maluc is a mere ten feet from the patch of roots. Maluc looks over to the roots and realizes that there are no more rocks between him and the roots.

Maluc whispers to himself, "I hope this is my lucky day."

Maluc gets down on his stomach and starts to slowly crawl towards the roots. The demon continues to move towards the far side of the cavern. Maluc holds his breath the entire ten feet to the roots. He reaches out and pulls one root, then a second and puts them in his pouch.

Steph whispers, "He has them."

Maluc slowly crawls back to the rock and waits a couple seconds to catch his breath. As the demon turns, Maluc starts to move out from behind his rock. Suddenly, a poison dart hits the rock next to Maluc's head. Maluc stops, not knowing what the dart is all about. He slowly peeks around the side of the rock to see the demon moving towards him. He takes a deep breath and watches the demon closely. When the demon turns his head, Maluc moves quick to a rock closer to the group.

The ground shakes as the demon steps closer to where Maluc is at. Maluc watches for another chance to move, and when the demon looks away, Maluc is one rock away from the group. Maluc takes a deep breath as the huge foot of the demon lands right next to the rock he is hiding behind. Maluc completely freezes, not moving a muscle.

Chaed whispers, "He is trapped."

Alexandra whispers, "Gaelin, do you have anything to help."

Gaelin shakes his head, "Not against that."

Robin whispers, "I might have something."

Robin peers out across the cavern at the patch of roots. She taps her staff on the ground as quietly as possible and vines come up out of the ground where the roots are at. Robin points her staff at the vines and moves her left hand around as if telling the vines what she wants them to do. The vines pick up a small rock and throws it over by the edge of the lake of lava.

The demon turns back to the lake, hearing the noise. The demon starts walking back towards the lake of lava. Maluc sees his opening and he runs over next to the group.

Maluc hands the pouch to Alexandra, "Here you go. Now, can we please leave?"

Kyvez nods, "I must agree."

The group makes their way back out of the cave and to their horses. Everyone unties their horse and climbs on.

Kyvez speaks, "We should get almost all the way back to the hut before we will need to stop."

Alexandra nods, "Then lets get moving."

Everyone falls in behind Kyvez and they start back the way they came.

The group has stopped and everyone except Solur and Kyvez are getting some sleep. The horses are tied up to some burnt trees. Everyone finds the ground rather uncomfortable to sleep on. Kyvez is sitting on one side of the camp and Solur is sitting on the opposite side. Alexandra wakes up and slowly looks around. She slides out of her bedroll and sees Kyvez. Alexandra walks over to where Kyvez is sitting.

Kyvez looks up at Alexandra, "Having trouble sleeping?"

Alexandra sits next to Kyvez, "I cannot help but think about my father, and if he is even still alive."

Kyvez is intrigued by Alexandra, "I still cannot believe that a Princess has made it all the way here. If your father is anywhere as strong as you, I am sure he will be fine."

Alexandra smiles weakly, "I have had a lot of help, especially Solur." She pauses, "I envy you. Solur is everything I would want in my husband. He loves you completely."

Kyvez smiles, "He is very special, but do not worry. You will find a wonderful man that will love you will all his heart."

Alexandra nods slightly, "Hopefully. You know, if someone would have told me back before all this started that I would one day be sitting with a vampire and talking about men, I would have thought the person was crazy. It is amazing that people from such different ways of life can get along if they just get to know each other."

Kyvez nods, "I look forward to getting to know all of you better." She glances over and sees Solur motioning to her, "It is time to wake the others."

Alexandra nods and the two ladies stand up and walk over to the group. Solur, Kyvez and Alexandra wakes the others. Everyone starts to get up and slide out of their bedrolls.

Maluc rubs his neck, "Between the hard ground and the smell in the air, it was a great sleep."

Everyone smiles and shakes their head. At that time, they hear an odd, unexplainable noise over by the horses. Everyone gets up and walks over to where the horses are at. Out from behind one of the horses, a couple feet in front of the group, comes a floating eye, about the size of a basketball with thin tentacles hanging down about two feet.

Kyvez speaks, "A beholder."

In a flash, Solur draws his sword and cuts the beholder in two.

Kyvez continues, "We must hurry."

Chaed questions, "What is wrong?"

Solur speaks up, "Remember, I told you that what a beholder sees, the Lord of the Undead knows."

Maluc speaks very depressed, "The Lord of the Undead knows we are here."

Solur nods, "Yes, and the undead army will be coming for us soon."

Robin speaks up, "Then lets waste no more time talking about it."

Alexandra nods, "To the horses."

Everyone gathers up their things and hurries to their horse. The group climbs on their horses. They fall in behind Kyvez and after a couple miles, they ride past the hut where they met Kyvez at. The group doesn't even slow down. They get another mile closer to the coast and they stop on the top of a small hill. The ten of them look out at the glow of what looks like hundreds of torches in the distance.

Alexandra speaks up, "Solur, see what we are up against. We will be waiting here."

Solur rides off and the others just sit and wait.

————

The group continues to gaze across the charred, barren lands of the Island of the Dead. Their faces are weary from the long journey. Alexandra's left hand gently rubs the pouch tied to the front of her waist as they await Solur's return. A few more minutes pass when they see Solur approaching fast. Solur stops next to the group.

Alexandra questions, "What are we looking at?"

Solur explains, "Two death knights and one hundred skeleton warriors are headed straight at us. The other eight death knights, four hundred skeleton warriors, the lich and the Lord of the Undead are moving for the coast. It appears they are trying to get to the skiffs before us."

Alexandra questions, "Can we avoid the first army?"

Solur shakes his head, "It would take time. The other army would beat us to the skiffs."

Chaed speaks up, "Then we ride straight through the first army. It is the only way."

Kyvez chimes in, "That does seem to be the only way."

Alexandra lets out a sigh, "Then that is what we do. Do not slow down and try to stay on your horses."

The ten of them ride hard, straight at the first undead army. They each think to themselves, this could be the end. As the undead army comes into view, everyone draws their weapons. The skeleton warriors, which have chain mail armor hanging from their bones and a helmet on their skulls, draw their short swords. Some skeleton warriors draw back bows with arrows. The two death knights, dressed in all black plate mail armor, draw their medium swords.

A volley of arrows lands all around the group as they get fifty yards away. Behind Solur, the group rides straight into the mass of skeleton warriors.

Solur works his sword on his right, cutting down skeleton warriors that get too close. Chaed comes up on Solur's left, taking down skeleton warriors as fast as he can work his sword. Alexandra falls in behind Chaed and Kyvez falls in behind Solur. Both ladies work their swords as fast as they can as the skeleton warriors just keep coming at them.

Another volley of arrows come at them as swords cut at the horses. The rest of the group follows in behind the others. Then, Kyvez's horse takes an arrow in the neck. The horse falls and Kyvez is thrown to the ground. Kyvez rolls to a knee as she hits the ground. Ayron takes an arrow in the left shoulder and he falls from his horse. Steph's horse is cut by a sword and the front legs buckle. Steph goes over the front of her horse, hard to the ground. Chaed's horse takes an arrow and falls. Chaed hits the ground hard, losing his shield and medium sword.

Kyvez spins with incredible speed, cutting down a couple of skeleton warriors behind her. She leaps into the air and lands behind another skeleton warrior, quickly bringing it to an end. Solur pushes his way through the masses to get to Kyvez. Solur rides up and kicks a skeleton warrior away from Kyvez. Kyvez climbs on Solur's horse and the two of them are off again.

Chaed hurries over to his horse and draws his magical long sword. He turns fast, cutting down two skeleton warriors. Then, a death knight approaches. The death knight cuts in fast from the left, but Chaed blocks the deadly sword and counters. The death knight blocks Chaed's counter and thrusts in. Chaed spins around the sword and removes the death knight's right leg, just below the knee. Chaed spins back the other way and drops the death knight with another massive cut. At that moment, Alexandra rides up to Chaed. Chaed climbs on her horse and they start on through the crowd of skeleton warriors.

Steph spins her staff with deadly speed and skill and crushes skeleton warriors that get too close. Then an arrow zips in and hits Steph in the right thigh. Steph cries out as she falls to a knee. A skeleton warrior steps up behind Steph and readies to strike with his sword. Suddenly, the skeleton warrior's head is removed as Zak stops his horse next to Steph. Steph climbs on with Zak and the two of them start after the others.

Maluc and Gaelin push their way through the mass of

undead. A sword comes in and cuts Maluc on the left leg as an arrow comes in and hits Gaelin in the right shoulder. Gaelin nearly falls, but he holds on to his staff and his horse.

Robin tries to push her way through to Ayron. Ayron cuts down a skeleton warrior, then the other death knight cuts Ayron across the back. Robin tries hard, but there are still too many. Ayron spins and brings his sword around. The death knight ducks and cuts Ayron deep across the stomach. An arrow flies in and hits Ayron in the lower back. Ayron cries out and before he can recover, the death knight drives his sword into Ayron's chest.

Robin screams, "No!"

The others look over to watch Ayron fall. Robin fires a magical arrow into the death knight's chest. Robin tries to get to Ayron's body. Solur rides up and grabs her reigns.

Solur yells, "It is too late!"

He pulls her reigns away from Ayron's body. Robin turns her horse and follows Solur through the remaining skeleton warriors. A last volley of arrows fly in. Alexandra moves her head left at the last second and an arrow scratches her on the right cheek.

The group clears the undead army and continues riding hard for the coast.

The group gets closer to the coast as the undead army closes in, a mere hundred and fifty yards off to the group's right. Everyone sees the skiffs and the water ahead as the undead army closes to a hundred yards. The group stops fast and dismounts. They start for the skiffs.

Solur yells, "Look out!"

Everyone drops to the ground as a fireball from the lich, now only seventy five yards away, flies pass them.

They watch as it hits one of the skiffs and the skiff explodes. The group scrambles to their feet.

Solur speaks, "This is bad."

Alexandra questions, "What do you mean? Lets go."

Chaed chimes in, "At most, the skiff can only hold six."

Kyvez speaks up, "Lets hurry. We are in range of the lich."

Chaed looks at the water, "We will be defenseless once we are in the water, unless Gaelin's magic can protect us."

The undead army closes to sixty yards.

Gaelin speaks up, "Three must stay behind and hold them off. It is the only chance we have."

Zak chimes in, "Whoever stays must be able to hold their own."

Steph speaks up, "Alexandra and Gaelin have to go."

Chaed nods, "They will need you and Zak to find their way back to Glenfin."

Solur looks at the undead army, not fifty yards away, "I will stay."

Kyvez looks at Solur, "If you stay, then I stay."

Chaed speaks up, "I will stay with you."

Solur shakes his head, "No. They will need your sword to get back."

Robin speaks up, "It has to be me. My magic works well against the undead and they already have Gaelin."

Solur nods, "It is settled. The six of you go, now."

Everyone except Alexandra climbs into the skiff.

Alexandra protests, "There has too be another way."

Solur looks into her eyes, "Go, before it is too late."

Arrows land all around them as another fireball hits the water about twenty feet behind the skiff.

Alexandra gives in, "We will never forget you three." She looks at Robin, "I am going to miss you so much."

Robin bows her head, "It has been an honor, my

lady."

Alexandra climbs into the skiff. Solur pushes the skiff into the water.

Chaed places his left hand to his heart and looks at Solur, "You are the bravest warrior I have ever known. It has been an honor."

Solur nods his head as the skiff starts away from the coast. Robin, Kyvez and Solur turn back to the undead army which is now only twenty five yards away. Solur takes off his cloak and drops it on the ground. He draws his sword and dagger. Kyvez draws her sword and Robin readies her staff. The three of them look at each other as if to say, goodbye.

———

Alexandra and the others watch as the undead army closes in on their friends. A volley of arrows comes down at Solur and the others. Solur cuts one arrow from the sky as it comes at him. Then, the skeleton warriors and the death knights draw their swords.

The Lord of the Undead, standing nearly six feet tall with black armor and a skull helmet on, draws his medium sword with his right hand, "Kill them!"

Robin steps back and raises her staff, "May the dead, be gone."

A golden ripple of light moves out of Robin's staff and into the charging army. When the light hits the first ten skeleton warriors, they stop instantly. The skeleton warriors cry out in pain as they slowly crumble to dust. The lich, a decayed human wearing royal looking rags and holding a long staff, launches a fireball at Robin, but Robin dives away to safety.

Robin rolls to a knee and creates an ice ring as the lich prepares another fireball. Robin launches the ice ring. Before the lich can launch his fireball, the ice ring slams into him. The lich crashes to the ground. Robin seizes the opportunity and sends another ripple of golden light into the undead army. This time, ten skeleton warriors and the lich are turned to dust. Robin spins around and ducks under a skeleton warrior's sword. She hits the skeleton warrior in the ribs with her staff and the skeleton warrior crumbles to the earth.

A sword cuts across Robin's back. Robin cries out in pain and turns to see a death knight standing there. She brings her staff around quickly, but the death knight blocks with his sword. The death knight kicks Robin in the stomach. Robin loses her footing and falls to her back, losing her staff. The death knight drives his sword down into Robin's chest.

Kyvez comes up behind the death knight and thrusts her sword in between it's shoulder blades, piercing it's heart. She turns quick and cuts down a skeleton warrior on her right. An arrow flies in, but like a flash, Kyvez dives away and rolls back to her feet. Another skeleton warrior steps up and cuts in at Kyvez. She blocks quickly and her counter cuts down the skeleton warrior.

Kyvez senses someone behind her and she spins around. She finds herself face to face with the Lord of the Undead. Kyvez thrusts in, but the Lord of the Undead parries. The Lord of the Undead counters, but Kyvez hops back to safety. She cuts in from the right, but the Lord of the Undead drops under her sword and cuts Kyvez deep across the stomach. Kyvez lets out a groan of pain as the magical sword draws her immortal blood. Kyvez swings again, but the Lord of the Undead blocks and sweeps her feet out from under her. As soon as Kyvez hits the ground, the Lord of the Undead drives his sword down. His blade pierces Kyvez's heart.

Solur turns to see Kyvez fall, "No!"

Solur shoves away two skeleton warriors as he runs at the Lord of the Undead. The Lord of the Undead sees

Solur coming and motions for some skeleton warriors to move in front of him. Three skeleton warriors step in front of Solur. Solur spins by the first sword and cuts down one skeleton warrior with his sword. As another sword comes at Solur, he kicks the blade away with his left foot and drops the skeleton warrior with his dagger. The last skeleton warrior cuts in at Solur. Solur brings his sword across and blocks. He spins around and takes the skeleton warrior's arm off at the elbow. Solur keeps spinning and he comes around again and removes the skeleton warrior's head with his sword.

Solur gets closer and a death knight moves to stop him. The death knight thrusts in, but Solur is not to be stopped. He spins around the sword, ending up behind the death knight. Solur cuts the death knight's throat with his dagger. Then, Solur turns and locks eyes with the Lord of the Undead.

The Lord of the Undead prepares himself for Solur. Solur closes to a few feet and starts to thrust his sword in at the Lord of the Undead. The Lord of the Undead brings his sword across to block. When the two blades touch, Solur spins to his left and his deadly blade comes around in a flash. In the blink of an eye, the Lord of the Undead's head flies a few feet across the battlefield.

Solur rushes over and kneels next to Kyvez, "My love, I am here."

Kyvez speaks with her last breath, "I love you."

Suddenly, a sword drives into Solur's lower, left back and out his front. Solur, winces in pain and turns. He cuts down the skeleton warrior as it withdraws it's blade out of Solur. An arrow flies in and hits Solur in the back of the left shoulder. More skeleton warrior's close in, but Solur manages to hold them off. Then, another arrow flies in and hits Solur in the front of his right shoulder. Solur turns right and drops another skeleton warrior, but a death knight steps in on Solur's left. The death knight drives his sword into Solur's stomach.

Solur grabs the blade as it is still inside him. He brings his sword around and removes the death knight's head. With the strength he has left, Solur pulls the sword out of his stomach. Then, the fatal arrow flies in and hits Solur in the heart. Solur drops to his knees, dropping his sword and dagger. Solur crawls over to Kyvez and Solur falls next to his love.

The others watch the battle from the skiff. They see Robin fall and Kyvez. They cross into the sunlight just as the last arrow finishes off Solur.

Maluc speaks up, "I cannot believe they are gone."

Zak nods, "Gone, but never forgotten."

Chaed nods slightly, "True. Legends will speak of this day for centuries to come."

Gaelin looks at Alexandra, who is staring off into the clear, blue sky, "Are you okay, my lady?"

Alexandra replies, "Yes. I am fine."

She closes her eyes and takes in the sunshine and fresh air as for one moment, Alexandra blocks out the world around her.

And in the darkness, Alexandra's voice can be heard, "It was so hard for me to believe. With all the scholars of the kingdom at my disposal, I learned more from the undead, an elf, a thief, the rangers and my friends. The days back to Glenfin were long and we never forgot the sacrifices of our fallen friends. It still amazes me that we were able to accomplish so much given our diverse backgrounds, but I guess anything can happen if people just put their differences aside. I may never have another quest, but that is okay. I doubt another quest would ever fulfill me like the Quest for the Dragon's Eye."

Epilogue

THE SKY IS CLEAR BLUE IN THE OPEN FIELD back in the lands of Glenfin. The serene view of a crystal clear lake is breathtaking as a waterfall is not too far in the distance. A slight breeze is in the air, carrying the fresh smell of flowers.

Zak is standing by the lake. He is dressed in a formal green tunic and trousers, with brown boots. His clan leader stands with him, also dressed in a formal tunic. Chaed is standing next to Zak. Chaed is dressed in his shiny, plate mail armor with his helmet off.

The rest of the clan is seated about ten feet away. Then, Alexandra walks up and stands opposite of Zak and Chaed. She is wearing a beautiful flowing yellow dress. She smiles at Zak and Chaed. A few seconds later, the string instruments start playing. Everyone stands as Gaelin and Steph step out. Gaelin is dressed in his formal white and gold wizard robes. Steph looks like a dream in her hand made, white dress. She has a flower in her hair. Zak just stares at the beautiful woman who is about to become his wife.

Gaelin walks Steph up to where the others are standing. Once they stop, Gaelin bows his head to the clan leader and passes Steph over to Zak. Zak and Steph just stare at each other, not really hearing what the clan leader is saying. The clan leader talks for a couple of minutes.

The two of them come out of their gaze when they

hear the clan leader, "Shall we continue."

In the front row, King Romlay stands, dressed in his formal robes. Next to him is Maluc, also wearing a nice tunic and trousers.

King Romlay nods, "Continue."

The clan leader speaks, "Do you, Zak, take Steph to be your wife? To have and to hold, to love, honor and cherish for as long as you live?"

Zak smiles, "I do."

The clan leader continues, "Do you, Steph, take Zak to be your husband? To have and to hold, to love, honor and cherish as long as you live?"

Steph smiles and sheds a tear, "I do."

The clan leader speaks, "Then in the eyes of our Lord and our King, I now pronounce you, man and wife."

Zak and Steph share a passionate kiss. The King stands and bows his head to Zak and Steph, and once again, peace reigns throughout the kingdom.

THE END

www.ingramcontent.com/pod-product-compliance
Lightning Source LLC
Chambersburg PA
CBHW060354030726
47497CB00003B/701